# ONCE UPON A MARRIAGE

MARJ CHARLIER

# ONCE UPON A MARRIAGE

MARJ CHARLIER

SUNACUMEN
PRESS

Published by Sunacumen Press
Colorado Springs, CO
Printed in U.S.A.
ISBN: 979-8-9914967-7-3

# DEDICATION

To Ben

My best friend, my husband,
my first reader, my travel companion,
and my conscience.
You will be in my heart forever.

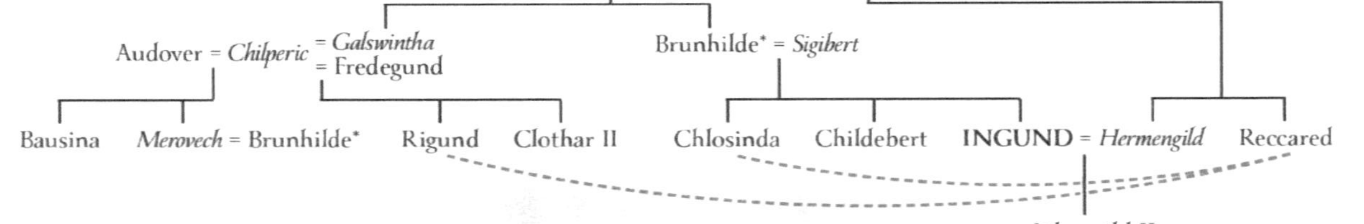

MEROVINGIANS
Aregund = Clothar = Ingund
Audover = Chilperic = Galswintha = Fredegund
Gundowald
Chairbert
Sigibert = Brunhilde*
Guntram
Bausina
Merovech = Brunhilde*
Rigund
Clothar II
Clotild
INGUND = Hermengild
Chlosinda
Childebert
Athnagild II
Theudebert
Theuderic
* additional marriage
.... illegitimate
--- engagement but no marriage
murdered by family member
VISIGOTHS
Athanagild = Goswintha = Leovigild = ?
Audover = Chilperic = Galswintha = Fredegund
Brunhilde* = Sigibert
Bausina
Merovech = Brunhilde*
Rigund
Clothar II
Chlosinda
Childebert
INGUND = Hermengild
Reccared
Athnagild II

German
Oceana
Gallicus
Luticia (Paris)
Merovingian
Gaul
Ingund and
Sebastianus
Lombard
Kingdom
Tolosa
(Toulouse)
Sostomagus
(Castelnaudary)
Carcassonne
Narbo
(Narbonne)
Caesaraugusta
(Zaragoza)
Ingund,
Sebastianus,
Nicole, and
Hermenegild
Toledo
Visigothic
Iberia
Ingund,
Sebastianus,
and Nicole
Barcino
(Barcelona)
Sardinia
Hispalis
(Seville)
Corduba
(Cordoba)
Malaca
(Malaga)
Ingund, Sebastianus, Nicole, and Athanagild
Carthage
(Tunis)
Mauretania

# INGUND'S JOURNEY INTO HISTORY

*Time travels in divers paces with divers persons.*
— William Shakespeare, As You Like It, III, ii, 328.

*For us believing physicists, the distinction between past, present and future is only a stubbornly persistent illusion.*
— Albert Einstein

# PROLOGUE

B ack from Cyprus," he texted.

According to the physics department secretary, Sébastièn was supposed to be on a research sabbatical. There was little reason for a physicist to be on an island in the Mediterranean. Maybe the Hadrian accelerator in Switzerland. Maybe the Atacama Cosmology Telescope in the high desert of Chile.

Here in Minnesota, he was Sébastièn, a cynical, down-to-earth scientist – his feet frozen in academia and a smirk on his face. But she had come to believe he was also Sebastianus, the driver of a Visigothic queen's carriage, which might make sense if he had said "back from Constantinople" or "back from Carthage." But Cyprus?

Hell, it didn't matter where he had been. She slammed her laptop closed, kicked off her clogs, stripped off her pajamas, and threw on a skirt that stopped well above her knees. It was time for him to explain himself, here in the twenty-first century.

She didn't wait to scrape the windshield of her car. Navigating snowy streets through an icy window was in her Midwest DNA. Waiting for the car to warm up was for wimps.

Since she came back from the sixth century, she had tried to reach the physics professor, hoping he would explain what had happened to her. How did she – and he? – end up in the Visigothic Kingdom fifteen hundred years ago? And how had five years passed in ancient Spain when only five months had passed back in Minnesota?

After her adrenaline-fueled adventure in medieval Iberia, she had returned to modernity to finish her dissertation. For a month, limp with ennui for all but the ancient past, she stared out the frost-smeared window next to her desk, her fingers frozen on the keyboard, wondering if she could have – should have – gone on to Constantinople with Sebastianus and Queen Ingund.

Why had she turned her back on the last chapter of that time-defying leap into late antiquity?

Because Sebastianus had insisted. If she had not come back, she would die in the sixth century. She would never be born in America, never graduate from the University of Iowa, never be curious about Saint Ingund. She would never board a plane for Paris or Toledo.

She never could have fallen in love with the same man in two distant centuries.

I

When Nicole lived alone during her graduate studies in Iowa City, she cooked what she wanted, read books as late into the night as she wanted, and kept her apartment simple and clean. But she was lonely much of the time. Or so she had thought.

Now, pulling into the garage of the bungalow she shared with Justin since they had moved together from Iowa, she tried to shake off a wave of dread. Lonely was underrated. Solitude was easier. Certainly, it was more productive. She had papers to grade, a lecture to prepare for tomorrow, and her dissertation to finish, but Justin would beg her to watch a rerun of the day's golf tournament. "Bill Murray is a hoot!" he'd declare, trying to infect her with his enthusiasm.

Sitting in the car, listening to the click of the cooling engine, Nicole took deep breaths and reminded herself how lucky she was, living with Justin.

He kept his mess of clothes and shoes and old sports magazines on his side of the bedroom. He did his share of dishes and cooking. He was trim and handsome, with wavy black hair and a sexy, persistent five-o'clock shadow. He was athletic—a great golfer—

which, as a poor golfer herself, Nicole could respect, even envy a bit.

Compared with some of her friends' husbands and boyfriends, he was "a catch," as her friend Katie had said. Katie's husband, Doug, was a stage hound who called himself a Marxist and dominated dinner and party conversations with a relentless dialectic that kept everyone on edge. He ran a non-profit on campus and strived to prove that no one in their social circle could claim a greater commitment to saving the world. Compared with him, Justin was normal.

On the other hand, at times Nicole felt suffocated by Justin's "normal." Lately, he was spending occasional evenings and weekends with Kevin, his best golf buddy, taking some of the pressure off their relationship. But his car in the garage indicated this was not going to be one of those times.

"Hey," she greeted him, throwing her briefcase on the entry table. "How was school today?" She unwrapped the scarf from her neck and accepted a peck on the lips. Hiding her irritation, she headed directly into her office.

"Toby acted up again," Justin said, following her and leaning his butt against her desk. "I had to call his mom at the clinic."

"Toby's the one who…"

"Yeah, he's the one." Justin talked so much about this Toby that Nicole didn't need to finish her sentence.

"Anyway, I am going to talk with the principal about him. So disruptive. I think the other kids would be happy if he just went away." Nicole scrolled through her messages as Justin continued talking about Toby and other details of his day.

An email from her mother caught her attention. "Oh, good!"

Justin stopped talking, leaned around, and looked over her shoulder. "What happened?"

"It looks like Mom is coming up again right after spring break."

"Again? Wasn't she just here? Maybe we should have moved farther away." Justin snorted. Their parents had always been involved in their lives to an extent that made her students' helicopter parents look neglectful. But her mother's proximity was another reason Nicole had agreed to take the job at McIntosh Univeristy in St. George, only four hours from Iowa City. Her mother was aging fast, suffering a growing list of disabilities. Nicole was grateful she could see her often.

Fuming, Nicole returned to her inbox. But then Justin said the kind of thing that always made her feel guilty for her irritation: "I imagine you need to get some work done. I've thawed out some chicken thighs. I'll make dinner. If your mom's coming, you'll need to get ahead on your work."

"Thanks," Nicole said, uploading the latest draft of her dissertation. "I've really got to figure out why I can't make Ingund feel real."

NICOLE REREAD THE SECTION SHE had finished the weekend before, and, just as she had then, she stared at the blank screen that followed it. She couldn't figure out how to proceed. The stage had been set: She had introduced Ingund as the first of the three cousins betrothed – one after the other – in the sixth century to Visigothic princes of Iberia. The cousins were daughters of the Merovingian dynasty, the extended, dysfunctional family that ruled Gaul before the time of Charlemagne. Nicole had studied their history for so long that she could sketch a family tree of five generations of the large, incestuous, and murderous dynasty from memory.

For her dissertation, she was focusing on arranged marriages of royalty and nobility in medieval times, like Ingund's. Only fifteen when she was betrothed to the Visigothic prince Hermenegild, Ingund was expected to serve her parents' imperial ambitions, forming an alliance through marriage and children. What intrigued Nicole about Ingund was her role in converting the Arian Visigothic empire to Catholicism.

Nicole didn't want her dissertation to end up as another moldy paper, stuffed away in the university archives, read by fewer than a dozen readers. She wanted people to know about Ingund's sacrifice. Her PhD advisor at Iowa approved her decision to write it as a novel.

Now, when she wasn't in class, preparing for class, or grading student essays, she dove into writing.

But her fascination with Ingund wasn't helping Nicole bring the young woman to life on the page. Historians recorded little more than the basic facts of her engagement and her fight with her mother-in-law. Nicole struggled to put flesh and bones on the story. Giving up, Nicole turned off her computer and went to the kitchen to watch Justin cook.

"I'm going to have to go to Paris and Toledo," she said, sitting across the kitchen bar from him. "I can't get a feel for the setting or the characters sitting here in snowy Minnesota."

"What? I don't understand how going to France and Spain in 2023 is going to help you imagine what life was like in 570," Justin responded, not looking up from the chicken thighs frying in half an inch of sizzling oil.

"Well, their libraries have more primary sources, and maps, sketches, artwork. Maybe books on clothing of the times, food, transportation. I mean, did everyone ride horses then, or just the nobility? Was cross-country travel common? I just don't know these things."

"So, you've been studying the Middle Ages since when? Kindergarten? And you don't know these things? You haven't imagined them?" She could hear his sarcasm; usually he hid it better. He often rolled his eyes as she described some compelling anecdote of early medieval history, evidence of her nerdy obsession.

"History books are full of wars and politicians, not the quotidian details of life," Nicole said, sneaking a carrot slice from the salad Justin had fixed.

Justin shook his head over the fry pan. "Well, if you have to go to Europe, then go. I just don't know when you're going to have time. Aren't you teaching again this summer?"

"I probably have time at spring break. And there's a few weeks between the spring and summer sessions," Nicole said. "The bigger problem is money."

"Borrow from your folks. They're loaded."

Nicole bristled. Her parents were comfortable financially but certainly not "loaded." Underlying his quip was Justin's belief that her family's good fortune was undeserved. Nicole's grandmother had sued the physician who treated – or actually, didn't treat – Nicole's grandfather for a heart condition and wound up with a few million that her parents inherited. His parents had scraped and saved to amass their sizable nest egg.

"I don't want my father to hold more debt over my head," Nicole said, swallowing her irritation. "He never stops reminding me how much he spent on my education."

"Put it on credit cards then," Justin said. He turned off the burner and spooned the chicken onto a pile of paper towels. "Once you get a real job, it will be easy to pay it off."

Oh, boy. Another trigger. "Real job." Since she took the assistant professor position at MacIntosh, he had hinted it wasn't a "real" job. Yes, it paid poorly. As badly as high school teachers were paid, he made twice as much teaching high school history and coaching golf as she did lecturing in college. But, she insisted from the beginning, it was an investment in their future.

Again, Nicole stifled her reaction. Arguing at dinner was something she hated, having witnessed many uncomfortable dinners as a child of constantly warring parents. It did seem odd, though, that Justin was suddenly amenable to building up credit card debt. From his parents he had inherited a belief that credit cards led families down the road to perdition.

"I'll see how much room I have on my credit cards. Maybe I can go over Easter break." She sighed. "I just can't figure out how to write this book without getting over there."

# II

At the start of spring break, Nicole flew to Paris. She had only a few days for research, but the trip would help her determine how to spend her time in France the three weeks between the spring semester and summer school. She hadn't been in Paris for years – not since an undergraduate semester as an exchange student. Although she believed a 2,500-year-old city couldn't change that much in nine years, her friends told her it had. The scooters that once took over sidewalks and dodged through traffic had recently been outlawed, but America was everywhere, her friends said. Burger King, Facebook, t-shirts, and Levis.

Still, Nicole had a sense of *déjà vu* on the cab ride from the airport. Paris didn't feel that different. The traffic was still insane, even though the cars were different, and the monuments she remembered were where they'd always been. From her hotel window near the Sorbonne on the Left Bank, she could see the Tour Eiffel in the distance, still unobscured by tall buildings. Looking in the other direction, she grimaced at the scaffolding surrounding the Catédrale Notre-Dame de Paris, but it wouldn't affect her research. Construction on the cathedral started in the twelfth century. She was interested in what occupied the Île de la Cité long before that.

The next morning, she surprised herself by waking just as the sun rose. She showered, gulped a café Americano in the hotel breakfast nook, and headed for the Musée de Cluny. She hadn't visited the museum when she was in Paris as a student, surprisingly, given that her major in college was history and her specialty medieval history. She spent most of her time those four months in bars and cafés where she could imbibe beer and wine that a 19-year-old couldn't order in Minneapolis. Clearly, opportunity had been wasted.

She started with a tour of the massive, flamboyant Cluny Museum's permanent collections of tapestries, paintings, sculptures, gold objects, and stained glass, much of it brought in from outside of Paris in the thirteenth to sixteenth centuries, well after the years Nicole was interested in. But two displays held her attention and helped fuel her imagination: gold crowns from the Visigoths of sixth- and seventh-century Spain, and an ivory statuette of Ariadne, a goddess associated with the Roman god Bacchus. The jewel-encrusted gold pieces displayed the fine craftsmanship of the so-called "barbarian" tribes that moved through Gaul and Iberia after the fall of Rome. And the sculpture's depiction of a pagan figure from sixth-century Constantinople proved that many people in the sixth century still worshiped the old religions despite the increasing predominance of Christianity.

By noon, she was yawning in the hushed halls of the museum. After another café Americano at a nearby sidewalk café, she returned to the museum's underground bathhouse built in the first two centuries after Christ. The 2,200-year-old grand Frigidarium's vaulted ceilings rose fourteen feet above the stone floor, typical of the grandeur of Roman civic buildings. It struck her as odd that the Romans used the bathhouse for only a couple of centuries two millennia ago, but still looked substantially serviceable.

Leaving the museum's hushed ancient ruins, she was stunned by the bustle of the busy street. It was as if she had jumped from the fall of Rome to the twenty-first century in a single step. Which she had, in a way. The honking cars, shouting vendors, and lively side-walk cafés were disorienting after the subterranean tranquility of the baths. Despite her exhaustion, Nicole felt lighter than she had in months. Now she was certain she could find what she needed if she came back before the summer session. The fear that she'd never get Ingund's world right had vanished. She knew she'd discover even more in the archives of the Sorbonne's libraries.

Sauntering back to the hotel for a nap, she stopped to marvel at the solid, classic simplicity of a mercantile set back a bit from the street. It was old. Very old. The stone blocks of the façade were etched by centuries of weather. She put her hands up to the sides of her face and squinted through the cloudy glass. It was a costume shop — not like an American Halloween costume store, but more like a museum of period clothing. Closest to the front window, a Victorian dress with a pinched waist and large round bustle hung suspended on a rod, swaying slightly. Behind it, she recognized a nun's habit from the eighteenth century. Could the store have earli-er costumes — perhaps from as early as the sixth century?

As Nicole entered, a small woman wrapped in a crocheted shawl approached. The drafty shop smelled of old wool and cotton, of dust and old paper.

"*Bonjour, mademoiselle. Comment-allez vous? Est-ce que vous voudriez quelque chose en particulier?*"

"*Bonjour, madame.*" Nicole smiled genuinely. "*Parlez-vous Anglais?*" She could speak decent French in America, but she couldn't speak French like the French do.

"*Un peu,*" the lady said, bowing her head slightly as if to empha-size her understatement. Nicole knew the French typically under-sold their command of other languages.

Nicole felt huge — too large to fit in the store's crowded spaces. At five-foot-eight, she towered over the clerk. Perhaps accustomed to being the short one in adult encounters, the woman didn't ap-pear intimidated. She was older than she had appeared at a distance. Deep wrinkles lined her cheeks and long creases from her eyes to her temples testified to a lifetime of delight at greeting strangers.

"Would you have any costumes from the sixth century?" Nicole asked.

"Woman or man?" the clerk asked, turning to lead Nicole into the dim room. The shop was long and narrow, arranged so that walking into its depths took Nicole further back in time.

"Woman. Perhaps Merovingian? A queen or a royal daughter?"

"Ah, you know your French history," the woman said, holding out her hand. "I'm Elise, and I don't meet too many Americans who have an appreciation of Frankish dynasties."

"I'm Nicole, a history professor from Minnesota. I study Merovingian and Carolingian women."

"And what do you say about them?" Elise motioned for Nicole to continue following her.

"Well, I'm trying to establish that even in medieval times, many women sought ways to escape the limiting roles they'd been assigned since the Bronze Age."

"Oh." Elise shook her head slightly. "I'm not sure about that," she said, stopping next to a display case that held two-piece brooches like those Nicole had seen in late Roman and early medieval textbooks. "I'm not convinced that women were adventurous back then. If they were, it was forced on them by circumstance, like Jeanne d'Arc. The times were already difficult."

Nicole considered disagreeing. Certainly, Fredegund and Brunhilde – the "dark queens" whose daughters were subjects of her research – were adventurous. They won autonomy over their male relatives and fought for the sovereignty of their sons and grandsons. But Nicole wasn't there to rehash the same arguments she had with her colleagues back in Minnesota.

"Here are some accessories, from the period you asked about." Elise opened the glass lid of the case. "Most of them are reproductions, but we have a few original pieces in the vault." She handed Nicole a flyer with sketches of the ancient items. No prices, just *"faire un offre."*

"These are spectacular," Nicole said, sweeping her arm over the display. "I didn't know there was such variety."

"But you said you were looking for dresses, *n'est-ce pas?*" Walking farther back, Elise pointed to three mannequins dressed in medieval clothing. One wore a plain, brown habit of an early Christian nun. Next to the nun was a Frankish warrior with bowl-shaped metal helmet over his long hair, a vest of finely woven metal over a blousy shirt, a knee-length leather skirt over cloth breeches, and leather straps crisscrossed up his calves from his boots. He held a long spear in one hand and a heavy dagger in the other.

"That is a recent reproduction," Elise said. She gestured to a tall mannequin of a woman. "But this one we think was made at least two hundred years ago, perhaps for some historical pageant. Perhaps it is much older than that."

Nicole walked around the dummy, surprised the woman was so statuesque. Long, curling locks flowed down her back and an ivory pendant hung on her chest. A perfectly preserved dark blue, heavy wool vest, nearly as long as the silk dress underneath and secured with a brooch, bespoke royalty. Only medieval elites could obtain such rich blue dye from the Far East.

"Could this be what Ingund looked like?" she asked.

"You mean Brunhilde's daughter? Quite possibly. We don't know, of course. There are no images made of her from that time. She probably wasn't blond." Elise shrugged.

Nicole studied the costume. It provided just the image she needed to flesh out how the protagonist of her novel may have dressed. She reached out to touch the wool and jerked her hand away. "*Je m'excuse!* I suppose I shouldn't touch," she whispered, embarrassed.

"Oh, no." Elise laughed. "All the costumes are for sale. You may even try it on, if you wish. It looks like it might fit a tall woman such as you."

"Really?" Nicole's heart raced at the idea. "I'd love to!"

She put her briefcase down as Elise unfastened the brooch and slipped the vest off the dummy's dress. "You can dress in there," she said, pointing to a door. "Start with the dress, and I'll bring you the rest."

In the tight closet, Nicole pulled the silk shift over her head; it fit like it was made for her. Elise fastened the hooks on the back and set the vest over Nicole's shoulders, just as a jingle indicated a customer had come into the store.

"I'll be right back," Elise said. "When you're ready, come out and look in the mirror."

# III

I placed the brooch in the spot on the vest where the mannequin had worn it and stepped out of the closet, looking for a mirror. Disoriented, I nearly tripped over the front of the skirt. The room looked entirely different. Thick, uneven stones had replaced the worn wood floor. The mannequins were gone, and in their place were trunks, their open lids revealing jumbles of linen shirts and undergarments, fur capes, and floppy leather boots. More than anything, the room resembled a backstage closet for a medieval play.

I followed the sound of Elise's voice through merchandise I hadn't seen before. Shovels, straw-covered bins of root vegetables, and bags of flour crowded the floor. I stumbled, confused, toward the now dim light at the front of the store. The windows looked like they had been smeared with grease. Could this be the same shop I had walked into? Were there two doors in that closet? Had I come out the wrong one – one that led into a different store?

I stopped, shocked at what I heard. Elise was speaking Old German, or some dialect of it mixed with a vulgar Latin. The Franks had only been in Gaul for a little more than two centuries, and Old German had yet to evolve into Old French. I hadn't heard the ancient German language since I took classes in early medieval dialects in college, and then, we didn't speak it as much as we read, wrote, and analyzed it for the way it influenced modern German. I'd been a prodigy then, picking it up quickly, as I did most languages. But until this moment, I'd never heard anyone speak it fluently. Even more curious: I understood Elise as if I had been born in medieval Paris.

Behind Elise, shelves rose to the ceiling, filled with bolts of silk, linen, and wool. She had pulled out a half dozen for a woman's perusal. I knew the stash hadn't been there before.

"I will get some silk from the Gupta region in a month or so," Elise told the shopper. "You might want it. I believe we will get some in that dark ruby color that Brunhilde so desires."

"Yes, I will. None of this is rich enough." The woman fingered a bolt of pale-yellow silk the clerk held out to her. "For now, I will take just the wool for Ingund's cloak."

Brunhilde? Ingund? I felt dizzy. I didn't believe in time travel. But then, what was this? It seemed as if I had, somehow, between entering the store and coming out of the dressing room, stepped through a portal to the sixth century. Had I, who needed nothing more than to meet women who knew – perhaps worked for – Brunhilde and Ingund, just done so? Was this exactly the vivid imagination Justin accused me of not having? Or a dream, perhaps, enlightened by my visit to the museum?

The shopper turned to me, and I stopped, afraid to step closer and lose the illusion. She looked me up and down slowly, and I could tell she was taking in the deep dye of the vest I was wearing and the quality of the silk in my dress. She curtsied, and it occurred to me that she might think I was a member of the nobility, if not a relative of Queen Brunhilde or King Sigibert. My clothing indicated someone of such high status. And this woman, apparently a dressmaker, would certainly know that.

I nodded, but with little confidence in my Old German, I said nothing. I turned around to retrieve the briefcase, purse, and clothing I had left in the closet dressing room, chagrined at my lack of courage. Wasn't this just what I came to France looking for? A bit of the sixth century, however unreal?

"Are you the cousin from Carthage that Brunhilde is expecting?" the seamstress asked as I was retreating. "Ingund's new escort?"

I stopped. Whether I was dreaming or not, there was no question that this was the opportunity of a lifetime, whatever "lifetime" meant under these strange circumstances. My mind raced through a kind of risk-reward analysis. What did I know of Carthage, or of Brunhilde's far-flung cousins? If I said yes, could I fool everyone? On the other hand, if I got that close to Ingund, my research problems would be solved. And then, on the other-other hand, if I were really back in the sixth century, what would it matter? I wouldn't be writing my novel anyway.

There wasn't time to figure it all out. I decided that I had no choice. If I were in the sixth century, where I knew no one, had no home, what could I do other than follow this woman, this seamstress, to Brunhilde's home – castle – whatever it was?

"Yes," I answered. I managed to pull a few Old German words out of my memory. "I am the cousin from Carthage. And you are?"

"Ingoberga, seamstress to Brunhilde and her daughters. I have a wagon waiting. Would you like to ride to the palace with me?"

This time, I didn't hesitate. "Yes." I remembered from my research that Sigibert had built a new palace near the church of St. Stephen on the Île de la Cité shortly after his brother Charibert died and he had inherited Lutetia, as Paris was known at the time. No one in the twenty-first century knew what this building had looked like, and I would get to see it. Or at least imagine it in this dream. "I will gather my belongings and come with you."

The woman nodded and turned back to Elise. I threaded my way through the ancient merchandise to retrieve my things, but I couldn't find the closet door. The wall where I thought the door had been was now covered with heavy hooks, weighted down with thick coils of chain and rope. I panicked. What would I do without money? Without my briefcase?

Money? I slapped myself on the forehead, momentarily distracted by the realization that my bangs had disappeared. I felt the top of my head. My hair was piled up in a huge knot, secured with a tangle of ribbons. I looked around for a mirror.

Silly! I admonished myself. Mirrors hadn't been developed yet in sixth century Gaul. The best I could possibly find would be a polished slab of pewter, and none hung on the walls.

Sillier yet? Thinking my U.S. dollars or my credit card, my driver's license, my cellphone, my passport — any of it — would be of any use to me here in medieval Paris. Losing my briefcase was the least of my worries. How to pull off the ruse that I was a royal cousin, familiar with Carthage, or that I was a capable escort for a young princess? That's what I needed to worry about.

I spun around and headed back to the front of the store. I didn't understand what was happening. I was no longer in control of whatever came next, I decided, so I might as well get on with it.

"I will come for my trunk later," I said, bluffing. Elise — if that was still her name — looked confused. What "trunk" was I referring to? she must have wondered.

"Meanwhile, perhaps we can find whatever you need at the palace," Ingoberga offered. "Brunhilde has far more frocks than she will ever wear."


WALKING OUT ONTO THE STEAMY street with Ingoberga was no less shocking than stepping out of that closet had been. I would have been frantic if I hadn't been reveling in the notion that this experience was much richer than any sane person could imagine. It may have been a dream, but it was certainly as useful as a few afternoons sitting in the Sorbonne libraries.

"So, this is Lutetia," I said to myself. It wasn't anything like the Paris I had just left less than an hour before — or what I thought was Paris just an hour ago. I chuckled to myself, remembering what Justin had said: How would visiting modern-day Paris help me figure out what it looked like in 570?

If he only knew!

I hadn't known how rough Lutetia would be. San Francisco in the Gold Rush days had nothing on Paris in the sixth century. Horses and donkeys pulled carts and wagons in no organized fashion down the muddy street. The teamsters yelled and shouted for the right of way as their animals and loads nearly ran headlong into each other. Wagons swayed wildly over the ruts in the street and scraped against those going the other way. They rumbled past us, splashing up the muddy sewage that ran down the middle of the road.

Vendors with loaded push carts called out to the passing pedestrians and riders as they wove through the mud and traffic. Vegetables? Meat? Whores? I had no idea what they were selling; the words were not ones I recognized. In the hot, humid air, flies swarmed above and behind their carts, and I was reminded how dangerous simply eating would be in a time with no antibiotics and no germ theory of disease. Fat rats ran across the road and down the gutters, and I remembered how frequently plagues had swept across the continent, iteration after iteration.

As we stood on a narrow, leaning boardwalk next to the shop, men stepped around us, out into the street, most of them dressed more shabbily than the people I had seen in homeless camps in Minneapolis. But there were others, too, dressed as merchants or businessmen, who weren't willing to cede their line. They bumped into us as if we were invisible.

I was sweating profusely as I inhaled staccato breaths, absorbing the scene. Eighteen centuries. This is what Paris looked like eighteen centuries ago! Or what it looked like "now"—the "now" I was "now" living. I must have looked pale; perhaps I swayed a bit with dizziness and from the sideswipes of passersby. Ingoberga put her hand on my shoulder and pulled me back, closer to the building.

"Lutetia is bigger than Carthage?" she asked, her face sympathetic. "Busier?"

"Oh, yes," I stammered. But I had no idea. In all the time I had studied the history of Gaul, the barbarian invasions, and the

Merovingian dynasty, I had not thought much about North Africa. That was a problem with academia. Before long, you knew only a tiny slice about anything, whether you studied bugs or string theory or feminist history.

Down the slope of the city in front of us, I could see the old Grand Pont, the original bridge built by the Parisii and later improved by the Romans, where the modern-day Pont au Change would later stand, leading over the Seine onto the Île de la Cité. And looking over low, wood buildings down the street that would eventually become the Boulevard Saint Germain, I spied the large limestone building that centuries before had contained the Roman baths, and just an hour ago in my life, housed their ruins. Most of the huge blocks of the structure were intact, despite as many as five centuries of brutal Gothic and Vandal raids and frequent conflagrations.

Too bad the Roman paving stones hadn't lasted as long, I thought, as another filthy, haggard donkey pulled a cart close enough to scrape the edges of the boardwalk, rocking the cart and eliciting what I assumed were swear words from those streaming past us.

I knew that some ten thousand people inhabited Paris in the sixth century, but I didn't expect so many of them to crowd onto this one street on the Left Bank at the same time. And then I remembered: Sixth-century Lutetia, despite its robust population, occupied only a tiny portion of the geography Paris would in the twenty-first century. Limited by marshes on one side and farmland on the other, its streets were narrow, and its small houses were scrunched up against and atop of one another. In Sigibert's day, it was a busy crossroad for trade and for the armies that marched in and out at his command and the armies his brother Chilperic sent to harass him.

I stepped back as far as I could to avoid a heavy, swaying wagon-load of passengers as Ingoberga bravely stepped out to wave to the driver of her wagon. Negotiating his way to the boardwalk where we were standing, the man tied the reins to his seat, hopped down, and opened a gate of sorts on the side of the wagon. He offered his arm to Ingoberga, but she swept her hand to invite me to enter first. I accepted the proffered forearm, climbed in, and sat down hard on the wooden seat. Ingoberga followed and the driver closed the gate.

A canvas tarp over the top muffled the street noise, blocked out some of the stench, and shut out most of the light, if not the heat. Even inside the wagon tent, I sensed the narrowness of the streets and the closeness of humanity. I had trouble breathing. I sat back and fought the urge to pull the canvas back enough to peek out, but I worried that my curiosity might seem strange to a woman accustomed to this world.

"Tell me how it is to cross the big sea," Ingoberga said as she settled into the seat across from me with her packages. "Do you see monsters? What is the ship like? How long does it take?"

I knew none of those things either. To cover my ignorance and avoid further questions I chose my answer carefully. "It was exhausting," I said, lowering my voice to a near whisper, as if it would serve as proof, still surprised at my near fluency in Old German. "I haven't had a decent sleep since I left. Do you mind if I look out? This is my first visit to Lutetia, and I guess I won't be here long."

Ingoberga looked at me with a half-smile. "You realize that Ingund knows nothing about her engagement, don't you?"

"Oh, yes!" I lied again. "I will say nothing about it. When will the queen tell her?"

"It could be soon, but the girl must be curious about why we are preparing such a large trousseau for her. Or why you are coming. Of course, we have many guests all the time. And maybe she knows more than I think. The palace halls are full of gossip."

I was relieved that her language was coming back to me so quickly. Even though I didn't catch all the words Ingoberga spoke, I could make out enough. I figured a few days of near muteness, using my "exhaustion" as an excuse, would enable me to pick up even more. That was if I stayed here and didn't slip forward to the twenty-first century, just as unexpectedly as I had slipped back to this one.

What she'd told me so far, helped me put a date on my time travel. Sigibert was still alive if Brunhilde and Ingund were still in the palace, and he and Brunhilde had held the capital for only a handful of years. Therefore, I was in Lutetia sometime between 570 and 575. But I still didn't know how I got here or how I would get back. I kept telling myself, "Go with the flow," and reasoned that even if I was dreaming, I should make the most of this imagined scene. What I was dreaming might not have been accurate, but it certainly was evocative.

Taking a deep breath despite the putrid air, I sat back and tried to enjoy the experience. I marveled at the generative ability of my sub-conscience. When I had been sitting at my desk, I hadn't come up with any of these images. I hadn't seen the crowd of horses and wagons or the dirty pedestrians or the mud and or the sewage running down the middle of the streets. I hadn't felt the humid air or smelled the stench of an early medieval town. Where did this sensory overload come from? Had I known it all this time, and just had never let it flow to the surface? Was it simply the trip to Paris and the Cluny that had conjured it up for me?

I pulled the tent flap aside just enough to watch as the wagon bounced over the Grand Pont onto the *Île de la Cité*. I knew the Seine would be badly polluted by the raw sewage and waste of the city, but I hadn't expected it to look and smell as wretched as it did. A city full of rotten eggs would be pleasant in comparison.

I wondered if my contemporary American environmentalists knew how long ago the world had lost its swimmable, fishable rivers.

As we rolled through the seven-foot-high stone ramparts that guarded the banks of the Île onto the better streets of the island, I considered what I had gotten myself into by climbing into this carriage. Depending on how long I stayed, I might have to accompany a spoiled, naïve young woman on a weeks-long journey through dangerous territories infested with highway men and warring Merovingian cousins to reach her betrothed in Iberia. And what if the real cousin from Carthage showed up before we left? How would I squirm out of that?

I imagined that as an escort, I would be expected to know more about survival and customs in these times than I did. What did I know? Just what I had read in books and academic journals. And the authors generally relayed nothing except what they read in the chronicles written by kings and bishops and army commanders—nothing about how women dressed, what people ate, how governesses behaved around royalty like Ingund, let alone around kings and queens. I started to suspect I was about to make a shitload of mistakes. I hoped at least I wouldn't end up like many of Brunhilde's slaves and servants did: broken on the wheel or burned at the stake. Even if it were only in a dream.

# IV

We pulled onto a wide cobble-paved yard and stopped in front of an impressive stone building, the first substantial structure I'd seen that didn't look like it would burn down in minutes if a lantern fell from a wagon. Here, the shadows of the narrow streets receded, and the sun reached the ground. It was easier to breathe again.

Ingoberga motioned for me to get out of the wagon first, and as the gate opened, I stepped cautiously on the running board. I felt a warm hand cup my elbow. I glanced up into the eyes of a tall palace guard. He gazed past me as if looking at my face were a serious offense. Given the improbability that he would notice my curiosity, I looked him up and down as I dropped down onto the pavers. He had the shoulder-length hair and full beard I expected from Merovingian men, but his dark, simple uniform was clean and pressed like no clothing I'd seen in Lutetia up to then. I guessed his job didn't entail much mucking around on the streets of the Left Bank. I smiled broadly, and I saw his eyes dart to mine and away again. I caught a sly smile that lasted a split second before his face turned to stone again.

The palace before us was ornate compared with the buildings

we'd passed so far, but it was nothing like France's more famous late medieval and early Renaissance palaces like at Versailles. The low-pitched tile roof was crowned with a small octagonal turret with windows on each side. Arched windows, crisscrossed with iron mullions and fitted with small panes of precious glass, punctuated the flat, two-story façade. Angels and ersatz columns were carved into the frame around the large, copper-plated door. Stamped into the verdigris were scenes of battles, more angels, and crowned figures of kings and queens.

A tiny, hunchbacked woman had run out to gather Ingoberga's bundles. As I followed Ingoberga into the palace, I glanced back, hoping that the good-looking guard's eyes were following me. His back was turned toward us, though, and he spoke in hushed tones with the driver who was still settled on his high seat. Only one of us had been impressed with the look of the other.

A doorman opened the wide door for us, and we stepped inside. "Wait here," Ingoberga said, "and I will send someone to show you your room. I'll be up shortly with some dresses you can try on. Brunhilde will never miss them!"

As she disappeared down a dark hallway to the right, I wondered if that were true. Little had been written about Brunhilde except for the evil deeds she and her fiercest enemy and sister-in-law, Fredegund, had committed in their quests for power and the supremacy of their sons. How could I be sure that she wasn't as protective of her wardrobe as she was of her son, young Childebert? But I had no choice. All I had at that moment was the clothes on my back, as the cliché would have it. But in this case, it wasn't just a cliché. It was true. Ingoberga was taking a bigger risk than I was. She could end up on the wheel or at the stake, whereas I probably wouldn't. Not as a cousin. As long as they believed I was a cousin.

I didn't dare leave the wide foyer for fear of getting lost or stepping into a forbidden place, so I stayed put and looked around. In a large arch above the carved wooden doors in front of me, a tesserae mosaic portrayed a parade of saints in plain linen robes carrying gifts to a seated king. Gaudy battle scenes painted on walls to the left and right of the arched mosaic were each topped with a floating figure carrying a cross draped with a bloodied cloth. I made a mental note to spend more time with medieval art when – if – I returned to twenty-first century Minnesota. I had spent too much time studying queens and kings and philosophy and religion and not enough time with architecture and art. No wonder I had trouble creating vivid scenes for Ingund in my novel. She was much more likely to see these paintings and mosaics than to witness first-hand her father's or uncles' bloody battles.

I looked up at the arched ceiling, which was covered with a star-studded mosaic that filled the space between the thick wooden moldings at the top of the walls. Rubbing my stiffening neck, I lowered my gaze to study the large portraits of Brunhilde and Sigibert – or so I assumed – that were tethered by wires to the moldings on either side of the foyer. No contemporary images of Brunhilde or Sigibert had survived into modern times. Even if I didn't eventually meet the king and queen themselves, I now had a better idea of what they looked like. Of course, I didn't know if they were as beautiful as they were depicted in the paintings. Surely an artist would make them attractive. If the king and queen weren't happy with their images, even a royal artist might be executed for the insult.

Sigibert, in particular, looked like a maternal twin of the guard who had helped me down from the carriage. His long aquiline nose may have been exaggerated in the portrait since such a proboscis was considered a sign of an aristocratic nature at the time. His long hair flowed to his shoulders beneath a heavy, bejeweled and many-pointed crown like those I had seen at the Cluny, and a thick beard covered the bottom half of his face. His dark blue robes bore star patterns and crosses, and a scepter leaned against his shoulder. He looked more holy than fierce.

Brunhilde was depicted with a similarly long nose, which undoubtedly was a Frankish affectation, as she was a Visigoth by birth. Her face didn't look anything like others I had seen depicted of

Visigothic royalty, including Queen Goswintha, her mother and In-gund's grandmother. Of course, I had no way to know if those por-traits of the Visigoths, too, hadn't been painted to serve some Fran-cophile concept of beauty. Brunhilde's hair, ears, and neck were covered with a cloth that draped down from the small crown on her head. She wore a robe of dark burgundy trimmed with a wide strip of woven gold over a plain dark green shift, belted at the waist with a golden braid. She looked saintly.

Again, I was amazed at the detail this dream had produced. Granted, I had studied the Middle Ages long enough to have a con-cept of what a Merovingian palace might look like, but the picture I was getting was so complete and so profound, I was impressed with my own memory. I must have read about all of this at some point and had forgotten it. What a gift to remember it, if only while asleep! How much of it would I retain when I woke up?

I jumped at the sound of footsteps echoing down the dark hall-way to the left. I felt my throat tighten as I feared I might face the first test of my veracity. What if someone – maybe Brunhilde herself – asked me how her dear Aunt So-and-so was doing with her gout? What if my light blue eyes and red hair gave me away? I was of Irish descent, not French. Not Visigoth. Not even German.

Worse, what would happen if the real cousin showed up and ratted me out? All I could hope for was that severe weather over the Mediterranean might delay her until I figured out how to get back home or wake up.

I stood with the most regal posture I could imitate and met the eyes of an approaching child. She looked ten, maybe older. I wasn't sure how fast children matured in a world without modern nutrition or meat spiked with growth hormones. Or, given their expected lifespans, how fast they had to grow up. She wore a floor-length simple linen shift under a wool vest not unlike the one I was wearing.

She walked into the foyer and stopped.

"You are the cousin I was told would come," she said in vulgar

Latin, looking up at me without a hint of shyness. "What manner of hair is that? Does the sun of Carthage take the color from your skin? Why are you so old? I thought you would be younger, more like me." She walked around me, looking me over with an air of superiority that seemed inappropriate in one so small and young. "Why did you come here? Why would you leave sunny Carthage for these clouds?" She gestured toward the door and emitted a tiny snort.

I smiled at her impudence, her non-stop questions. If this was Ingund, as I guessed, she was not the shy, restrained princess I had imagined in my novel. Perhaps spoiled, but hardly repressed.

Before I had to answer her rapid-fire questions with my more formal, but long-neglected Latin, an aproned woman with a scarf wrapped around her head rushed down the opposite hall. She bowed slightly and motioned, wordlessly, for me to follow her. I turned to nod to the girl, but she was already running back the way she came.

I followed the slave or servant, whoever and whatever she was, down the dark hallway to a narrow stairwell and climbed after her to a well-lit corridor on the second floor. She opened a tall wood door and stood aside for me to enter. Several cots lined the walls between the mullioned windows in the large room, and a small table and a chest were pushed up against the wall next to the door. Ingoberga stood over a pile of dresses scattered on one of the low, narrow beds. She lifted one up to inspect it and sniffed the underside of the sleeve.

"I think these will do," she said, turning to me. "It has been some time since Brunhilde wore any of them, and even if you see her, she won't remember them."

I wondered why Ingoberga was so willing to help me and risk Brunhilde's wrath. From what I had read about the queen's hot temper, a "challenge" was probably too mild a way to describe anything done in her service. Maybe Ingoberga was eager to get Ingund betrothed and out of her hair. If the girl was as strong-willed as I already sensed, she might have been as hard to please as Brunhilde.

"You can wear your own dress if you sup with the queen tonight," she said. "But slip it off, and I'll brush it while you rest a while."

I didn't want to take off the gown in front of her because I was unsure of what undergarments I might be wearing. I didn't want to shock her with my modern bra and bikini panties. But it would be foolish to lie down on my cot with the mud and sewage of the street still clinging to my hem. I stood, uncertain of what to do.

"Hurry now," she admonished me. "I must get down to the sewing room and show my girls what we will do with my purchase today before they put it to the wrong purpose."

I turned my back, pulled off the vest, and untied the belt. She reached up behind me and unhooked the dress. It fell to the floor, and I was relieved to see I was still well covered with a simple full-length linen slip. I now remembered putting it on in the closet in the store, and I was grateful for its coverage. I dove for the cot and quickly slipped under a blanket without turning around. Ingoberga gathered up my soiled dress and slipped out of the door without another word.

I lay there thinking about what I knew about these people's futures — things they had no way of knowing. Ingund and her sister would suffer long separations from their parents, whose warring and raiding took them away from Lutetia for months. And then Ingund would be sent with no one but servants to accompany her to Iberia. And after that, so much tragedy to come.

# V

Given the circumstances I found myself in and my already dreamlike state, I surprised myself by falling asleep. Perhaps it was the heat, perhaps exhaustion. But I awoke some time later to a knock on the door. I looked around and realized I was still in a time-slip. Before I could pull any Old German out of my foggy brain, a woman entered with a pitcher and bowl and a small square of fabric I took to serve as both a towel and washcloth. She bowed slightly and backed out of the door, nearly running into the girl I had met earlier in the foyer.

"Cousin," the young girl said, slipping past the maid and sitting down on the edge of my cot. I was taken aback by such familiarity. "I should tell you I am Ingund, first child of Queen Brunhilde and your cousin, King Sigibert. I am sorry I was so rude to you earlier."

"I am pleased to meet you," I said, not knowing if that was what I should say to a royal daughter or if my Latin would pass muster. But I was probably going to make so many mistakes before I got out of there; I couldn't worry about it.

She leaned over and placed a small kiss on my cheek. This was a different child than the one I met in the foyer—more vulnerable, softer. "I'm sorry I called you old before," she said, bowing her head apologetically. "I know why they sent for you, although they act like I don't know."

I tried to shake the cobwebs out of my brain. I could barely follow what she was saying, let alone form my own Latin sentences. It would be easier to talk in Old German, as I had with Ingoberga, so I did.

"Why do you think they sent for me?" I asked. Ingoberga had told me the answer, but I wanted to know what Ingund knew.

"I will be betrothed soon," she said. Her Old German was as fluid as her Latin. She lay back across my legs and stared up at the ceiling. It seemed like such a grown-up move — exhibiting a pensiveness, a weariness that I wouldn't expect to find in a pre-teen in my day.

"How old are you?" I asked gently.

"Ten." She folded her hands over her waist and sighed. "I am the oldest. Chlosinda is seven and Childebert is two. I suppose once I am married, you will escort Chloe next. She is an easier child than I."

Such self-knowledge. At ten. No wonder medieval parents married their daughters at such an early age. Perhaps this was the answer to my earlier question: amidst the hazards and conditions of the era, children did grow up faster.

I thought about the body image I had when I was her age. Marry before menses? Marry when breasts were only buds and pubic hair unsprouted? I would have been frightened to death of sex, of intimacy. And ignorant of pregnancy.

I reached down and put my hand on her shoulder. She turned her head toward me. "Where will they send me?" she asked.

"You don't know?"

"The only reason I know I will be married is because I'm ten and because you have come here. And the gossip in the slave quarters."

"You go there? To the slave quarters?"

"I have friends there, but my mother doesn't know." She rolled over on her side and smiled at me. "You won't tell her, will you?"

Once again, I was hit by the realization of the danger I was in. I didn't want to disappoint this sweet, young girl, but I didn't want to end up on the rack, either. The more Ingund took me into her confidence, the better my novel would turn out to be. But the more I withheld from her mother, the greater the punishments I might face at the hands of one of the most notorious dark queens of all time. The choice seemed simple.

Until I saw the tears in Ingund's eyes.

INGUND LEFT AFTER A TIME. I assured her that I would keep her secrets, unless I felt that she was in danger. She pouted for a minute about my qualification and then kissed me on the cheek again. When she left, she had reclaimed the bounce in her step that I saw in the hallway earlier.

I was summoned to dinner by another servant or slave who helped me dress in one of the fine costumes left by Ingoberga, who had not returned my dress. As I followed her down the stairs and through the palace, I considered whether there was much difference between servant and slave. A female servant might ostensibly be able to quit working, might marry without permission, and might earn and save money—all things unlikely for a slave. But both were at the mercy of their master's demands all the time. Of course, sometimes that worked out fine. It had for Fredegund, who was Ingund's aunt and Brunhilde's archenemy. She had ascended from a handmaid to be Chilperic's wife after killing his first wife, Brunhilde's sister.

The dining hall looked like it could accommodate about four dozen guests. Long cushioned benches ran along the walls and large, rough tables sat in the center of the room. I had forgotten that most early medieval nobility and royalty consumed their meals while half-reclined on the benches, even though the lower classes ate standing up or sitting on stools at tables.

I didn't know how I'd fare eating on a bench, especially since forks hadn't been invented yet. Luckily, the meal comprised a simple porridge and a slab of bread big enough to make me bloat. The porridge lacked salt and spice, but a fine sheen of grease floated on the top, indicating that some meat or meat juice had contributed to its preparation.

Ingoberga had been wrong. Only Ingund and Chlosinda dined with me in the big hall. I was relieved. As much as I wanted to meet Brunhilde, I wasn't ready. I didn't want to face her until I had a good night's sleep and got accustomed to the culture. Cowardly, I was hoping all our encounters would be at a distance. Most historians would kill for a chance to be among these characters and ask them questions, even if they might worry that their interactions could change history and their world back home.

Chlosinda was her sister's opposite: shy and seemingly uninterested in who I was or where I came from. She ate her gruel with her head down and when she was finished, she curtsied clumsily and fled the room.

"Is she not accustomed to guests?" I asked Ingund as her sister disappeared.

"Oh, we eat with the maids and servants mostly," Ingund said. "But I wanted her to meet you, so when I am gone, she'll be familiar with you. Do you know how soon I will have to marry?"

"Do you want to marry soon?" I asked, taking the safe path of answering her question with a question.

"Not really. I am a little afraid. What if my husband is mean to me? What if he decides to kill me so he can marry another?"

That made me wonder if she knew Fredegund had murdered Brunhilde's sister, Galswintha, to marry Chilperic. After that, Brunilde and Fredegund would plot each other's demise over and over, always unsuccessfully, and their armies fought until Fredegund died and her feud with Brunhilde passed down to Fredegund's sons, grandsons, and great grandsons.

"Is your father in the palace?" I asked.

"He is fighting. That is what kings do. They fight."

"Yes, it seems so," I agreed. "Is he with Guntram Boso?"

"I do not learn of all the battles, there are so many," Ingund said with another precociously mature sigh.

I knew if her father was now allied with Boso, he would soon defeat Chilperic near Tournai. Immediately after that, Sigibert would be murdered by the most clichéd of weapons – a poisoned dagger – and Chilperic would take over Paris. Brunhilde would smuggle Ingund's baby brother out of Paris and send Ingund and her sister to Austrasia. Chilperic would catch the girls and imprison them and Ingund's betrothal would be delayed.

I shivered, wondering what would happen to me if I were still there when all of this occurred. I couldn't share any of my knowledge with Ingund. If I were time-traveling and not just dreaming, I worried about the impact my meddling in the sixth century would have on the course of history. If I did anything proactive, would I wipe out entire future generations, including my own family?

Ingund's governess came to retrieve her, and I was left to find my own way back to my room. I'd put off the call of nature as long as I could, and if I weren't magically whisked back into the twenty-first century in the next few minutes, I had to find a toilet soon. Even in a place this lavish, interior latrines were unlikely, so I went in search of a door that would open to the back of the palace. I walked down a long corridor and glanced through an open door to a kitchen with tiled walls and floors, a huge oven and cook top and a copper sink that was big enough to accommodate a hand pump. A fat man in a filthy apron looked up from the table where he was kneading bread and frowned. I scooted on down the hall, turned a corner, and saw what I was looking for. I pushed the brass latch, and the door flew open, startling a guard sitting on a bench outside. From the look on his face, I guessed I had awakened him.

Just beyond, a long, low building with a door on one end sat at the bottom of a small decline. It made sense that the latrine would be below the palace. Who wanted the waste to flow toward their house? I pointed ahead to where I was going, but the guard's distant, stoic gaze made it clear he didn't care to know my destination. I walked down and waited for someone come to out—man or woman. No one did.

I entered and thanked my luck; it was unoccupied. The ceiling was open to the sky – the better to air out the stench, I supposed. A tiled bench along the long wall had five holes, each about two feet apart. I didn't expect toilet paper but wondered for the first time in my life about its origins. A neat stack of rags sat on a small square platform in one corner, and a basket underneath held a crumpled mass of them that I left uninspected. I grabbed a clean piece and quickly squatted to do my business. I tossed my rag into the basket and wondered whose job it was to gather and wash them. I had never been so thankful for toilet paper; if I ever got home, I wouldn't take it for granted any more.

Too exhausted to investigate more of the palace, like I should have, I followed the hallway back to the front foyer and found the stairs to my bedroom. Three of the other cots were already occupied, and I tiptoed in. A soft snore rose from one of the beds, but curious eyes stared at me from the other two. I stripped off the dress, laid it across the foot of my cot, and climbed under the covers in my slip.

And then it occurred to me that if this was a dream, I might have just wet my bed. I felt under my bum; it was dry. If I had somehow peed in my sleep, I'd have to deal with it in the morning.

# VI

Nicole's first thought when she awoke was how much more comfortable the bed was than it had been the night before. She opened her eyes and knew why. She was back in the twenty-first century hotel room in the middle of modern-day Paris where she'd been before leaving for the Cluny Museum—whenever that was. A brief wave of disappointment quickly yielded to relief. Elation, even. As interesting as her dream had been, it was so much easier to be back in reality, in real time. She didn't have to worry about ending up on a rack at Brunhilde's command.

She tried to recall falling into this bed, but she had no such memory. And that dream she had! How strange! How real! How helpful! She now had details, right or wrong, to fill out the Paris chapter of Ingund's story.

Still, wouldn't it have been more helpful if she could have stayed in the dream long enough to have taken the trip to Toledo with the marriage-bound Ingund? But that would have taken five years. No one can dream about five years in one night.

Stretching her arms over her head, she sat upright and surveyed her room. There was her briefcase. Her shoes. Her cellphone, plugged into the outlet with the European connector she purchased in the airport in Paris. Apparently, she made it back with her belongings from that costume shop. But eighteen hours between the dressing room at the shop and waking up in her hotel room in 2023 had vanished.

She swung her feet out from under the covers and stepped into her fuzzy slippers. Justin had laughed when he saw her put them in her suitcase, but they were just what she needed after a vivid, disorienting, dream-filled night. Comfort. Ease. A touch of home.

Nicole looked into the full-length mirror on the wall across from the bathroom. Yes, she still had bangs, not the aristocratic up-do she'd worn in her dream, but now she wondered if she shouldn't change her style. Wouldn't it be more appropriate for a woman teaching medieval history? She pulled her shoulder-length hair up in the back and swept her bangs off her forehead, glancing left and right to assess the look.

Wrapped in a big hotel bathrobe after a quick shower, Nicole opened the closet, hoping that even if she didn't remember doing it, she had hung up the shirt, pants, and coat she had worn the day before.

Yes, there were her clothes, neatly hung on hangers as if put away by a fully conscious, fastidious dresser. But hanging next to them was an exact replica of the clothing she wore in her dream: the silk dress and the dark blue vest. Just like the costume she'd tried on at the shop.

Were they hanging there yesterday? She didn't think so. She must have bought them at the shop. Nicole looked for a price tag on the sleeve of the long dress. Could she take it back?

She couldn't find a tag on the dress or a receipt for it in her briefcase. She pulled a plastic dry-cleaning bag off the closet shelf and carefully folded the dress into it. The dress shop would take it back. She could explain. She had been exhausted, so exhausted that she didn't remember buying it. Or leaving the shop. Or walking back to the hotel. … Any of it.

Except the dream. She remembered all of that.

STOPPING AT THE HOTEL FRONT desk and addressing the clerk with a pleasant "bonjour," Nicole asked in French if she could see the manager. He wasn't at work yet, the attendant said in English. "What is the problem? Perhaps I can help."

Nicole proffered the bag and pulled out a corner of the vest. "I found this vest and dress in my closet," she said. "Do they belong to the hotel?"

"I assure you they do not." The attendant looked amused but not surprised, as if tourists found such vintage costumes all the time.

"Perhaps it belongs to the woman in the room before me?" She tried again to speak in French.

"That is possible," the attendant said, in English, flashing a conspiratorial smile. He winked. "But I promise not to tell your husband."

"What?"

"Whatever you wish to buy in Paris is our secret," he whispered. "I hope you find just the right party for it back in —" he looked down at the register on the desk " – in Minnesota, if I'm correct?"

Stuffing the vest back in the bag, Nicole swallowed her retort and thanked him.

Outside, the streets were already crowded with buses, taxis, and bicycles, but the sidewalk was only comfortably populated – enough to make Nicole remember how much she loved walking through big cities like New York. But unlike in New York, where she had spent a summer as an intern at Smithsonian Magazine, here none of the patrons who sat over tiny espresso cups and croissants at little metal café tables on the sidewalk seemed to be in a hurry.

Why was she in a hurry? Her flight home was not for another day, and all she had to do was return the dress, check out a library at the Sorbonne for a future visit, and do a bit more wandering at the Cluny. Nicole stopped abruptly in front of an attractive patisserie, causing a young man on a skateboard behind her to swerve off the curb and hop back up again, never breaking his pace. He flung his hand out behind him as he sped up and demonstrated the impressive length of his middle finger. She imagined him muttering a French version of "fucking Americans" to himself. She guessed she probably deserved it.

Eyeing an empty table near the patisserie's entrance, she drew her bag close, shimmied through the crowd, and sat down with a contented sigh. This is what it meant to live in a civilized city. It wasn't that St. George was uncivilized. There were sidewalk cafés even there now. The pandemic had engendered a proliferation of them as alternatives to scary indoor dining a couple of years ago, and the students had quickly come to adopt them, even in the winter.

The difference was the pace of life. Every French citizen certainly didn't embrace *joie de vivre* and a laid-back insouciance twenty-four hours a day. But, here, it didn't feel like everything, every moment had to be about commerce, about getting things done, about success. Here it could be talking with friends, even at 10 in the morning, at which time her colleagues in Minnesota would already be in the office or in the classroom, and her friends would be at their desks, swearing under their breath about bosses who were asking too much and paying too little.

The espresso and a croissant she ordered were as much about fitting into the scene as satisfying hunger. She sipped the dark, bitter coffee and pulled off bite-sized chunks of the pastry, chewing very slowly, savoring the buttery flakes. For the first time since getting out of bed, Nicole let herself think over the dream she'd had the night before.

The odd thing about it was that she could remember it all. Usually, she remembered only random snippets of her dreams, or vague notions about them, and those tended to evaporate soon after she woke up. This memory was more vivid and long. It felt real. Was it the dress that had stimulated such an experience?

Pulling out her notebook and balancing it on the edge of her tiny bistro table, she jotted down some details. The filthy and crowded streets. A man limping down the cobbled alley hauling a heavy bag of grain over his shoulder. Brunhilde and Sigibert's portraits. The seamstress's bad teeth. The dinner, the palace, the latrine.

And how young Ingund looked, and how tiny her feet! Nicole had known that the girl was only thirteen when she was betrothed to Hermenegild and fifteen when she married, but she hadn't known that a sixth-century ten-year-old would look so much like a modern-day preteen. She reached in her bag for her copy of *La Tragedia de San Hermenegildo*, a sixteenth-century Jesuit play about Ingund's husband Hermenegild, to review how the Spaniards described "Ingunda." She ordered a second espresso and sat back, contentedly. It was a relief to read Spanish, the first language she studied, starting in high school. It was much easier than French or Old German.

Old German! She had understood and spoke it so well in her dream. Did she really remember that much of it? Had she learned it that well back at Iowa?

Glancing up from her book and notes, she spied a man across the patio who was watching her over his newspaper. He lowered the pages and smiled. He seemed familiar, and it took a moment before she recognized the face of the guard who had helped her down from the wagon at the palace. But without the beard.

Well, she admonished herself, turning away from his gaze. They're all Franks. Didn't Sigibert look like him, too, at least in his portrait in the foyer? It was highly likely that every day she would see someone in Paris who would resemble him. When she worked up the nerve to look back, he was gone. So was his newspaper. In fact, there was no evidence he'd even been there: no empty mug, no dirty plate or napkin.

She snickered at her runaway imagination. Maybe Paris was a magical place, but more likely she was overreacting to the exotic stimuli of a great city.

# VII

Well, that is strange," Elise said when Nicole opened the bag and drew out the vest and dress on the counter at the costume shop. "Yes, we have these things. You tried them on yesterday, but they're still here. Come. I'll show you."

"Where do you think this one came from, then?" Nicole threw up her hands.

"I have no idea. Let's go and look at ours again." Elise led her back to the same area where they had gone the day before, and where an identical dress and vest hung on the mannequin. "We thought we had a one-of-a-kind item. Very old. Unique."

Elise was right. The dress hung elegantly on the slim mannequin. Nicole held her dress up next to it. It looked like a perfect duplicate.

"Well, I wish I could explain this," she said, shaking her head. She looked at Elise. The clerk's lips were curled with amusement.

"I don't understand it either," said Elise. "Bonne chance, peut-être? Mais, clearly you now own a vintage medieval reproduction. What will you do with it?"

"Take it back with me and show Justin, I suppose," Nicole answered, unsure.

"And who is Justin?" Elise asked, looking amused by the incident.

"Justin is my fiancé."

"You do not smile when you say that," Elise said. She paused and tipped her head thoughtfully. A sly smile spread across her face. "It is not my business. But perhaps you should stay here in Paris. You must have more research to do."

Nicole chuckled at the clerk's witty empathy. She felt the urge to share her dream with Elise. Perhaps the clerk had known other people to be inspired by the old items in her store. But she pushed the temptation aside.

"Thank you," Nicole said. "I'd love to stay longer. But I have classes to teach in two days. I will come back, perhaps between semesters."

"Oh, you must," Elise said, leading Nicole back to the front of the store. "And you must stop to see me again. Perhaps we can find more items that will help you write your story."


NICOLE HAD A GUT FEELING that her relationship with Justin would only get worse when she got back. Maybe it was less a prediction than the accumulation of evidence over time.

Her middle seat in the back of the plane was too uncomfortable for sleep. She'd never slept well on airplanes anyway, and now her anxiety about her return was layered on top of exhaustion from the trip. Getting away and being on her own in Paris had been liberating, not to mention interesting, and coming back to Justin's constant pressure to set a wedding date was going to grate on her nerves.

It had been bad enough before she left. He constantly pestered her as she prepared to go to Paris. "You know, we're trying to save for the wedding. How much is this going to cost again?" he had asked as he drove her down to Minneapolis to catch her flight.

"You have asked that question about fifteen times in the past week," she said.

"Oh, no." He snarled. "It must have been a hundred times. Or two hundred. Probably I asked it a thousand times," he said. It was a common strategy of his to mock her hyperbole with a greater exaggeration. She grimaced and blamed herself for not learning to avoid it.

"Okay, but it's not the first time you brought it up. And I thought it was your suggestion that I pay for it with credit."

"Well, how much?" He persisted.

"I used some airline miles, so the flight was only $600, and I'm flying coach."

"And...?"

"Well, the rooms were expensive, so they'll probably come to about a thousand for three nights, and then meals."

"So, we're talking a couple thousand dollars," he said. "How long will that take to pay off?"

"I don't know," she said, reaching over to turn down the car heat. "I don't understand where this is going."

"It's not going anywhere." He turned the thermostat back up and frowned at her. "I just hope you've thought about it because you're not likely to have a decent salary until you finish your dissertation."

"That's exactly why I'm going," she said, her voice rising.

"You don't have to yell." He looked at her, his eyebrows knitted. He turned back to the road just in time to swerve around a two-by-four someone had lost in the middle of the freeway lane.

"Maybe you should think more about driving and less about my expenses," she retorted, immediately regretting it. He was already unhappy with her, and like most men she'd ever known, commenting on his driving pissed him off more than anything. He jerked the steering wheel back and forth a few times, swaying the car over the lines on both sides of the lane. "There is that better?"

Nicole seethed and said nothing more the rest of the drive. When she got out of the car, he stayed in the driver's seat and let her grab her suitcase from the back seat by herself.

The second reason for her trepidation about returning to St. George was the dream. She still hadn't figured it out. The vintage dress she was bringing back only complicated things. She would want to talk about it, but Justin would blow it off. A man solidly anchored in the physical world, Justin couldn't even tolerate mainstream religion, calling it "superstition," let alone things like time travel or dreamtime. She'd have to rely on Katie. Or her mother, who taught literature classes on fantasy and mythology, and regularly visited a psychic – not hard to find on the flaky side of Iowa City.

Third was sex. For a time after they'd started sleeping together, she would return from any trip longer than a day to a very horny Justin. And they were still experimenting with lovemaking up to about two months ago. Suddenly, his ardor had cooled. Now, she was lucky to keep him awake long enough to make love more than one night a week. She was afraid it was likely to stretch to once a month unless something changed.

How important was sex to holding their relationship together? She wasn't sure, but she didn't think she'd be satisfied with only once a month, at least until she was much older, and she didn't know how to turn his disinterest around. She hadn't changed her look or her dress, hadn't lost or gained weight, or made any other changes that she could blame on his flagging sex drive. So, what could she do?

And then, there was her conversation with Kevin.

Early in the flight, somewhere over the Atlantic, the man sitting in the aisle seat next to her rose and walked away. Taking advantage of the opportunity, she unbuckled her seat belt and walked up the aisle. She needed to calm down or she would arrive in Minneapolis in an exhausted snit. She turned around at the curtain that separated coach from business class, and walked back slowly, looking for familiar faces – people she might know from Minneapolis.

Her seatmate had returned, so she passed by her row and waited in the short line for the toilet. In the last row of the plane, she saw someone she recognized, Justin's golf buddy from Oklahoma

State's golf team, now a pro at the inexpensive Minneapolis golf club where Nicole and Justin belonged.

"Kevin," she said, pulling his attention from his magazine and getting a big grin despite the interruption. "I didn't know you were in Paris!"

"I wasn't," he said. "I was in Provence. Aix-en-Provence and Avalon. Scoping out golf courses for an alumni trip."

"College alumni or high school?" she asked.

"College. Hasn't Justin told you about it?"

Nicole struggled to wipe the surprise off her face. Smiling, she nodded. "Sure," she lied. "But I forgot when this was supposed to be."

"Sometime this fall. Early enough that we can plan on warm weather. Justin didn't say if you were coming along. Are you?"

"I haven't decided," she said. That wasn't a lie. She hadn't known she needed to decide. "It will depend on how my dissertation is going, I suppose."

"Oh, yes. Justin told me you were struggling to write. I guess that's why you were in Paris?"

Struggling to write? Is that how Justin saw it? Perhaps this explained his displeasure with her trip. If he thought she was struggling with writing instead of needing to do research, then he probably didn't think a research trip was going to speed her work along.

"Yup, research."

She pointed toward the opening lavatory door. "I'd better scoot in there while I've got the chance."


AT FIRST, JUSTIN PUT ON a good show. She texted him when the plane landed, and he greeted her with a hug and a quick kiss at baggage claim. He grabbed her suitcase and carried it to the car for her.

"How was Paris? Did you find what you needed?" he asked as he steered his Subaru through the parking garage and out the airport exit.

"Well, I found a great deal of information that will help, especially some details about Lutetia—that's what Paris was called back then."

"So, you won't have to go back, then?"

Nicole chuckled. "Ah, no. I only had three days. There's a lot more research I need to do." She decided not to mention her dream right away. She'd work it into the conversation slowly, and only if his interest in her research lasted long enough.

It didn't. Long before they reached St. George, he had exhausted his curiosity with sixth century France and had switched the subject to his plan to go back to Oklahoma State for the summer to help the new golf coach with the incoming freshmen recruits.

"I didn't know anything about this," she said.

"Oh, I'm sure I mentioned it a few times."

"I don't think so. And I knew nothing about your alumni trip to Southern France, either."

His head swung to face her, a puzzled frown on his face. "Where'd you hear about that?"

"Kevin was on the plane. He told me he'd been in Provence looking at courses."

"Oh, I forgot he was going there so soon," Justin said, his face flushing slightly. "Didn't I tell you about that?"

"Uh, no."

"I'm going to stop at Holiday for some beer," he said, as if the subject had been exhausted, and turned into the gas station parking lot. "I'll be right back."

"What are we having for dinner?" she asked, but he had already walked away.

# VIII

Justin was far from alone in questioning the value of her research. Her colleagues in the history department rewarded her discussion of her investigations with crooked smiles and barely concealed rolling eyes.

Just a week before she had left for Paris, as the faculty discussed the status of their research and publishing efforts, or the progress on their dissertations, Jonathan, the other PhD candidate in the department, wondered aloud if her thesis wasn't "more hysterical than historical."

The smear had come toward the end of the meeting. Nicole's face burned, but she had learned not to respond to such slurs—especially Jon's. Over the past year and a half, Nicole came to see his reproofs were born not out of disrespect, but out of competitiveness, as if when it came to academic credibility, only one of them could succeed. She would gain nothing from engaging in his battle for status. Further, arguing with anyone here wouldn't change this crew's fossilized opinions about women in history.

She thought the incident had gone without notice, but the day of her return from Paris, she was startled by a loud shout behind her in the hallway to her office.

"Nicoletta!"

Nicole stopped, squeezed her eyes closed, and took a deep breath before turning around to face the head of the history department as he ambled down the hall toward her.

"Yes, Timothy?"

Timothy. Not Tim. Never Tim.

The man insisted that the faculty address each other by their full given names inside the history building. No Tim, no Nicole. Only Timothy and Nicoletta.

The falsetto that he used when he called out bugged her more than his insistence on formality. He used that high pitch only when addressing her, the sole woman in the department.

"Nicoletta, I've been meaning to catch up with you." The squat, bald man didn't act like he was trying to catch up to anyone. He sauntered toward her in his usual way, chest out, chin high, expecting the world to wait for him and revel in his company.

Nicole forced a smile and adjusted the heavy load of student papers in her arms, surprised again by the realization that he was not bad looking despite his stature, girth, and bald head. It wasn't unusual for women to gather around him at university cocktail functions, hanging on his words and chuckling receptively at his quips. She didn't find him particularly interesting or funny herself and figured that his bright eyes, square jaw, aristocratic nose, academic status, and fine salary were bigger draws than his repartee.

"Nicoletta," he repeated, stopping a few feet away. "You should know that I didn't approve of Jonathan's comment at the faculty meeting yesterday. I have spoken to him about it."

He paused and looked at her expectantly. Did he expect her to thank him for that? If he "spoke" to her fellow associate professor about his slight, what had he said?

Timothy stood, expectantly. For a moment, Nicole considered simply nodding and walking away. But her continued employment—contract or not—depended on him. He wanted to tell her what he said to Jon.

She took a deep breath and succumbed. "And what did you say to him?"

Timothy's face wiggled like he was fighting a grin, trying to look serious. "I told him it was pretty clever, but probably not appropriate this day in age."

This day "in" age? Clichés were bad enough; messing them up was ever worse. But Nicole let that slide, too. There were bigger issues at stake.

"Was it ever appropriate for a faculty to make that kind of sexist comment about another professor's work?" she asked instead. She heard her pitch rise and blanched at her own testiness. "Look," she said, holding up a hand. "It doesn't matter. I'm not going to change minds around here anyway. I'll be gone long before attitudes …"

She stopped abruptly. This was one of her self-defeating behaviors: spouting off about Neanderthals in the department. To belittle the faculty's attitudes was to insult them, not to mention the human cousins of 40,000 years ago, and there was no upside in that.

She brushed the hair back on her forehead and started again. "No, I mean, thanks for saying something. I am grateful that you recognized the misogyny in his comment. I know you expect better of your colleagues."

"Of course!" Timothy said.

There was no "of course" about it. But at least he had recognized Jon's overt sexism. Even if this entire department's faculty needed to be slapped upside their heads, not gently reprimanded.

Dropping the papers on her desk, Nicole sank into her huge, upholstered desk chair and spun around to look out the window at the brick wall of the humanities building. The big, fat chairs her male colleagues favored didn't suit her slight frame; hers made her back spasm.

Nicole had known when she accepted the position at the University of MacIntosh Department of History in St. George, Minnesota, that her colleagues were unlikely to share her taste in desk chairs, let alone be soul mates. They were all men, to start — a rarity in academic departments these days. And Timothy Wilson's historical specialty — well over-represented at MacIntosh — was military campaigns, not the origins of the patriarchy. Without having read a word of it, the other professors had asserted at one time or another that her dissertation's argument about feminism, even though it wasn't called that, in the Middle Ages was nonsense. To them, feminist thought and desires were a modern construct. And Nicole suspected most of historians would agree with them. Once she finished her dissertation and passed her orals back at Iowa, she would look for a more suitable academic environment, but it would take some time to find a history department where her perspective on the Middle Ages would be welcome.

She had accepted the job at MacIntosh for two reasons: it was close to her mother in Iowa City, and her fiancé, Justin, got a job teaching history and coaching golf in the city's largest high school. They would move once she accepted a tenure-track position elsewhere, but she knew it could take some time to find a history department where her perspective on women in the Middle Ages would be welcome.

OVER THE NEXT TWO WEEKS, Nicole tried to make sense of Justin's prickliness at home. The easy theory would be an affair. But she started to wonder if it had something to do with her disinterest in his life. What did they really have in common anymore? He played golf. She buried her head in the sixth century.

Further, Justin in an affair was hard to imagine. Neither he nor she had ever had a serious relationship with someone else, as far as she knew. They'd been best friends from birth, and he was her first sexual partner. He had told her she was his first, too, and she believed him. And, as a high school teacher and coach, he had to be above reproach, and in a town as small as St. George, an extramarital dalliance would be both hard to hide and career suicide.

On the other hand, if he had never had sex with anyone else, perhaps he was starting to think he had missed out on something.

His friend Kevin wasn't married and, as a professional golf instructor and shameless flirt, had his pick of partners among the young women who took lessons from him. Perhaps watching Kevin enjoy himself had stimulated Justin's imagination.

The situation required a decision: was there enough of a reason, enough love, enough mutual interests to sustain a marriage? But she needed to delay it for a while. She needed to finish the dissertation, get comfortable with what had happened in Paris, see her mother when she could, and finish the semester with good evaluations that would help her land a better faculty position somewhere else. She would make Justin sit down and talk it over sometime. But not yet.

It had only been a couple of months since everything had seemed fine between them, but her visit to sixth-century Gaul—something she couldn't talk with him about—made it obvious that it would never feel right again.

Over the next week, Nicole returned his neglect with her own. She pretended to be asleep when he came home after his work on the golf course with Kevin. She quit asking about his day just as he had quit asking her about her dissertation. Even in their better moments, sitting over dinner, their cellphones put aside, when they let their conversation wander, unhurried, she felt they were both holding back, superficial discussions keeping them from being honest with each other.

It wasn't as if she wanted to break up or start swiping through a dating app to find someone else. She needed no more distractions. She wanted to work. She needed to expand the notes she'd taken about her Paris dream and write them into her novel before she forgot the details.

But the calamity that burst into her life next was even more distracting than her conflicted feelings about her engagement. It threatened everything.

# IX

Her mother arrived as planned the next Friday, looking tired, ten years older and twenty pounds lighter than she had just a couple of months before. When she showed up at Nicole's office, Nicole had to force herself not to gasp. She noticed for the first time how much her mother's hair had thinned. She had quit dying it years before, and now it was nearly white. Her pink scalp showed through the strands.

"Something's wrong, Mom. Sit down. You look exhausted. What is it?"

"Let's talk about that later," her mother said. But she did sit down, practically falling into Nicole's guest chair. "Tell me about your trip to Paris."

Her mother had asked about it on the phone, but Nicole hadn't mentioned the dream. It was too complicated for their usual twenty-minute chat. But finally, she had someone to talk to about it.

"Yeah, well, I already told you a little. But I didn't tell you about my strange experience," she started. "First, I think we could both use a cup of coffee. I'll be right back."

Nicole hurried down the hall to the faculty break room and pulled a couple of community mugs down from the cupboard. She was pouring the coffee into generous scoops of non-dairy creamer when Timothy startled her.

"Hey, just the person I need to talk to," he said. She turned around to see him standing in the doorway with an unusual frown. He usually looked happy to see her.

"What's up?" she asked, stirring the coffees and trying not to read too much into his expression. "My mom just got here. Would you like to meet her?"

"Not right now," he said. "Would you be available Monday morning for a little tête-a-tête?"

"Sure. What's on your mind?" Tête-a-tête? Timothy's specialty was American military history, not French, and he'd never shown a predilection to use foreign phrases before unless they were battle or military terms.

"Best wait. It's complicated." Timothy's expression was dour as he turned abruptly and walked away.

"Well, that was fun," Nicole muttered to herself. Now she'd have another thing to worry about, and she'd have all weekend to imagine disagreeable possibilities.

Returning to the office, Nicole set her mother's cup down and stood with her back against the window, holding hers with both hands.

"Mom, it seems like you've aged ten years since I saw you," Nicole said. "What was that? A month ago?"

"Well, thanks!" her mother scoffed. "I don't need you to tell me how old I look. I have your father to remind me of it every day."

"I'm sorry." Nicole was. She turned back and sat. She knew how much her mother's appearance meant to keeping her department heads at Iowa from dismissing her as old and irrelevant. "I imagine the drive up here is getting a little tiring. Are you feeling okay?"

"I told you I don't want to talk about it," her mother waved her hand as if to clear the subject from the room. "I came up here to find out how you're doing on your dissertation and to get away from your father for a few days."

"Is he getting worse?" Nicole kept the question vague. Who knew what bad habits her father was fine-tuning lately. Was it his quick temper? Throwing out insults like he didn't care how much they stung?

"Sure," her mother smiled wryly. "That's what he does. He just gets worse and worse. But that isn't why I'm here. Didn't I just say that?"

No, Nicole thought. Her mother had just said she wanted to get away from him. Nicole looked away. Neither of her parents were easier to get along with now than they had been when she was growing up in their house. In fact, they both seemed to be getting less patient and quicker to anger. If she wanted to get through this weekend visit without her mother storming out of the house and driving like a maniac back to Iowa, she needed to take a punch or two without complaint. And putting up with her mother was a lot easier than fending off her father's slights.

"Ah, yes. So let me tell you about Paris. You'll love this. While I was there, I had the most vivid dream about Paris in the Middle Ages. It was so vivid that I remember every detail. Usually, I forget most of a dream as soon as I wake up."

Nicole told an abbreviated version of her dream. As she expected, her mother was intrigued. She had once taught a graduate seminar called "Dream Sequences from Greek Tragedies to Modern Romances." Nicole might have taken it herself, if the English department hadn't frowned on students taking courses from their parents.

"Maybe it wasn't a dream," her mother said.

Nicole smiled into her mug. "What are you saying?"

"Maybe whatever you experienced was real. Time travel, you know."

Nicole's mother had always toyed with flaky notions of reality. Visits to the psychic, her fascination with mythical creatures from the faeries of Ireland to the Valkyries of the Norse, and her experimentation with mind-altering mushrooms all continued unabated, even as she approached retirement age.

"Mom, you don't believe that any more than I do," Nicole said, laughing. "But I'm glad you listened. I suspect Justin will suggest I see a shrink."

"He's an awful lot like your father, isn't he?"

"Maybe." Nicole didn't want their conversation to go there. "But let's go home and get supper started. I want to forget this place for the weekend. And I have just the bottle of wine that will help us do that."

THE BOTTLE OF WINE THEY shared at dinner didn't make her mother look any better. Nor did it keep Nicole from worrying about what Timothy wanted to talk with her about. Was it budget cuts? No summer session? Reducing her class hours next year? Whatever it was, his comment that "it's complicated" didn't bode well.

Justin used the excuse of her mother's visit to take a spring golf trip to Minneapolis with Kevin, which made the weekend easier, but didn't help her sleep any better. By the time she watched her mother pull out of the driveway and head back to Iowa on Sunday afternoon, she felt as old as her mother looked. Can anxiety make your joints ache? she wondered.

Even though she dreaded what Timothy had to say, Nicole found walking into the history building the next morning a relief. Finally, the mystery would be solved. Perhaps not satisfactorily. But at least finally.

"Come in, sit down, close the door," Timothy said, not looking up when she knocked on his door.

"How'd you know it was me?"

"No one else wants to talk to me on Monday mornings. The whole department comes to work on Monday with a bad hangover." Finally, Timothy looked up, and as if to prove his point, he looked like he'd come in after a night of being overserved.

Nicole wondered if the fact they had to work for Timothy had something to do with her colleagues' weekend drinking habits, but she quickly decided not. He wasn't a bad sort, if a bit stiff.

"So, what's up?" she asked, trying to set a light tone.

He set aside the paper he was reading. "Uh, well, as I said, it's complicated."

"How so?"

Timothy leaned back in his thick leather desk chair and folded his hands in his lap. It was such a predictable posture that Nicole had to stifle a giggle. She forced her mouth to stay straight.

"Uh ... uh," he stammered. "Well, apparently, you've hit a nerve with a couple of students in your women's class."

Immediately, she knew which students he was talking about. It was the two men. Most of the students in the Women in the Middle Ages class appeared engaged and interested in her lectures, but most of them were women. They often stayed after class to ask Nicole to expand on a point or two. The two men, on the other hand, never looked up from their notebooks, took copious notes as if they were gathering evidence, and quickly left the auditorium at the end of class. Evidence of what? she wondered.

"What is the problem?"

"They talked with the dean about filing a formal complaint."

"A complaint? About what?"

"I'm not sure yet, but it's not about your behavior," he said, shaking his head as if that was going to make things better. "It's about the material you are presenting in class."

Nicole sat back. "But those guys have never said anything to me in class. Or after class. Or come to my office hours. If they have a problem with what I'm teaching, they should talk to me."

"What makes you think it was the guys?"

Nicole dipped her head and looked at him through her eyebrows. "Really, Timothy. You think I couldn't figure that out?"

He didn't get it. "If they never complained to you, how do you know it was them?"

She ignored the question. "Are you going to tell me what their complaint is?"

"I don't know what it is," Timothy said, raising his hands at his sides and shrugging. "The dean said he'll meet with the ethics committee later this week to discuss it before forwarding the complaint to us."

"The ethics committee? This is going to the ethics committee before I even know what I'm accused of? Don't I get to defend myself?"

"I don't know. I've never had one of these before." He looked aggrieved, as if this were something happening to him, not to her.

Nicole steamed. What she was presenting in class wasn't earth-shattering. It wasn't that controversial. In fact, it was derivative; many other authors and academics had said it all before, including a famous University of Wisconsin historian who wrote about the origins of the patriarchy. And in today's world, it seemed that the material and the speakers that spawned the most student pushbacks were the conservative ones, not the progressive ideas. But, she supposed, the men wanted to prove a point. What the point was, she had no idea.

She looked at her feet and took a deep breath before standing up. "Well, this is ridiculous. I don't know what these guys are complaining about, and I have to give a lecture today with them sitting right there in the classroom, obsessively taking notes. Excuse me. I think I need a cigarette."

"I didn't know you smoked."

"I just started." She walked out.

# X

Nicole was tempted to go home, open a bottle of wine, and sink into an armchair to soak into self-pity. But her heart wouldn't stop pounding and she couldn't sit still. She paced nervously in her office, and when the small space felt like it was closing in on her, she took her pacing outside. Without thinking about where she was going, she found herself quoting Timothy in Katie's office in the English department.

"I can't believe this," Katie exclaimed. "What the hell?"

"You mean 'what the fuck,' don't you?" Nicole plopped down in Katie's guest chair. Her heart rate had dropped. It helped to have someone else to tell about the complaint.

"When do you find out what's going on?"

"He said next week, I think. I don't remember. It's just so stupid. Silly, even. If these guys have a problem with me, why didn't they talk to me about it?"

"Because that would defeat their purpose."

Nicole cocked her head. "What?"

"Well, if they want to make a stink about your lectures, talking to you about them won't do it. They have to go public."

"But why do they want to make a stink?"

"Oh, come on, Nicole. You know why. Your lectures offend their sense of masculine superiority. Obviously."

"Well, it's not obvious to me," Nicole argued. But even as she said it, she knew what Katie meant. It was absurd that a lecture about female desire for agency and power in the Middle Ages had anything to do with how these young men felt about themselves. Young men were too easily offended. The real snowflakes.

The two women sat for several minutes in silence. Nicole appreciated Katie's ability to let her sit and think without trying to make things better, as so many people did. Nicole needed her company. Her unconditional support. Not advice.

"Hey, you know what?" Katie said, finally breaking their silence. "We should go to the faculty-grad student party next weekend. You've been working too hard, and we haven't been out in ages."

"Yeah, I know. But it's not just work that's made me antisocial. I have a lot on my mind."

"That's even a better reason to go," Katie said. She reached across her desk and put her hand on Nicole's arm. "You just don't seem yourself these days. We'll have a chance to talk about things, like your trip to Paris. I'm very jealous, you know. And you can tell me what else has been bugging you. Before this complaint thing, that is."

"I don't know if a faculty party is the best place to have a personal conversation," Nicole said.

"Actually, have you been to one of these parties? Everyone is so busy trying to impress each other with their research findings and their brilliant new advisees, no one will pay any attention to us. Guaranteed."

No, Nicole had never attended the spring graduate student and faculty get-together. The cocktail party was supposed to give the students a chance to peddle their dissertations to potential advisors in a relaxed but still official setting. No worries about what might be seen as inappropriate student-faculty meetings over cocktails at a bar.

Katie taught in the English department as a tenured professor and had attended a half-dozen of these parties over the years. She told Nicole that she usually dragged Doug along, but he had signed up for a Marxist retreat the coming weekend, and Katie didn't seem a bit disappointed that he couldn't go with her.

As the faculty advisor for one PhD candidate and a reader for two others' dissertations, participating in oral exams and teaching a regular load of classes gave Katie little time to sit around talking. Nicole was a little surprised she could spare an evening for a party.

Nicole shook her friend's hand off her arm. "Do you really have time for a faculty party?" Nicole squinted. "Or is there some reason you need to be there?"

"Nah. Nothing that interesting. But I could use a free cocktail or two. And as I say, 'all work and no play—'"

Nicole waved her off. "Okay, if you stop with the clichés, I'll go. I really could use the break from being in my head so much."

THE PARTY ON THE TOP floor of the student union building was redolent of the milquetoast history-department parties at Iowa. Her department in Iowa City was so big, it had its own parties. MacIntosh's history faculty probably couldn't organize a six-person dinner, given how few professors there were and how little they liked each other.

Nicole saw more khaki pants and button-down shirts in the room than she'd expect to find in an L.L. Bean warehouse. Only a few men sported jackets, and the women – a distinct minority, and mostly spouses – dressed only slightly better than the men: a jersey dress here and there, a few cotton skirts paired with ankle boots, and a few outfitted exactly like their male colleagues.

As they passed through the thin gathering to the bar, Nicole spied a couple of men from the history department standing next to each other, rocking back and forth on their heels, mute, staring at their phones, apparently with nothing new to say to each other. She waved and they nodded in her direction. She hoped that would be the sum of her interaction with them for the evening.

A portable bar was set up along one wall, and by the time Nicole and Katie got to the front of the line, the room had started to fill up. Wine glasses in hand, Nicole and Katie worked their way through the gathering crowd to gain breathing space in a far corner atop a small triangular dias, giving them an unobstructed view of the assembly.

"I have a distinct feeling that absolutely nothing is going to happen here tonight that will be remembered a week from now," Nicole said. She hadn't expected much, but the mundanity of the event was still disappointing.

"Is there anything more banal than a faculty party in the upper Midwest?" Katie asked.

Rhetorical questions needn't be answered, but Nicole did anyway. "Absolutely not. But it was your idea to come."

"Yeah. At least it's free wine."

"Do they pass appetizers?"

"Yup, but I'm not sure you want them. Figs wrapped in bacon? It's like combining the world's most objectionable sweet with the world's most objectionable dead animal product."

"Maybe we can skip out early and get a pizza," Nicole suggested.

"Hmm." Katie said. Focused on something in the opposite corner of the room, she shook her head and chuckled.

"What's funny?" Nicole said, following her eyes to a gaggle of male professors. Most of them were dressed casually, khakis and button-down shirts open at the neck. All but one — the good-looking one.

"See that guy in the oh-so-cliché tweed jacket?" Katie asked.

Nicole nodded. How could she miss him? "The tall one?" Even without his well-over-six-foot frame, he would have stuck out a bit, thanks to his oh-so-bespoke-academic attire and GQ-worthy face. Nicole noted the glass of brown liquid in his hand. Tweed and Scotch. Two clichés, not just one.

"He's a physics professor. You know, boring." Katie's voice

turned up at the end of the sentence, as if it were a question. "But he's quite the womanizer. Whatever you do, steer clear."

Okay, three clichés. Handsome prof in tweed jacket, drinking Scotch, and probably scouting for his next – in the post-#MeToo era, what did they call them? Conquests? Katie's "womanizer" sounded a little archaic. But Nicole wasn't sure; she'd never spent much time on dating apps. She had no command of the lingo.

Did Katie have first-hand experience with said handsome "womanizer?" Nicole decided not to ask, because, however bad his reputation, he was just the man she needed right now.

"Name?"

"Sébastièn Daguerre. French, apparently. Or so he claims."

He looked French. A bit like the man she remembered at the Parisian street café and the guard at the palace in her dream. And the painting of Sigibert. She supposed that if she hung around France long enough, eventually she would be able to tell Frenchmen apart a bit better.

Nicole tipped her wine glass toward Katie. "Well, excuse me, but I have something I need to talk to the Frenchman about. I'll be right back."

"I thought I told you not to—" Katie's voice got lost in the buzz of the crowd. She let Nicole go alone.

Nicole wended her way through clusters of partiers, trying to look like she was just wandering around, like she didn't intend to end up on the edge of the Frenchman's circle. She stopped behind one of the men across from Sébastièn and turned as if she were looking for someone.

"Would you like to join us?" Sébastièn called out past his companions, just as she was hoping he would.

"Uh, what?" Nicole acted surprised. "I was just looking for — "

"Well, maybe you just found him," the prof grinned. A flirt at least, if not a womanizer. "Come join us. We're just gabbing like the old hens we have become."

Ouch. Hens? "Chalk one up for latent misogyny," Nicole muttered to herself as one of the men stepped back to let her join the circle.

"What's the conversation?" she asked in full voice.

"Quantum string theory," the man who'd made room for her said, a drama-worthy serious look on his face. The other men burst out laughing.

"Don't listen to him," Sébastièn said. He had no foreign accent. Maybe he was of French descent, but he wasn't an immigrant. "We're just talking about the new head of the physics department. But the topic has been exhausted. Why don't you suggest something else we can talk about? These old coots haven't had an interesting thing to say all night."

"That's my cue to go find my wife," one of the men said. As if it were understood to be a recommendation more than a cue, the other men all gestured a toast with their glasses and peeled off as well.

Nicole felt guilty. "I didn't mean to chase off all of your friends," she said. She had to look up at Sébastièn. She backed a step away.

"I really have no friends," Sébastièn quipped. "Truly, very few people can stand me. I expect you'll be repelled in just a matter of minutes."

"It's possible." Nicole liked his humor, his self-deprecation.

"Now that we're rid of my boring colleagues, let me ask you this before I find out who you are," he said. "What is your favorite topic for discussion at a party? One that gets the conversation started if you've found interesting people to talk to, but leaves you abandoned if you've ended up with my fellow physicists?"

"Interesting question," Nicole said, and she meant it. "I guess my favorite question in the whole world, all the time is: why is there something instead of nothing."

Sébastièn grinned with one side of his face. "Very nice," he said. "You are now my best friend."

"Well, since you have no other friends, I won't let it go to my head. I'm Nicole, by the way," she said, holding her hand out to shake. "An assistant professor in the history department. I'm writing my dissertation on arranged marriages in the sixth century."

He met her hand with his. "I'm Sébastièn Daguerre, boring and lonely professor of physics. But I'm guessing you knew who I was already." He nodded at Katie watching them from across the room, taking advantage of the fact his head stuck pretty much above everyone else's. So, clearly, he wasn't fooled by Nicole's nonchalant walk toward him across the room.

"Yes, and I came over here with a very different question in mind."

"I hope it isn't about why Katie despises me. If it's not, do ask," he said, reaching out to place his empty glass on a tray carried by a uniformed server. "But let's walk over to the bar and I'll buy you a—what is it? Pinot Noir?"

"Good guess," she said. "Better than that overbearing California Cabernet they're serving, but not usually my choice." She followed him as he snaked through the crowd, breaking a path for her. The room had grown more crowded and more polluted with after shave and perfume over the past few minutes. She had no idea this spring party drew such a throng. She hoped the doors were open to the large patio where they might get some fresh air.

They got into the end of the line for the bar, and Sébastièn turned to her. "What is this question you wanted to ask me," he said.

"For a serious physicist like you, I suppose it might sound a little frivolous," she said. He gestured for her empty wine glass, and she gave it to him. "But this is it: Is time travel theoretically possible?"

"No. Because of entropy," he said immediately. He didn't act like he thought it was a silly question, but the quick response indicated it was an easy one. "Time can only move in one direction."

"I wish I knew why that is." She grimaced. Of course, his answer would be over her head. She should expect that.

"It's not that complicated," he said, "and a smart woman like you will understand." Finally, the seductive smile. She ignored it.

"Entropy and the second law of thermodynamics demand that randomness increases, and as it does, it takes tremendous amounts of energy to reorganize matter. Put it back together, so to speak. That dress you're wearing, which I like very much, I might add," he said, winking, "requires energy to spin those fibers, weave those fibers into fabric, and then sew the fabric into a garment. Putting the cotton back into a ball on a cotton plant, and then back into the ground as a seed or seedling would take even more energy. The accepted theory is that to go back in time and put everything back where it was would require more energy than exists in the universe. Just think how much energy it takes to clean your house when it gets messy." He paused and smiled that half smile again. "If it ever does."

"Oh, it certainly does." Nicole tried to let his winks and seductive smiles slip right past her, but he was good at them. "Thanks for the physics lesson. In just a half minute, I've learned more than I ever learned in high school physics. I was into the social sciences, as you might guess. I'm glad I warned you it was a ridiculous question." She screwed up her mouth and looked away.

"But," he added, leaning sideways to pull her gaze back toward him, "with quantum physics changing much of what we've always assumed about the universe, at least since Einstein, who knows? It's kind of an 'anything's possible' world now. There's certainly more we don't know than we do."

"So, it's possible?"

"I really doubt it, but why do you ask? Have you a fantasy that requires time travel? Something that you'd like to do over? A mistake you made in the past? Something you'd like to undo? Maybe you'd like to get rid of your boyfriend?"

"My fiancé, you mean?" There. She had now warned him. That should have helped keep things above board.

"Ah, you're engaged. Shoot. But that's to be expected. All the good-looking women are taken early."

"This seems to have regressed into the wrong kind of conversation," she said.

"Ha! You're right. My fault. Let's back up. You didn't answer my question. Why does time travel matter to you?" he asked, dropping the flirtatious tone.

"I was just reading a novel that relied on time travel for the plot, and I was curious as to what a physicist would think of it." It wasn't entirely untrue. She was curious about what he thought. And she had read Outlander, although "just" was a little misleading. It had been years.

They reached the front of the beverage line and Sébastièn ordered two Pinots, drew some loose bills from his pocket to drop in the tip jar, and handed her a glass.

"Let's step out on the patio," he said. "It's crowded out there, too, but at least we might be able to breathe."

"Are you sure I'm not taking too much of your time?"

"What else do I have to do? Talk with my colleagues about string theory? No. I have no agenda tonight, and I'm very happy to have met you."

Once again, he led the way through the crowd, which, perhaps due to his height and his classic tweed, parted easily for him.

"Now. Again. Why does time travel matter to you?" he asked as they reached the perimeter of the packed patio. "Sorry, but I don't believe it was just something you read."

Nicole hesitated. Whether she ever saw this man again or not, she wasn't sure she wanted to discuss something she hadn't even shared with Justin. She took a deep breath and decided, what the fuck? Besides her mother, she had no one else to talk with about it.

"What if I told you I had a bizarre experience that may have been something like time travel? Like I was back in the sixth century in a Merovingian castle." She half expected him to laugh at her, but instead, he narrowed his eyes thoughtfully.

"I think I need to know more. When did this happen and how much do you remember? Was the experience dreamlike or more tactile?"

Those were exactly the questions she'd been asking herself, and her answers hadn't helped her.

"I think it's probably just a dream, but I remember it in a way I never remember my dreams. The young girl I met, Ingund, was an important figure in early Christianity. I remember everything about her. I usually forget most of those things as soon as I wake up."

"Have you written it down? Did you take notes? Did you know what year it was?"

"I'm guessing I was there about 572."

"That's pretty precise," Sébastièn said. He rubbed his beardless chin as if straightening a beard that wasn't there. "Maybe it could provide the germ for a novel someday when you retire."

"Interesting that you should suggest that," she said. "I am writing a novel, and the time travel experience is directly related to what I'm writing about."

"Ah, a professor who has time to write novels! I knew I picked the wrong profession," Sébastièn said, displaying his half grin again. "Apparently history isn't as all-consuming as physics."

Nicole was a bit miffed at the implication: history wasn't as serious as physics? She didn't believe that. It just required a different set of skills.

"No, it's not a pastime," she said, lowering her voice for authority. "The novel is actually historical fiction, and I'm writing it as my dissertation."

"I didn't know fiction was a suitable platform for dissertations." He frowned. "Where are you finishing your doctorate?"

"Iowa."

"Oh." He looked impressed.

"Where'd you get yours?"

"MIT." Her turn to be impressed. "But it was several — " He stopped as something over her head caught his attention.

"Uh oh," he said. "Here comes the part of the evening I was dreading."

"What?" Nicole turned to see a skinny, freckled young man with a mop of red hair sluicing his way through the throng with purpose in his eyes.

"A graduate student," Sébastièn whispered, leaning close to her ear. "He's lobbying for his dissertation topic. I'm afraid I won't get away from him easily."

He stood straight to greet the intruder. "Joseph," he said, holding out his hand to shake. "This," he put his hand on Nicole's shoulder, "is a fascinating professor of medieval history whom I just met. Nicole, this is Joseph. He's a particle man."

Nicole shook the young man's hand, noticing how thin it was. "I'm quite sure I don't know what a 'particle man' might be, but nice to meet you." She had a flashback to some "Big Bang Theory" episode concerning particle versus string theories, but she had no intention of asking these two to elaborate.

"I'm afraid we're about to bore you to death," Sébastièn said, turning back to her. "But I'd love to hear about your experience. How about coffee some morning?"

Nicole caught the suspicious grin on the student's face. Up yours, she thought. It's just coffee.

"Yes. You know where to find me." She gave the grad student snake eyes and slipped through the patio back into the crowded room to look for Katie.

# XI

That she was still thinking about Sébastièn so much all week-end bothered Nicole, who wondered if it was an indication that her problem with Justin was of her own making, not his. She had put off sharing more of her time-travel dream with her fiancé even though she had now shared it with her mother and had hinted at it with a near-stranger. Surely there was something wrong with that picture, and it was her fault, not Justin's.

"Do you think time travel is possible?" Nicole finally broached the subject during dinner the Monday after the faculty party. If a physics professor could take a conversation about time travel seriously, maybe Justin would be more open to it than she had thought.

Instead, "Are you kidding?" was the response she got.

"No, I'm not kidding. Let me tell you what happened to me in Paris." She described the visit to the costume shop, the sudden shift to the sixth century, and then her arrival back to the present in her hotel room.

"And you think you actually went back in time?" Justin laughed, the kind of laugh that goes on long enough to betray itself as performance. Finally, he quieted. And then he looked at her and started laughing again.

She finished the food on her plate, waiting for him to finish his intended insult.

"Well, I really think it was a dream," she said, pretending not to notice how widely he grinned. "But it was incredibly real. I've been thinking about it a lot since, and I'm trying to make sense of it. I'm sorry you think it's so funny." She considered telling him that a professor of physics had treated her experience with greater respect than he was, but bringing Sébastièn into the conversation wasn't going to help.

"Honey, I think you really need to see a therapist," Justin said, his grin replaced with what looked like ersatz concern. "Maybe your obsession with the sixth century and your struggles with your dissertation are messing with your head."

"No, I'm not crazy," she said. "But I thought maybe you'd like to hear about it."

"Well, I'm not sure I liked what I heard. I'm really concerned."

Nicole's first reaction was: that's bullshit. Justin wasn't concerned. He wiped off his plate with a corner of a biscuit and picked up his phone. How concerned could he be?

Nicole felt her heart rate pick up and her face flush. She slowly, deliberately, put her fork down and took a deep breath. Unable to control herself, she shot back: "Concerned enough to tell me you're going to Southern France next fall?" She didn't realize until right then that she was still pissed that he hadn't mentioned it, that she had to find out from Kevin. Anger does that, she thought: it brings things to the surface you thought you'd let go.

"I'm sure I mentioned it," he answered, but his eyes didn't leave his screen.

"Mentioned it? Did you invite me? Apparently, Kevin thought you had invited me to come along."

"I don't know why he thought that. I haven't even decided if I'll go myself."

Justin refused to look at her as he said it. A lie. Enough, she thought. Enough of this conversation. She didn't have the energy to fight. She had too much on her mind already.

She got up from the table and put the dishes in the dishwasher.

NICOLE'S WEEK GOT WORSE BEFORE it got better.

She got another summons to meet with Timothy the next morning. "Here's the complaint," he said as she walked in his office. He handed the stapled sheets to her without rising.

Nicole sat down to read. Halfway down the page, after some basic facts she would have no problem stipulating to, was the meat of the complaint.

"Assistant professor Larson suggests that all men are responsible for what she believes is the misogyny rampant in our culture. Even though her lectures are purportedly about ancient and Middle Age history, she makes all men in her classroom feel embarrassed, belittled and culpable, which not only inhibits learning but sets these individuals up for ridicule by their female colleagues."

"Well, it's not very well written, is it?" Nicole remarked before continuing. "Not much of an argument." She looked up, but Timothy's stony expression indicated he didn't agree.

"But where's the proof?" she asked him anyway. "Don't they have to provide examples of how I implicated 'all men?' How I embarrassed them? They certainly take enough notes. And I'd like to know if any female colleagues have ridiculed them, or if this is just their imagination."

"I don't know anything about this," Timothy said, no apology in his voice. "Just finish reading it. I have to keep it on file."

"You mean I don't get a copy of it?"

"Not until the ethics committee makes its report."

"And when is that?"

"Probably sometime not until after the semester ends. I think they meet once a month. I'll let you know."

Nicole returned to the complaint. The rest of the page and a half of the text said little more of substance. And the signatures at the bottom had been redacted with heavy black lines.

"Ha," she said. "Do they think removing the names means I won't know who is making these allegations?"

"It could be some women in your class," Timothy argued weakly.

Nicole looked up at him and shook her head slightly. She had not expected him to abdicate his role in supporting her academic freedom. But clearly, he was not on her side. Even if he had been, he didn't have the guts to do anything about it.

"Is your budget really under this much pressure that you're going to sit back and deflect criticism by throwing me under the bus?" she asked. She threw the complaint on his desk.

"The budget has nothing to do with this."

"Yeah, right." She noted a thin sheen of sweat collecting on his forehead. The man was a wimp. A coward and a wimp. No wonder he would take the students' side. He was no more confident in his male superiority than they were. One five-foot-eight woman who stood up to their patriarchal attitude was too much. How fragile they all were!

"You know," she said, standing up and gathering her coat and backpack, "I don't know why they don't just take your military history courses if they're so intimidated by new ideas. They certainly don't have to worry about learning anything new there."

She didn't look back to see his reaction.

NEWS OF THE COMPLAINT WOULDN'T spread across campus until the ethics committee ruled, which gave Nicole a bit of breathing room over the next two weeks. The men had asked for permission to drop her Women in the Middle Ages class, and both Timothy and the dean had approved. If any of the women in the class noticed, they said nothing.

She knew it was unwise, but she didn't tell Justin about the complaint. It was a personal trait she didn't appreciate in herself: procrastinating to avoid potential arguments. When he found out, he would be angry. She doubted he'd be sympathetic, even though he'd always said he supported her research and writing. But now she wondered if he was as much of a feminist as she had thought. Could it be that being around golf and golfers as much as he was had eroded any progressive thoughts he had about women? Despite the incredible athletes on the LPGA, the sport still tolerated a significant amount of sexism, both on the course and in the clubhouse.

Distracted as she was by the students' complaint and by her continued confusion over the Paris dream, she was momentarily flummoxed by a phone call Tuesday after the faculty party.

She didn't recognize the man's name right away. "Who?" she asked.

"I know I'm not that memorable, but you have still hurt my feelings." The caller didn't sound hurt. "I thought you were now my best friend."

Ah. The physics professor.

"Oh, Sébastièn! I'm so sorry. Too much on my mind lately," she said in the most apologetic tone she could muster. "We said we'd go for coffee, didn't we? Although I think you answered my question quite well."

"So, no more time-travel episodes?" he teased.

They met in the student union, a safe place for two faculty members to meet. He was sitting at a corner table with a huge mug in front of him, reading a book. She leaned down to get a look at the cover. *The Three-Body Problem*. He looked up.

"It's science fiction," he said, "but the title refers to a physics problem – basically how three celestial bodies move given the speed and mass of each. A question of gravitational force. But the story is really more interesting than that. It's about aliens."

"Oh, aliens. That is interesting. Gravity, not so much." She put down her latte and pulled out her chair.

"Oh, shit," he said, standing up quickly. "I should have done that."

"But you were engrossed in your book. I don't take offense." She wondered when the last time Justin had even thought about pulling out a chair for her. But if he did, would she accuse him of a patriarchal act? "Is it a good book?"

"Absolutely not. Not a word about time-travel in it. It's almost the most boring thing ever written. Second only to my own textbook, of course. That is truly god-awful." He grinned.

Sébastièn put a leather bookmark in his book and laid it down. "Now you must tell me about your trip back in time," he said. He pushed his chair back a little and crossed his legs.

"We already talked about it. And we already agreed that it was a dream, anyway."

"I agreed to no such thing. Was it related to your novel?"

"Okay, I will tell you about it." She ran a hand through her hair, pushing her bangs back and letting them fall back on her forehead. Where to start? "It is related to my novel. I had gone to Paris to do research on the sixth century. What the city looked like, how people got around, that kind of stuff. I had gone to the Cluny Museum, you know, the museum of medieval history?"

He shook his head. "Nope. No idea what that is."

"Anyway, I was walking back to my hotel, and I stopped in this shop that had historical costumes in the window. I thought I might find something helpful."

Nicole continued retelling the same story she'd shared with her mother and Justin — each of whom had different reactions to it. As she recited it, Sébastièn nodded from time to time, and kept a slight smile on his face that she thought indicated he found the story amusing. When she concluded with "and that's all I know," he nodded more vigorously.

"I like it," he said. "It's a good story even if it isn't true."

"What do you mean, if it isn't true?"

"Okay," he said, uncrossing his legs and pulling closer to the table. "The physicist in me may not believe in time travel, but I'm not just a physicist. I'm also a bit of a romantic, to be honest. And it seems that your dream was quite helpful to your work, wasn't it? What do you think was the catalyst?"

"You mean the portal?"

"Well, yes. I guess I should leave the choice of vocabulary to those experienced in time travel," he said, laughing companionably.

"The dress. I forgot to tell you that I have the dress. Somehow an exact duplicate appeared in my closet in the hotel."

"Whoa!"

She couldn't tell if he was acting, but he seemed impressed. Sébastièn sat mum, and Nicole thought she caught a glimpse of amusement in his eyes. Did he think she was silly? He caught her questioning look, and his eyes turned sober. He stared thoughtfully into the distance as Nicole sipped her latte. Was he looking for a physics theory that might explain the appearance of the dress?

Finally, he shook his head and looked at her. "But this is still my question," he said, narrowing his eyes. "Is there some reason you're so interested in arranged marriages?"

"I just think they're fascinating. And it reveals so much about power and the importance of geopolitical alliances in the early Middle Ages."

"Hmm." He looked skeptical. "It doesn't have anything to do with your own engagement?"

"Oh, hell no! And you asked that before. I thought we'd already covered that."

"The lady doth protest too much, methinks."

"Yes, Shakespeare, I can see you think that. But no. Justin and I were childhood friends and neither of our parents had anything to do with the fact we became more than that as adults."

"'More than that?'"

"Jeez, you are nosy! Do you cross-examine all your friends this way?"

"I told you I don't have any." He laughed. "I just find the topic an interesting one for someone engaged to get married. I can't help but wonder if there is some subconscious thing going on there."

"Subconscious thing? You're a physicist if I remember. Tell me about your credentials, Mr. Freud."

"Nope. Sorry. I have none." He stood up and reached for her cup. At first she thought he was leaving. It seemed quite abrupt. But instead, he picked up, sniffed her empty cup, and asked, "Want another latte? It's on me."

She nodded and watched him walk away to the barista in the far corner, noticing a slight limp she hadn't seen when they were walking side-by-side at the party. She wondered where it came from. An accident? She didn't know him well enough to ask.

But he had raised an interesting question—for the second time: was there some connection between her thesis and her own marriage plans? Maybe there was. Was there much difference between a fated engagement like hers and an arranged marriage?

Nicole's mom and Justin's mom had been best friends since their freshmen year in Iowa City, and their husbands became besties shortly after that. They all taught at Iowa, her parents in English literature and his in finance. Growing up as close as siblings, Nicole and Justin—born in the same hospital on the same day—had ended up as lovers. No wonder Nicole had that cloying feeling that Justin had always been right there beside her. They'd been engaged since Justin returned to Iowa after getting his degree at Oklahoma State. He was her other half.

Perhaps she was trying to learn something from studying ancient marriage rites, something that might explain her own jitters. She huffed and shook her head at the thought. When Sébastièn came back, she'd insist on changing the subject.

"Non-fat okay?" he asked on his return, setting her cup down. "I forgot to ask."

"Well, yes, although I hope you didn't choose it because you think I'm overweight. Which I am, but ... oh, boy, I want to change the subject." She was blushing. Bringing up her weight was not what she wanted to do with near strangers.

"Certainly." He smiled sympathetically. "Want to talk about string theory?"

"Absolutely!" She had no idea whether she did or not, but it was better than where she had gone with the conversation. "What's new in string theory?"

# XII

At one point in midst of Sébastièn's description of string theory, Nicole decided that a physicist's Lockean world-view that the only real forces in the universe were those of molecule acting against molecule, of strings or particles acting against strings or particles was ultimately depressing. Unraveling the mystery of strings or particles could someday yield a unified theory of the universe – the physicist's dream – but she wondered if it left room or meaning for art or literature or beauty. Or morality.

"If there are no stories, no art, no lessons in human history that can't be explained as simple physics equations, does it really matter if it was strings or particles?" she asked.

"That's for you writers and philosophers to figure out," Sébastièn responded. "I can only do what I do. I'm quite limited that way."

Nicole was still smiling about that as she walked back to her office. "Limited" was a strange word to describe a person who could get his head around string theory or particle theory or any other physicists' inquiries. It was history, sociology, economics, linguistics, the so-called soft sciences, that the university's administration was eliminating from the curricula for having "limited" value to society.

Or to generating profits for corporations looking for their next well-primed employees.

She liked the physics professor. Yes, he was a flirt at times; probably his good looks gave him permission to be. But he had a sense of humor, and he seemed compassionate. Who didn't like someone who took their stories seriously? It was nice of him to be concerned, or act concerned, about her engagement to Justin, but admitting her issues with him would encourage Sébastièn to think of her as single. She didn't need that.

Besides, was anyone's love life perfect? Was any marriage all perfect alignment and bliss? Certainly, her parents' wasn't. It was becoming obvious that marriage to Justin could prove to be just as complicated and unsatisfactory as theirs, but in a different way, of course. All unhappy families are unhappy in their own way, she whispered, kind of quoting Tolstoy.

In any case, it wasn't any of Sébastièn's business.

ONCE THE SEMESTER CONCLUDED, TIMOTHY updated the ethics committee's schedule: it would be another two weeks before they made their determination on the complaint. Katie was traveling on a literary tour of the UK with her students, and Justin in Oklahoma for the summer. She had no reason to put off her return to Europe.

Sitting in her back-of-the-plane coach seat on the way to Paris, she worried how large the balance on her credit card was growing. It wasn't a great idea for someone suddenly out of work who had extremely poor employment potential to build up high-interest debt. But two tiny bottles of wine later, she decided she really didn't care how big her bill got or what Justin would be doing in Oklahoma. Sipping a third $15 bad Chardonnay, she vowed to put her own relationship problems out of her mind. Arranged marriages, not engagements of the twenty-first century, were her concern. She downed the wine and pulled the light airline blanket up to her neck and tried to sleep.

She spent the first several days in Paris, touring the Cluny

Museum and looking for books, maps, and illustrations in the Sorbonne, struggling to find anything as descriptive or graphic as the images she recalled from her visit – dream or time travel – to Lutetia. Frustrated, she woke up on the sixth morning in the hotel and decided to put on the sixth-century dress she'd brought with her. She didn't know if it would bring her back to her dream, if it really was her portal to the sixth century, but the dress seemed the most likely catalyst. And there didn't seem to be much of a risk in putting on a dress.

Catalyst. She chuckled as she pulled it over her head. That was the word Sébastièn had used. She wished he could have come along with her, and she'd see if he could reconcile the journey with his solid belief in the second law of thermodynamics.

# XIII

I was self-conscious as I opened my hotel room door to leave. My costume was likely to attract stares at least – perhaps laughter, perhaps ridicule – on the streets of modern Paris. I pulled the door closed and turned around to find the elevator.

I caught my breath. The dress was the portal! I was not in the hotel I was in just moments before. It wasn't Sigibert's palace, either. Where was I? And how much time had passed between my first travel back in time and this one?

The hallway I stepped into was as narrow as the one to my bedroom in Lutetia, but its floor tiles were made of bricks, not stone. Small birds chirped from their perches on the beams under a barrel-shaped ceiling. The corridor was illuminated by small octagon-shaped windows, open to the air. My research at the Sorbonne had schooled me a bit in early medieval architecture. Windows at the top of the walls was more typical of Byzantine clerestories than Romanesque.

The shock of the surroundings frightened me. Unsure if I was ready to venture into the sixth century again, I turned back to my room. Instead of a flat hotel door, I faced a weathered, thick slab of carved word with a heavy metal hook for a latch. I tried to release the hook, but it wouldn't budge. It was stuck, and so was I.

I took a deep breath. I'd survived before, I probably would this time. After all, I certainly had been alive in the twenty-first century, and that couldn't have happened if I died here, could it? And I had never heard of anyone dying in a dream. Falling off a cliff? Yes. But landing below? Never.

Unconvinced about my safety, but with no other choice, I headed down the corridor toward cheering and peals of laughter. The building looked like a monastery or a cathedral, but the noise made me wonder. The passage ended at a t-intersection, and I took another hallway toward the voices. I entered a narthex to what looked, from its modest size and decoration, like a parish church. An unruly crowd of worshipers were dancing and chatting and ignoring the priest who stood at the altar, doing his best to rein in the worshippers.

I had stumbled on proof of something I had read about: how the church had struggled to turn once-rowdy pagans into ritual-respecting Catholics early in the history of Christianity. Edict after edict was promulgated by church leaders to try to quell the enthusiasm of the new converts, but outside of Rome and some major religious centers, the church's authority was still shaky.

I put it together: I had somehow ended up in the southern provinces. Architecture on the coast of the Mediterranean in the south of Gaul was influenced by Byzantine styles more than buildings were in Lutetia. I knew Ingund had stopped in Tolosa, Toulouse in my time, on the way to Toledo, where her betrothed, Hermenegild, lived, and she had visited with Bishop Cyprian there, according to Gregory of Tours' histories. If I was destined to follow Ingund's life journey, it made sense that I had ended up in Tolosa as well.

If she was in Tolosa, it had been four or five years since I was in the sixth century before, and much had happened. This I knew: After Ingund's father, Sigibert, was murdered, his brother, Chilperic, stormed into Lutetia, only to be murdered himself. Ingund's little brother, Childebert, was crowned the baby-toothed king of Austrasia, and Brunhilde established herself as regent. Only then did she have the power to negotiate Ingund's marriage and, thereby, forge an alliance with the Visigothic kingdom.

I wanted to focus on the arranged marriage theme itself, not on the myriad Merovingian battles. And that meant I had to find Ingund.

I turned away from the dancing parishioners and wandered through the hallways with two questions on my mind. First, if I were reunited with the young princess, how would I explain my long absence or my return? Second, Old German wasn't going to work here in the province of Septimania. I was going to have to rely on my bad Latin.

I turned down a hallway that seemed brighter than the others and walked toward a large, square, manicured courtyard. The walkways along its four sides were lined with doubled Corinthian columns that reminded me of the images I'd seen of the cloister at the Iona Abbey in Ireland. The columns stood atop a short wall that prohibited me from walking out onto the grass and turning my face up to the sun as I wanted. It was that urge that made me realize how cold I was.

"Cousin!"

I turned and opened my arms to a charging Ingund. She was so much taller, and so much older. She had the body of a young woman, and a beauty that made me think of the line, "Was this the face that launched a thousand ships," that Christopher Marlowe had yet to write. Hermenegild was doomed to do her bidding!

"Ingund!" I replied, letting her wrap her arms around me and lean her head against my chest. "You are safe and well!" I exclaimed. "Are you ready to be married?"

I surprised myself. My words came out in completely respectable vulgar Latin, the same language she and her sister spoke years earlier. The easy assimilation that time travel enabled amazed me.

"Oh, yes," she said, pulling back, her eyes bright with optimism. All the tragedy in her life seemed to have rolled off her slim frame.

"I am ready to marry Hermenegild. But this morning we must first visit the bishop of Tolosa. He sent a message that he has something important to tell me. I am going to the monastery to meet him. Will you come along?"

How could I miss this opportunity? In my mind, her meeting with Bishop Cyprian was one of those events that changed the course of history. Of course, Ingund didn't know that.

"Yes, most certainly," I said, letting her take my hand and pull me toward the front entrance of the basilica where a horse and carriage waited.

Finally, I felt the sun's warmth. I closed my eyes and tipped my head to catch its rays.

"Cousin, you will ruin your complexion," Ingund scolded. "Where is your hat?"

"I lost it on the voyage," I said as I opened my eyes and followed her to a carriage that waited on the street. The carriage seemed anachronistic. I had always thought there were no such fancy transports back in Ingund's time. But I was wrong. This one wasn't as refined as those of the Late Middle Ages. It looked like the wagon that took me and the dressmaker to the palace in Lutetia, but instead of a canvas cover, it had sides and a roof made of wood. Shades were hung inside the open windows on the sides, but there was no glass.

"I lost all my belongings as well," I continued after swallowing my surprise.

"No, they aren't lost," Ingund assured me. "Your trunk arrived this morning from Narbo."

A uniformed man stepped around the horse and opened the carriage door for us. I was stepping up after Ingund when I glanced at his face and stopped. He was the same guard who had escorted me from the wagon the day I arrived in Lutetia. The one I thought looked like Sébastièn's twin.

I tried to get his attention, but he avoided my eyes.

"Come, Cousin!" Ingund poked her head out the door. "We

must not be late! And Sebastianus," she said, "be sure to bring my cousin her trunk when we return to the cloister."

Sebastianus? That was too much of a coincidence. My face must have expressed my surprise.

"Are you okay, Cousin?" Ingund asked as Sebastianus waited for me to climb in, and closed and latched the door. "You look bewildered."

"It is nothing," I said, sitting down across from her.

I tried to think of something to say that wouldn't elicit any questions about my absence. I thought that I had probably disappeared about the same time as news of her father's death had reached Lutetia. If that were the case, my disappearance would hardly have been noticed.

"How did you escape the palace when Chilperic arrived?" Ingund asked. She settled back on the cushioned bench and curled her legs up under her skirt. At fifteen, she still had a lot of little girl in her.

"Oh, my dear," I said, stalling. I had no idea how to answer. "How can you worry about me when you have been through so much?"

"But where did you hide?"

"In Lutetia," I lied. "But it was not as difficult as what you experienced." I was more eager to hear her story than I was to make up more of my own.

Ingund nodded and obliged with an abridged version. "Mother sent Chlosinda and me to Austrasia when my uncle took over Lutetia. She rejoined us in Metz just before I found out who I am to marry. I'm so happy that Chilperic didn't capture you. Did you hear that he was murdered? My mother thinks Aunt Fredegund did it. Just as she murdered my mother's sister and my father. Now that little bastard of hers will be king of Nuestria, but he will always be under his mother's thumb."

I was a bit surprised by how much she understood about the confounding politics of her mother and her aunt. She went on to talk about how her little brother was now a king, even though he probably could barely crawl up on a throne without help, and the rumor that Fredegund's daughter Rigund had also been sent to Iberia to marry a Visigoth, but the marriage was called off when Chilperic was murdered.

"My mother was relieved," Ingund said. "And my marriage will make her happy. She wanted the alliance with the Visigoths, as she was one, and she didn't want Fredegund to get it first."

I let Ingund ramble on while I organized my thoughts. The current Visigothic Queen Goswintha in Toledo was Brunhilde's mother. She had married King Leovigild in Iberia, after her first husband and the former king, Athanagild, died. Now she was stepmother to Leovigild's sons, Hermenegild and Reccared. When Ingund and Hermenegild married, Goswintha would be both Ingund's stepmother-in-law and her grandmother. No doubt that would flummox my twenty-first-century readers. Imagine drawing that family tree!

Ingund's story wound down, and I jumped in to encourage her to continue talking. I couldn't tell her where I'd been. "Do you know much about Hermenegild?" I asked.

"Not much. But he is only seventeen, just two years older than me, which I think is good. I would not want to marry an old man!" She giggled and I wondered how much her mother had told her about her marriage "duties." Married to King Leovigild's eldest son, she'd be expected to start producing heirs to the Visigothic throne right away. Was it my responsibility to explain to her what those "duties" entailed? I hoped not.

The look on my face must have given my thoughts away. "Oh, do not worry," she added quickly. "Mother told me all about the marriage bed. I am certain it will not be as awful as my mother said. After all, I know she and father slept together whenever they were in the same city, and she would not have done it if she did not like it." She giggled again.

# XIV

The carriage slowed down and stopped, and it rocked as Sebastianus jumped down from his seat and pulled open the door. The basilica in front of us was massive and impressive. I wondered if it were the ancient Temple de la Deurata, the golden temple built by the Roman Emperor Honorius for the god Apollo, the one that the Christians repurposed as a Catholic cathedral. A monastery was attached to the cathedral in Ingund's time, so it was likely Bishop Cyprian's home.

The front entrance of the church was flanked by squat Corinthian columns carved with grape clusters and leaves. We were escorted inside past a glass-bead mosaic, a niche decorated with small columns, and a large marble baptismal font. It was an impressive edifice, but Ingund followed a priest through it with hardly a glance to one side or another. Perhaps she'd seen enough temples and cathedrals in her time to be blasé about them.

We were ushered into a small office lined with shelves of leather-bound manuscripts. A small altar with a silver chalice, a candelabra, and a small, bejeweled cross bearing a carving of the crucified Jesus stood on the far side. The bishop rose from his desk, and Ingund knelt to kiss his ring. I stayed back by the door, thankful to be ignored, and tried to do nothing to interrupt this auspicious meeting.

The bishop's Latin was classic, and a bit hard to follow, but Ingund seemed to have no problem understanding him. She responded to his long lecture with humble nods and whispered monosyllables. I was impressed with her piety. It was a side of Ingund I had never seen, and I could tell it wasn't an act.

Gregory of Tours had written about this visit, so I had an idea what was transpiring, which helped me follow along. "You must not allow Goswintha to baptize you to her heresy," was the gist of it, along with "You must be diligent in your effort to convert Hermenegild to the one true Chalcedonian faith." His commands were embellished with predictions of the ways the Visigoths would try to coerce her to convert to the Arian version of Christianity.

Not being a religious observer myself, I had always found the disagreements between different denominations and religions perplexing. The Arian and Chalcedonian—or as I knew it, Catholic—religions were both based on the divinity and sacrifice of Christ; the major difference between them involved the characterization of Christ's nature: God and man from the beginning, or first man and then God. It seemed too trivial a difference to have incited wars and thousands of executions, but any student of history knew how many apparently innocuous religious disagreements had been settled, or not settled, by brutally destructive wars. Only empire builders, tuberculosis, and malaria-carrying mosquitos accounted for as much death over time.

After a long hour, the bishop rose over the kneeling girl's bowed head and blessed her travels with what sounded like a heartfelt benediction, and I saw that the man not only wished for the defeat of Arianism, he also genuinely cared for this young woman. From my research, I knew she would write to him later, when the onerous task of converting an entire empire to his faith threatened her life.

On the ride back to our accommodations, Ingund was uncharacteristically subdued. I could tell she was taking the bishop's advice and instructions seriously. But perhaps she also realized how difficult standing her ground was going to be. It would be a test of her will and the depth of her religious convictions.

We rode in silence, and when we parted for the evening, she kissed my cheek and bowed her head and walked away. She was only fifteen, but it seemed she had become an adult in that short meeting with the bishop. I believed it was the task he laid on her slim shoulders that had changed her.

I WAS UNPREPARED FOR THE scene we made when we left the next morning for Toledo. I gave up trying to count the number of wagons that Brunhilde had filled with treasure as Ingund's dowry. The queen had much to gain from her daughter's marriage. Her child-son reigned over one kingdom – Merovingian Austrasia – and now her daughter would be queen over another –Visigothic Iberia. This marriage and its expected offspring could bequeath her grandsons both thrones, and Brunhilde's legacy would be assured.

The caravan was led and followed by retinues of guards on horseback, and more rode back and forth along the sides of the wagons, watching out for highwaymen coveting a piece of the princess's fortune. We didn't encounter any thieves over the next four weeks, but in small villages along the way, peasants stood at the side of the road, often with a shovel or hoe in hand, watching solemnly as we passed. They didn't wave. We took to closing the shades at our windows so we wouldn't have to see their envious, sometimes cadaverous faces.

We rode in the same carriage we had used in Toulouse, and Sebastianus was back in the driver's seat. I tried to forget he was up there, but there was little along the road to distract me from wondering about him. Ingund was accustomed by then to riding long distances, and she snoozed most of the day. Before I stepped into the carriage the first day, one of her many handmaids handed me a piece of linen and an embroidery kit of thread and needles, which would have given me something to do if I had known what to do with them.

"My eyes are not good anymore," I explained to Ingund as I handed them back. "I fear I will lose my sight long before my years have warranted it."

We rode in silence for most of the morning, the carriage bouncing on the Via Aquitania, the ancient Roman road leading down to the coastal city of Narbo, later Narbonne, on the east side of the Pyrenees. Some of the road was stone and some gravel—the roughest ride was on the remnants of Roman stonework, as the fine blocks had weathered and shifted since the second century. With the Roman Empire's collapse, maintenance was left to warring and constantly changing rulers who preferred to use their resources to kill each rather than fix the infrastructure. I considered how little things had changed in fifteen hundred years.

Halfway through the morning, as the rocking cabin was putting me to sleep, Ingund nudged me.

"Cousin?" she said. "Are Carthaginians Catholic or Arian? You?"

"Uh, I am a Christian," I responded, shaking myself awake and making it up as fast as I could. "I put my faith in the rulings of the Council of Chalcedonia." I knew little about Carthage, but I had studied enough church history to have a grasp of Constantinople's influence over North African religion. In fact, I had no religious beliefs that were relevant in her world. "Catholic," I continued. "Under Emperor Maurice, the vestiges of Vandal Arianism in Carthage were eradicated."

"What did you think about the bishop's warnings? Do you think Hermenegild will agree? Will he convert?"

I knew the answer, but I had to stay away from facts and just give a vague opinion. "I believe if he comes to love you, he might. But you may have to worry more about others in his family. I do not know what King Leovigild will think of your intervention." I avoided mentioning Goswintha. Ingund would run into that force of nature soon enough.

It took us three days to reach Narbo. I had guessed this would be our route, so I had done some research at the Sorbonne on possible waystations along the way. And our first stop was exactly where I expected: Castelnaudary, a long-used staging post on the old Roman road. I wasn't sure if it was still going by its old Roman name, Sostomagus, but it didn't matter.

It wasn't much of a town, as it lay far from any sizeable river and wouldn't have existed at all if it weren't about thirty kilometers, or about a day's wagon trip, from Toulouse. Most of the two dozen or so wagons accompanying us stopped at the outskirts of town, along the road, and their drivers and guards set up camp. Even from where we stayed at an inn inside the unimpressive town walls, we could hear their laughter and games well into the night.

Our inn was a small, decently maintained, two-story stone building with a dining hall and tavern on the first floor and bedrooms on the upper floor. A stable groomsman next door accepted Sebastianus's horse and carriage.

The princess was treated with grave respect, which was a surprise to me. Then it occurred to me that there were probably advance sentinels riding ahead of our wagon train, ensuring that the royal entourage would be accommodated with a decent meal and acceptable wine before other, lesser travelers. Shown immediately to our room, I was pleased to realize I'd be with Ingund the entire time. I helped her remove her traveling coat, dress, and shoes and replace them with a long nightgown, slippers, and robe.

Several cots lined the walls of our second-floor room, but no one else was allowed to bed with us, which was a relief to me. My Latin had improved quickly, but I was more concerned about meeting a "fellow" Carthaginian who would want to discuss matters at home. I had avoided revealing my subterfuge so far, and the real aunt from Carthage had never arrived, as far as I knew. Perhaps she had arrived in Lutetia just as Chilperic had entered the city and had been killed or frightened away in the mayhem.

After our short exchange about Hermenegild's conversion, Ingund had said little. She was polite, and I was respectful, but she made it clear she was not in the mood for conversation. She sampled very little of the soup that was delivered to our door, and when she crawled into bed before the sun had set, I took advantage of the "time off" and wandered downstairs to the tavern. In spite of the considerable size of our caravan, only a couple of tables were occupied, so I found a seat and asked for a glass of wine. The innkeeper cocked his eye at me and assured me that although a princess was a guest, the inn did not possess glass.

"A cup, perhaps?" he asked.

I nodded and smiled demurely. "Yes, of course."

The heavy ceramic cup did not disappoint, however. The serving was twice what one would expect at a bar in Paris in the twenty-first century, and not much worse than the house wine served at most of them. I offered what I thought would be an appropriate amount of coins, the innkeeper refused it. He pointed to a man sitting at a table in the corner, whom I guessed was the caravan's bursar, the man responsible for covering the expenses of the entourage all the way to Toledo.

Sitting with him was none other than the mysterious Sebastianus, who, seeing me look their way, gave a small nod and immediately returned his attention to his dining companion. It was the first time I had seen him look directly at me. Up to then, he had avoided my eyes. I swallowed hard and looked away. Sébastièn would be able to trace his family tree directly back to this man, I thought, considering how similar they looked to each other. I guessed that it wasn't possible for an assistant to a princess and a future queen to directly address a servant, even one as highly placed and trusted as him. It was probably for the best, as focusing on anything outside of my role as an escort could have caused me to neglect my duties and the history I was there to absorb. I quickly downed my wine, thankful for the drowsiness it would bring, and retired to our room.

# XV

We stopped for a night inside the double ramparts at Carcassonne, a major fortress that had been in Visigothic hands for at least a century. Unlike the peasants we had seen along the road up to then, the citizens gathered and cheered as our caravan passed through the gates of the city. Ingund smiled at the reception, the first bit of joy I had seen reflected in her face since her meeting with the bishop.

The opposite of forgettable Castelnaudary, Carcassonne was awesome. Due to its prime location on the road that connected the Mediterranean and the Atlantic Ocean, and inhabited since the neolithic era, its history as a fortress stretched back to the Roman Republic. The Visigoths took it over in the middle of the fifth century. Attached to the double city wall, tall turrets rose high into the darkening sky, presenting an imposing authority and an effective defense against Frankish raids and sieges. We passed by a bridge over a moat around the largest castle I had ever seen. I counted a dozen towers, but I knew that eventually, the city came to possess fifty-three of them.

While I gawked at the sights, a solemn Ingund took in little of our surroundings. She didn't know the history of the city as I did.

She couldn't know that it would be the last holdout of the Cathars, a Christian sect, whose members were expelled or murdered by a papal army in the thirteenth century; or that one of its towers would house the Spanish Inquisition. I was humbled realizing she would never know of the Cathars or the Spanish Inquisition.

As we entered the basilica where we were to stay for the night, Ingund asked the priest if she could take the eucharist, and I began to realize how profoundly religious the girl had become since I left five years before. Perhaps incarceration at the hands of her uncle in Metz had transformed her from the young, impulsive pre-teen into this quiet, contemplative young woman. When I had first seen her on my return, I thought I was back with the vivacious, precocious girl I had left. But that childlike enthusiasm had quickly fallen away, and this solemn, devout Catholic woman had taken her place.

I would have liked to wander Carcassonne's streets to take in gulps of historic atmosphere, but after Ingund's communion and our unexpectedly extravagant meal of roasted pork, stewed beets, turnips, and thick bread, it was too dark to venture out alone. Despite the impressive fortifications of the city walls, the basilica was secured against intruders, and no one could get in or out.

We made it to Narbo the next day, where we stayed for three nights to rest the oxen and horses. The pause was good for humans as well. The Mediterranean air suited Ingund, I thought, and we took long walks on the beach east of the city, accompanied by a pair of guards in front of us and a pair behind us—sadly, I recognized none of them as Sebastianus. I was astonished at the size of the hulking vessels berthed at the docks, although I had to hide my surprise, as I had supposedly traveled from Carthage on one.

The sun and the walk along the beach cheered Ingund a bit, and as we left the port city, she wondered aloud what her wedding would be like. She opened the curtains on both sides of the carriage to watch our passage between the Pyrenees and the sea. At times we caught a glimpse of the Mediterranean coastline, the brilliant blue water churning to white foam on sandy beaches, and on the other side, towering, snowy peaks in the distance that would serve as a land barrier to Nazi Germany's incursions far in the future.

We rode five more days to Barcino, Barcelona in my time, and six more days across the inland road to Caesaraugusta, which was Zaragoza to me. Ingund was quiet—too quiet for my comfort. She stared out the windows for hours at a stretch. I would have preferred that she let me know what was on her mind. Was it her upcoming marriage? Was it Bishop Cyprian's request? Was it leaving her mother, sister, and brother behind in Gaul? Occasionally, I asked a question, using my most empathetic voice, but she either pretended not to hear me, or her heavy thoughts blocked her ears.

One day, as we neared Caesaraugusta, she finally turned away from the view and looked at me in a way that implied I was guilty of something.

"Cousin," she said, "I think I know something about you that you do not want anyone else to know."

"What's that?" I said, momentarily certain she had figured out I wasn't really her aunt.

"You can read. I saw you looking at the words on the wall at the inn in Narbo, and I saw the way your eyes moved across the lines. People only move their eyes like that if they can read."

"How do you know that?" I asked, admitting nothing.

"My father could read, and my mother cannot. For years, I have watched her glance at a piece of writing as if it is one solid block, while he followed the lines just the way I saw you do."

"You are right," I ventured. "I can. My father taught me. He wanted me to enter a convent, and he knew that I would be expected to learn to read and write, so he was helping me prepare." I was getting proficient at making things up on the spot. But I didn't know why she thought this was important.

"So, if you can read, have you read anything of the Visigoths? Do you know anything about Leovigild and my grandmother, Goswintha? Can you tell me something that can prepare me like your father did?"

I paused before answering. Could relaying a bit of history about the current empire in Spain change history? Could it hurt? I considered the butterfly theory: a butterfly flaps its wings and changes the future of everything on Earth. Or something like that. I wished I had Sébastièn there to help me explain it.

If I told her a bit of history of the Visigoths, would it change the way she reacted to her mother-in-law or her husband years down the line? Or was I already a part of history, and what I would tell her had already had its consequences?

I decided that it would help me secure her friendship, and my impact on the future was unlikely if I kept to information that her husband would already know. I took the chance.

I told her how the Visigoths were given the southern coast of Gaul, Septimania, by the Romans who were eager to get them out of Italy. Pushed south by her father's people, the Franks, her mother's people, the Visigoths invaded much of Spain, acquiring lands once held by the Vandals and Alans, but failing to drive the Suevi out of the northeast corner of the Iberia. Her grandfather, the Visigothic king Athanagild, overthrew his predecessor thirty years before she was born. His rebellion destabilized the peninsula and allowed the Byzantines to take control of the southeastern coast, something I thought might still be a touchy topic in Toledo.

The story of the royal family in Iberia was no less convoluted and twisted than Ingund's own family tree in Gaul, so I was patient as I repeated much of what I'd discussed with her earlier: When King Athanagild died, a noble named Luiva was elected king, and he gave his brother Leovigild most of Iberia, keeping the northern territories for himself. When Luiva died, the Visigoths were reunited under Leovigild. Leovigild and his first wife had two sons, Hermenegild and Reccared. When that wife died, Ingund's grandmother, Goswintha, who had been Athanagild's wife, married Leovigild.

As I told the story, I realized my dissertation would benefit greatly from a sketch of the family tree. I knew this was a headful of information, but I tried to keep it as simple and uncontroversial as I could for Ingund. She nodded as I talked, stopping me occasionally to get names straight. She took it all in, and then, when I was finished, she sighed and returned her gaze to the passing countryside.

"It seems that Fredegund's Neustrian Franks and the Visigoths have always been at each other's throats in Septimania," she said. "By marrying me to Hermenegild, I guess my mother will make things harder for my aunt Fredegund. She'll have enemies on the north and south."

She had come to grips with the big picture already. There was no love lost between Brunhilde in Austrasia and Fredegund in Neustria. "That is possible," I said, which was as close as I could come to agreeing.

It took us another seven days from Caesaraugusta to reach the outskirts of Toledo. With obvious relief, we were finally ready to enter the capital of Leovigild's kingdom. Ingund had endured nearly three months on the road with little knowledge of what her new life would be like, what her new husband would look like, how he would treat her, or how her new family would or wouldn't embrace her. Impressed as I was by the courage required of a medieval princess (as if she had a choice), I knew that her challenges so far would pale compared with what she faced over the next five years.

# XVI

At a large, sprawling country villa the night before our entrance into Toledo, several handmaids swarmed into our room to prepare Ingund for the introduction to her grandmother the next day. She would meet Hermenegild as well, but I knew the real test of her success as Visigoth royalty would be how she faired with Queen Goswintha, her grandmother and soon-to-be step-mother-in-law. If nothing else, she needed to appear as a cultured and respectable bride for the king's oldest son.

The servants struggled to bring a large tub up the stairs to our room, and a dozen men carried pitchers of steaming water up to fill it. I stood outside the room, listening through the open door to the laughter and lively chatter of the women as they praised Ingund's beauty, her porcelain complexion, her thick and wavy hair. I smelled jasmine, and I knew no expense was being spared in these preparations. There was only one variety of jasmine native to Europe, so it was possible the incense had been imported from the Far East by her mother and sent with the caravan for this night. When the maids were leaving her room, Ingund spied me standing outside and called me in.

"Cousin," she said. "Please come in and pray with me."

I swallowed hard. Here was another thing about the Middle Ages I hadn't studied: the structure of Catholic prayer. But I walked in and closed the door behind me. Ingund was propped up on several large pillows in bed, her hair curled and piled on her head, and a necklace of rosemary and thyme wound around her neck. She turned her eyes toward me; they were swollen with tears, and her nose was pink from crying.

"Oh, dear princess," I said, sitting down on the edge of the mattress. "Why are you crying? Isn't tomorrow what you've been waiting for?"

Ingund nodded but didn't answer.

"Remember when we first met?" I said, nearly whispering. "You were nine or ten. And you told me you knew I had arrived for this purpose — to take you to your husband. We're here now. Why the sadness?"

She let out a heavy sigh and wiped her eyes with a wadded handkerchief. She could flip back and forth from a playful child to a perceptive woman in a matter of seconds. She had to decide which she wanted to be, and I imagined it was as hard for a young woman in the sixth century as it was for any young woman at any time. Maybe harder for her, now that an entire kingdom — a dynasty — depended on who she would become.

"I do not know," she whispered. "I know I should not cry, but I am afraid."

"Afraid of what?" I asked softly. Now that she was out of the reach of her murderous Aunt Fredegund, she'd never been safer in her whole life.

"I am afraid that I will no longer be able to sing when I want to. I will not dance or play with the dogs or run in the trees. I have never had control over what happened to me, but from now on, I will not control one minute of my day."

Aha! I thought, quite selfishly. This was just the kind of independence and agency women have always wanted, even if they haven't always been able to have it. It was exactly what I had been describing in my classes on medieval feminism. If only my protesting students could hear her! But this wasn't the time to gloat over my feminist perspicuity.

I nodded in agreement. "You will have to fight to maintain what small freedoms you will have," I said. "But I believe your husband will fall in love with you, and he will strive to preserve the joy that radiates from your soul. He will want you to dance. He will want to hear you sing."

"How do you know this, Cousin?" she asked, blinking away some more tears.

I didn't know, but I wished I could tell her I did. History was mute on the subject of Ingund and Hermenegild's love, but it was possible to read between the lines and imagine them facing their coming battles with a strength that could come from only two places: love and faith. I knew she had enough faith for both of them. And I couldn't imagine how any young man could resist her beauty and her spirit and not love her.

"You need your rest," I said, avoiding her question. "But first, I will listen to your prayers. They will help you realize your finest dreams, because I will know what you ask, your God will grant you."

I saw a tiny smile turn one side of her lips, and I was relieved. I closed my eyes, and I heard her whisper, "Blessed Christ, thou hath given your life to absolve my sins and risen to the righthand of the Father, with whom you share dominion over the world. Forgive me for my selfish concerns. Guide my heart to find communion with that of my husband. Grant him the kindness and the love that I will depend on as we travel through our lives together."

Or something like that. It was actually much longer. I was tearing up as I listened. I wanted to rush back to my room to record her prayer before a word of it was lost from my memory, but I had no tools to write with nor parchment to write on. I was expected to be as illiterate as every woman but a cloistered one was at the time. I took her hands in mine.

"Bless you, child," I said, knowing I had no authority to bless anyone. I wasn't even sure what "bless you" meant to her. She nodded and closed her eyes, and I hoped her prayer and my presence had comforted her. I rose and kissed her forehead and took my leave.

It was the last time I saw hints of the princess as a child. She seemed to grow up the rest of the way to womanhood that night. I never again heard her beg me for assurances. From then on, when she asked for predictions, it was with the authority of a royal princess, and later as a queen. I never saw her cry again until we parted for good.

I'd never seen anyone grow up so fast. But then, Ingund wasn't reared to be just anyone.

WE ROSE EARLY, AND FOR the first time, Sebastianus escorted Ingund into the carriage by herself. I boarded a crowded carriage with the handmaids, who quit chattering as soon as I stepped in. They lowered their eyes, and it reminded me that I was supposedly a member of the royal family. Only Ingund's first cousin-once-re-moved, but still due respect.

The caravan had barely started to move when the shouting started. I wondered if this was some kind of regular ritual, perhaps the community coming out to greet their new princess. Our carriage stopped abruptly, toppling my traveling companions and me over each other, and we fought to keep from falling on the floor. One of the handmaids scrambled to her feet and opened the carriage door to peer out.

"What is happening?" she called up to the driver. I squeezed out past her and looked up to second the question. He simply shrugged and pointed to the princess's carriage in front of us.

A young man on horseback had ridden up and was speaking to Sebastianus. He was dressed in a fine uniform, an impressive sword hanging down the side of one leg. He was gesticulating excitedly as several companions rode up behind him, all grinning as if they were sharing a joke.

Sebastianus jumped down from his perch and opened Ingund's carriage door. A crowd of guards on horseback and a dozen travelers from our entourage gathered around, murmuring with curiosity, and I jumped down to walk up near the front of the carriage. I wanted to be within striking distance if she called for my help. The young man dismounted and knelt in front of the open door, holding his hand out, his sword propped against the ground behind him. I couldn't hear what he said, but a moment later, Ingund stepped out, gingerly, and put a gloved hand in his and curtsied, her head held high.

I was probably the last one at the scene to figure it out: The prince Hermenegild, himself, eager to meet his new bride, had usurped his stepmother's intended order of introductions, and had come out to escort her to Toledo.

I couldn't think of anything more romantic, and I hoped it was a harbinger of a true love I thought was rare in arranged marriages. I was thinking that I might have to change the theme of my novel from the dangers and disasters wrought by these forced unions to the miracles that can occasionally, even if not permanently, transform the fateful tale of a betrothed young woman into a love story.

I knew how this love story ended. Still, for a moment in time, long before the horrors of medieval military and religious conceit bore down on this young couple, the kingdom shone on them, and my heart swelled for them. I felt my eyes sting with tears and looked away in time to see Sebastianus wipe his face with the back of his glove. He returned my smile and winked. I felt my face flush, and I ducked back into the carriage.

STILL FOLLOWING INGUND'S CARRIAGE, NOW with Hermenegild riding alongside, protectively, perhaps possessively, we passed through impressive city walls and rumbled down a rough, cobbled street built by the Romans, probably as far back as the first century B.C. Most of the wagons parted from us just inside the city walls, and only our carriage and Ingund's followed Hermenegild up the stone street to the palace.

At the doorway of a solid Gothic building stood Queen Goswintha, and she did not look pleased. As her son dismounted and a stableman led his horse away, she stood, legs wide, arms crossed. An attendant stood on either side of her holding armloads of what I supposed were gifts for Ingund.

Hermenegild stepped up to his mother, bowed discreetly, and spoke to her. We were too far from them to hear what she said, but it was clear she was angry. Her arms flew out to her sides, and I got my first—but far from my last—glimpse of her temper.

"What is the problem?" I asked the handmaids who were all glued to the windows, afraid to get out of the carriage until the disagreement had been resolved.

"She would be angry that Hermenegild showed himself to Ingund first. It was the queen's privilege to greet the princess and welcome her to the kingdom." I guessed they learned that from Brunhilde's handmaids, who would have given them instructions for how to behave on their arrival. I had only joined the entourage in Toulouse, so I missed whatever orientation there might have been. Now I didn't know if I would be allowed to stay with Ingund. I guessed it would be possible only if Ingund demanded it, and even as close as we had become over the long journey, I wasn't sure how much it would matter in this new place. As a relative of Ingund's father's Merovingian side, and not her mother's Visigothic side, I might be seen as a possible spy, marriage alliance or not. I hoped I wouldn't be turned away because there was so much more of Ingund's story to come.

Finally, Goswintha waved her hand to dismiss her son, and Hermenegild, head down, walked around to the side of the palace where the groomsmen had taken his horse and disappeared. Only then did Sebastianus hop down and open the princess's carriage door.

As Ingund stepped out with Sebastianus's help, I grimaced, thinking it wouldn't be fair if Goswintha took her fury at her son out on Ingund. But my worry was short-lived when the grandmother walked toward Ingund and held out her arms. Ingund was swallowed in the long, wide sleeves of the queen's coat, and I let out my breath. Maybe things were going to be all right after all. At least for a while.

The home of King Leovigild and Queen Goswintha resembled a monastery more than a palace. Only a single arched doorway flanked by Corinthian columns interrupted the façade of finely joined gray stone masonry. How modest it looked compared with Sigibert's palace in Lutetia! A small entry foyer opened to a wide corridor, its high barrel-shaped stone ceiling carved with human and animal figures. On either side, doors led to about a dozen rooms that I didn't have a chance to peek into, as we rushed to the living quarters at the back of the palace, hurried along by Leovigild's guards.

I was led into a small chamber with a serviceable cot and a small armoire next to Ingund's bedroom on the second floor. She would keep her own room, even after the marriage, and would be invited to join Hermenegild in his bed only at his summons and only after the wedding.

"She is as scary as my mother," Ingund whispered to me as I helped her remove her traveling clothes and wash her face and hands in the large bowl on a dresser. "I guess I should have expected that. She is my mother's mother."

I huffed a small chuckle and left my response at that. Until I got better at reading her new in-laws, I thought I should keep my observations to myself.

Besides the dresser, her room was nicely furnished with a large bed, an armoire, a chest, and a small table and chair that could serve as a dressing table. Hanging behind the table, a thick sheet of pewter served as a decent mirror, polished and reflective as any I had seen in the sixth century. A rug from the Far East cushioned the plank floor. The window faced the entry courtyard. Pushing aside the curtains at the window provided an unobstructed view of the entry courtyard below.

I looked out to watch Sebastianus and a couple of groomsmen conversing before he climbed back up on Ingund's carriage and drove it around the corner of the palace.

"What are you looking at, Cousin?" Ingund asked, leaning against my back.

"Nothing." I quickly dropped the curtain.

"Really? Nothing?" she teased. I wondered if I had given myself away, as unabashedly as I had stared at Sebastianus the past few days. He had only once met my eyes, but I thought I could feel them on my back at times. Perhaps my attraction to him was reciprocated. But he wasn't letting me know.

# XVII

The extravagance of the marriage ceremony didn't surprise me much, except by its four-hour length. I was teetering and yawning from boredom, cramping legs, and the stuffy air of the cathedral long before it was over.

As I had seen in paintings of medieval weddings, the bride and groom took their places on either side of a two-sided kneeling bench on the level of the altar. The priest stood between them, behind the bench, trading huge liturgy texts, a Bible, and goblets back and forth with an acolyte who stood beside him. Ingund was dressed in a suffocatingly heavy robe of wool, lined with ermine and gold, and she kneeled demurely for nearly the entire time. Hermenegild wore a long, dark blue vest over a tunic and britches, which looked considerably more comfortable than her outfit, but he only knelt at the end, when they received the final benediction of the ceremony and each drank from a gold chalice. I was glad she didn't have to stand for four hours in that costume, but I could imagine her knees buckling from pain when she got up.

I understood little of the archaic Latin the priest recited and sang, and little of the responses from the attendees, the noblest of whom stood crowded around the platform. I stayed well back with the highest-ranking soldiers, lower-ranking nobles, and a few servants of the household. I knew hundreds more peasants, servants, and slaves were huddled outside of the front door, getting as close as they could to the historic moment.

Finally, the bride and groom stepped down from the raised platform in front of the altar and exited by a side door. I had expected them to walk down the aisle between the assembled celebrants, but I was misled by not having seen anything but twenty-first-century weddings before then. Apparently, the priest would deliver more advice and instruction to the newlyweds before they'd be allowed to leave the sanctity of the church and join the royal party in the palace.

The wedding banquet that followed, held in the great hall of the palace, was more extravagant than the wedding. Three long tables had been placed in a U-shape, with the head table away from the entrance. Stools were arranged on one side of the legs of the U, and cushioned benches were set along the head table.

When the doors were opened and some fifty of us were slowly ushered to the tables, Ingund and Hermenegild were still missing. The queen and king were already sitting at the head table, and the king was guzzling from a big goblet while the queen looked on, disparagingly. I, as a low-ranking royal cousin, sat at the very end of the head table, which didn't please me as it didn't give me a clear view of Ingund, who would sit between the king and queen with her new husband. The nobles and some wealthy merchants filled the stools, men and women alike, although by the time they'd all drunk enough, it was hard to pick out who might have been married to whom, as they all clung to and fell over each other lustily.

We had all been seated when Ingund and Hermenegild were escorted into the room by his brother, Reccared, and a woman I didn't recognize. I assumed she was a royal relative, more important than I was, supposedly a real cousin. Before the newlyweds sat, they were greeted by Leovigild and Goswintha with a toast that I couldn't hear over the din in the room. Past the royalty at my end of the table, I could see that Leovigild was already swaying from his celebratory gulps.

The meal went on for at least five hours, and I knew the celebration would continue for three days. I had acquaintances in my time who would brag about their capacity for liquor, but they couldn't hold a candle to the celebrants at a Visigothic feast. I watched guests occasionally stand, stumble outside, and regurgitate to make room for more food and drink, before returning to the table. I wasn't enjoying myself. The elderly woman sitting next to me in a long silk gown, a huge fur coat draped over her shoulders, had turned her back to me to talk with the man next to her, and never once looked back. I searched the crowd unsuccessfully for Sebastianus to see how he was behaving, but either he had not been invited or had turned down the invitation out of good sense.

The parade of servants bringing food and tankards of wine and beer had not stopped by the time I excused myself three hours later. I was more drunk than I'd ever been in my lifetime, but I was also likely the most sober person in the room.

As I stumbled clumsily to my room, I felt disgusted at myself and the scene I'd just left. It would take centuries before this royal wastefulness would come to its rightful punishment—in the French Revolution, the Haitian Revolution, the Irish Rebellion, and more. Watching the partygoers' behavior made me wonder why the reckoning hadn't come sooner.

I knew my displeasure was a privileged form of cultural intolerance, privileged by post-industrial liberalism and democratic notions. What was appropriate in twenty-first-century polite society would not be appreciated by Ingund's guests either—the mixing of races and people of different classes, for example. Possibly, the top 1 percent of my world celebrated as wantonly and lewdly as the upper crust of Ingund's century. I had just never witnessed it.

I fell into bed with my dress on and decided I'd skip the next two days of feasting. I'd help Ingund get ready if she needed me. But if she protested my truancy, I'd feign stomach upset and a headache.

As it was, she didn't even notice my absence. She was already madly in love.

I DIDN'T KNOW HOW LONG the love that had burst out of their marriage, full force, from its first moments, would last, but I had never seen a new bride so enamored of her husband or a husband immediately besotted with his wife. Yes, theirs was an arranged marriage, and most of them were negotiated before the bride and groom met, let alone fell in love. But this one was working. At least for now.

Hermenegild and Ingund were, within hours of their wedding, inseparable except for the times he had to spend with his father and she with her mother-in-law. I suddenly had too much spare time and was considering going back to the twenty-first century for a break. The only thing that held me back was that returning was no sure thing, and the best parts of Ingund's story—or should I say, the most dramatic parts—were still ahead of us.

I wasn't welcome around the handmaids, who were either embroidering, or tending to Ingund's clothing and grooming, or in some way bustling around in every room, all the time. They didn't exactly snub me, but I realized I was making them uncomfortable when they quit chatting and gossiping when I walked by. Growing up, I was taught to never hold myself above anyone who cleaned, cooked, or cared for children, or did what we called pink-collar or blue-collar work. So, I didn't, but things were different, oh, so different, in sixth century Toledo. I tried loitering in the small garden back of the house, but the gardeners scowled and quit working, leaning idly on their tools, anytime I invaded their territory, as if on strike, even though I only wanted to sit for a moment and listen to the birds.

I found myself wandering to the stables just to get out of the house. I had never been a horsewoman, much. I could ride if I had to, but I didn't really care for it. After a week of my brief stable visits, Sebastianus stopped avoiding my eye and slipping away whenever I approached. Still, he said nothing in greeting. But after a second week, he watched me approach, handed me a curry comb, and pointed at the chestnut mare in the stall next to him. I was surprised. She was his favorite horse, the one he rode when he wasn't driving Ingund's carriage. That he would let anyone else groom her was surprising. It felt like I'd been awarded a gold star. That he, a servant, would ask a member of a royal family to do manual labor for him was even more surprising.

When I had brushed her to a fine sheen, he pointed me to another stall, but this time instead of sticking to his own tasks while I worked, he sat on a bale of straw and watched me. I felt his presence as viscerally as if he were standing close enough for the hair of his arms to tickle mine. My heart pounded, and my breaths grew short and uneven by the time I was finished. I turned to him for my next assignment, but he stood up and stuck out his elbow to escort me out of the barns. I flushed, put down the brush, and accepted his invitation.

We walked around the stables, me on weak knees, and I lifted my skirts so I could match his long stride down a wooded path toward a small stream that I hadn't visited before. A simple plank had been set on stumps next to a little rapids where the sun glittered off the falling water and wet rocks. If I'd known about this place, I probably would never have started hanging out at the stables.

I let go of his arm and sat on the small bench. He sat next to me. In that setting, I should have been the most relaxed I'd been since I left Minneapolis. But with him so close, I relived the many times I'd watched him, noting the fine shape of his body, yearning for such a man's touch.

"Tell me the truth," he said in fine Latin, looking at the water, not at me. "Who are you and where did you come from?"

"I am Sigibert's second cousin," I said definitively. "I came from Carthage to escort Ingund to her new home."

"No. No, you aren't." he said. "I don't think any of that is true, but I have to give you credit for doing such a good job of faking it."

"Faking what?"

He turned to me with a sly smile. "You're not a cousin, and you're not from Carthage."

"What makes you think that?" My heart beat harder now, not from his proximity, but from fear of discovery. Was he going to rat me out—or whatever they called tattling in the sixth century? Obviously, he was right, and he knew that when he handed me the curry comb.

"You are no Vandal, no Frank, no Byzantine," he said. "You don't look like one, and you don't act like one. When you curtsy before the queen, it's not with reverence but with awkwardness, like you don't think you should have to do it. You don't think she's better than you."

I didn't answer right away. He was right. I was trying, but my mannerisms were all wrong. Despite all the ways I had tried to fit in, from bowing to a king and curtsying before the queen to speaking Latin and being at Ingund's beck and call, I knew someone was likely to notice how ill-suited I was for it all.

"You've been watching me."

"I'm not going to get you in trouble," he said, gently laying his hand on mine. "I let you groom my horse, whom I admire more than any woman, except you. But to you, I am only a humble servant, and you are royalty."

I saw the glint of humor in his eye; he was teasing me. He knew I wasn't royalty. He probably wasn't a humble servant. In fact, when I thought about it, he didn't act particularly demure around the real princes, princesses, queens, kings, and their cousins either.

"You are a bit out of line for a humble servant, aren't you?" I teased back. "What right do you think you have of talking that way to a relative of the king, an escort to a princess?"

"That would be a good question," he said, "if it were true. Now, are you going to tell me who you are, or will I have to try to find out in some other way?"

What other way could he find out? Would he start asking others who I was? I wondered for a moment whether it made sense to tell him the truth or make up a more believable story. I knew I couldn't tell him I came from the future. How would he react?

He was still looking at me with his crooked grin, his bright blue eyes squinting with wit. I hesitated, my eyes glued to his, and sensed heat rising up my spine. Instead of answering him, I did what I wanted to do more than anything else. I leaned forward and put my lips to his. He didn't seem surprised. He slid a hand around to the back of my neck and held me there.

When we pulled apart, he looked no more apologetic than I was. I recognized an urge to pull him to the ground with me, stunned at how much I wanted more from him, someone I hardly knew. We stared at each other for a few moments before he pulled my face back to his again. I grew dizzy, hardly able to breathe, as his lips caressed mine, his beard tickling my chin. When we stopped, I leaned my forehead on his shoulder and closed my eyes.

"I have been waiting for you for a long time," I whispered. It was the most honest thing I had ever said in the sixth century. "But why should it be you?"

As an answer, he stood up, took my hand, and led me back to the stables.

# XVIII

After that, we came together most afternoons, lying on a scratchy blanket stretched across bales of straw. Familiar with the groomsmen's routines, Sebastianus knew when we would be alone. I trusted him, even knowing the price of getting caught would likely be banishment from the palace, at best.

His touch was both tender and confident, and with him, I discovered lovemaking for the first time. Before then, I knew sex, but not lovemaking. Not until Sebastianus and I made love.

After we exhausted each other, we lay nearly naked and perilously exposed, often coming close to staying longer than we should, talking quietly, Sebastianus's hand on my breast or my stomach, my head on his chest or his shoulder. As many questions as I had about who he was, he revealed nothing other than to explain away the long scar on his left arm as a "minor war injury."

He knew little about the Merovingians, which I thought was strange, since he had fought for them, and he knew even less about the history of the Visigoths, the Byzantines, and the Vandals. I summarized their stories and probable legacies for him, stopping my tales at our then-present, AD 579. If he wondered how I knew so much, he didn't ask.

I told him my real name.

Neither of us spoke of love.

We met daily for weeks. Time passed as irrelevant. I was surprised and ecstatic, and yet, conflicted. I was in the sixth century, either for real or in a long, vivid dream, but I was still engaged, wasn't I? Didn't the promise of marriage apply even if I didn't make it for another fifteen hundred years? What if this was only a dream? Are we responsible for what we do in a dream?

And a suspicion had started to take root that I couldn't shake. Was it possible that Sebastianus and Sébastièn were one and the same? They looked alike. Was he as much of a time traveler as I was? In Minnesota, his scientific realism was his cover, and here in Toledo, he pretended to be nothing but a manservant. I had my doubts, but I kept them to myself. I loved what we had, and I didn't want to ruin it.

Meanwhile, Ingund and Hermenegild spent hours together behind his bedchamber's door, learning to make love, too. She moved around the palace as if floating, as if she didn't need legs or feet, a small, persistent smile on her dreamy face.

"You are happy?" I asked her not quite rhetorically one evening as I was helping prepare her for her regular evening meal with her husband. She sat on a stool at the dressing table in her bedroom, her hands in her lap and a dreamy, distant look on her face. I was brushing her hair to a sheen.

"Yes. Yes. So happy," she whispered. "I did not know that marriage would be so wonderful. My mother had me prepared for misery and pain. But this is better than I dreamed it would be."

That made me wonder about Brunhilde's marriage to Sigibert. Had it been miserable? Is that why she prepared her daughter for the worst? Like Ingund, Brunhilde had been shunted from one kingdom to another as a diplomatic tool, and she and Sigibert didn't meet until just before the wedding. But her husband, unlike his brother Chilperic, never took other wives or bore children with other women, although he would have had the opportunity.

Perhaps Brunhilde had been happy in her marriage, and yet, all I knew about her was how powerful and power-hungry she was. Historians didn't care about marital satisfaction. For them, marriage was only interesting if it secured territory or advanced a religion.

"What about you, Cousin?" she asked, turning to look up at me. "When will you have happiness? You are too old to marry, but perhaps there is still a chance for love."

I was only twenty-six! But in an era when marriages were arranged before the bride reached puberty, and even some weddings took place before it happened, I was old.

I ignored the unintended insult and nodded. "I am certain I will find love in my life," I said, not committing to any place or century.

"How about Sebastianus?" she asked, smiling at me in the pewter mirror. I fumbled and dropped the brush. I bent to pick it up and as I rose, I saw her grinning face in our reflection.

"Why would you think of him?" I choked out as an answer, knowing that my clumsiness and my red face gave me away. I stared at her hair, the brush in my hand motionless over her head. "He's not of royal blood, is he?"

"No, but neither are you," she said, grinning conspiratorially.

"What are you saying?" I quit pretending to brush her hair and sat down on the stool next to her. Was my subterfuge being called out for the second time in just weeks?

"Cousin." She winked. "I call you that so you will be welcome and treated as you deserve to be. But I have known from the start you were not a cousin. It is a good thing my mother never met you. One look at your hair and your skin, and she would have sent you to the rack as soon as you arrived. Lucky for us, everyone was happy to go along with your deception, as long as I accepted you. I guess I had been a fairly difficult child, and you didn't seem to mind that. And I believe we could easily have been cousins, as kind as you have been to me."

My mouth was so dry, I couldn't form a word. My sight blurred, darkly, and for a moment I wondered if I'd go deaf from the ringing in my ears. If Sebastianus and Ingund both knew I wasn't who I said I was, who else would figure it out? Who else had?

My next thought was this: if I ever lost Ingund's favor, I was toast. I wouldn't survive another day in Goswintha's household. And why had she mentioned Sebastianus? Had she seen something? Had I been too careless with my daily visits to the stables? Did she overhear some household gossip? Had someone spied on my daily disappearance? It wouldn't take long for such a salacious tale to spread in a royal house.

When I could finally speak, I chose my words carefully.

"Sebastianus is an attractive man, but I do not think it is right for me to think about him. You are my first responsibility. My only responsibility. You should not be concerned about me. I am to be concerned about you."

"I am doing fine," Ingund said, spinning around and taking my hands. "When I am with child, which should be soon" – she blushed a bit at that – "I will need you more. Right now, I have little time to spend with you. My husband devours my days and fills my thoughts. You should go away for a while. Go to my father-in-law's villa. Relax and think about what I said. Now that I know what love is, I want you to have it, too."

So, she didn't know about our daily trysts. She only wished for them. Perhaps my furtive glances at Sebastianus had been reciprocated behind my back, as I had felt, and the observant Ingund had recognized them for what they were.

I knew at that moment she was right: I needed to go. But I needed to go home, not to a villa outside of town. My affair with Sebastianus was puzzling and consuming. I had fallen in love with a man in the sixth century, and that was crazy. And now, if anyone besides Ingund suspected it, it was also dangerous. It could shorten my future with Ingund and Goswintha if not my life.

And I needed to decide what to do about Justin when I got home and see if I still had a job.

But before I had a chance to leave, I witnessed one of the most famous scenes in Visigothic history, which postponed my trip.

# XIX

I guessed it before anyone but Ingund. But we kept mum until she was sure.

When she was certain, and Ingund and Hermenegild announced that she was with child, another great feast erupted in the palace. Although medieval times were difficult, and the peasants as hungry and deprived as historians thought, the abundance of food and drink consumed later that week told a different story. Huge platters of roast pigs, chickens, and geese, surrounded with turnips, greens, beets, and tiny cabbages were carried into the dining hall by a parade of servants and slaves. Wooden tankards fairly littered the tables, and I watched Hermenegild down more than a dozen goblets of dark, undiluted wine. In contrast, Ingund drank little, although perhaps as much as her queasy stomach could take. She'd been joyful but had turned nearly green with sickness every morning for a week or so. She stayed with the revelers as long as she could before asking me to escort her to her bedchamber.

The baby was good news, but the imminent arrival of an heir to Leovigild's throne didn't appear to overcome Goswintha's hostility toward Ingund's stubborn adherence to Catholicism. She and her husband, King Leovigild, believed their Arian religion was part of what held the kingdom's governance together, even though the people of the tribes that predated the Visigoths had largely converted from paganism to Catholicism already. Goswintha bickered about Ingund's refusal to convert as they walked in the halls and over their meals. She wasn't concerned if anyone heard her nagging, and the handmaids tried to avoid them when they were together. If I saw one scurrying down the hall toward me in panic, I guessed that Ingund and Goswintha would soon follow. Ingund answered her grandmother only by lowering her eyes and shaking her head. I admired her tenacity and courage. I could not have stood up to the queen with the composure she did, but then, I had no idea what it was like to have such a strong religious conviction.

I was with Ingund when the queen summoned her to the courtyard.

"What does she want?" Ingund asked me as, hand-in-hand, we wended our way through the palace to the chilly open air. I suspected this would be the moment memorialized in history books: a spectacular confrontation about conversion. But I couldn't interfere with history.

"I don't know. Her handmaiden didn't say," I answered, feeling guilty about my foreknowledge and my decision that I shouldn't stop what was about to happen.

I could tell Ingund was nervous, but she tried to smile. I slipped my hand out of hers and put it on her shoulder, and she sighed. "I'm sure it will be nothing," I lied. "You have been getting along well, other than your religious differences."

When we walked out onto the stone plaza of the courtyard, tension hung in the humid air. A priest stood next to Goswintha, a sly, conspiratorial smile on his face, a big leather-bound manuscript clutched to his chest. Ingund stopped. She looked at me with wide eyes, and I thought she might run, but Goswintha pushed me aside and grabbed her arm.

"You have defied me and our kingdom long enough," the queen said. She jerked Ingund toward the fountain in the middle of the yard. Ingund tried to pull back, but the older woman was bigger and stronger. The priest slid behind Ingund's back and gave her a gentle shove forward.

Stopping in front of the fountain, Goswintha held tight to Ingund's arm, as the girl squirmed to get loose.

"I am with child, Queen Grandmother!" she yelled. "You could harm Hermenegild's heir. What is this?"

"You will renounce your heresy and be baptized as an Arian," Goswintha demanded.

"No!" Ingund strained against her grandmother's grip. "I cannot! I believe in the Trinity, that the Son is divine. I will not forsake my salvation or my child's salvation for you or your kingdom!"

I thought that last part was unwise, and I stepped forward to intervene, but Goswintha shot out her arm to block me and flung me a look that told me it could be fatal to get between them. And then, she did what I knew from history she would: she pushed Ingund into the fountain.

The girl plunged into the water on her side, screaming and floundering, struggling to get to her feet. She got to her knees, but slipped and fell again, and I feared for her life and that of her baby.

Even the priest seemed shocked at Goswintha's violence. The old queen held Ingund's head under water and gestured to the book in his hands.

"Read the sacrament now," she shouted.

The priest backed away. "I cannot baptize a person who does not accept the faith willingly," he said, nearly in a whisper. He may have been afraid of Goswintha, but he may also have been afraid of his God's wrath if he debased the sacrament.

Ingund managed to raise her head enough to gulp some air. Scowling, Goswintha lunged forward and pushed her back underwater. At that point, I had no choice but to act. Ingund was not supposed to die then, I knew, and if I let it happen, I would risk allowing a major break in the trajectory of history. Perhaps, I thought fleetingly, I was meant to be here. Perhaps I was destined to travel back in time to save her from this very danger.

I put my knee on the edge of the fountain and reached out to the struggling girl. She grabbed my sleeves, and I pulled her upright. Goswintha stood back and watched, a self-satisfied smile on her face, shaking water from her hands.

"There. It is done," she said. Clearly, she didn't think the reading of the sacrament was necessary. She had accomplished what she wanted without the help of the priest. She considered Ingund baptized in the Arian faith. She turned and strode away, leaving the courtyard the way we had come out without a glance back at her sobbing, drenched granddaughter.

The priest stood, watching us as I helped Ingund stumble out of the fountain, her dress soaked and her hair dripping. I looked at him, the obvious question on my face. Was she now baptized as an Arian?

"No," the priest answered my unvoiced question. He looked neither apologetic nor victorious. "She who does not go to the fount in humility and intent has not accepted the faith or been baptized." He turned and followed Goswintha into the palace.

I wrapped my cloak around the shivering Ingund and walked her back to her bedroom. I realized how fortunate it was that I hadn't yet returned home. Who would have saved her if I hadn't been there?

INGUND CAME TO ME THAT evening, exhausted and red-eyed. I rose at her knock, and she let herself in. She walked into my arms, and I held her for a few long minutes. Finally, she pulled back, her face distorted with pain, perhaps more emotional than physical.

"I told Hermenegild about what Goswintha did," she said. "He said he will chastise his mother, which is not good, as she will hold it against me."

"But at least he stands behind you," I said. "He is trying to protect you."

"Yes, but he ignores my pleas to convert and save himself from damnation. Why should I retire for eternity beside the blessed Jesus if he is not with me?"

I had no answer. It wasn't a question I had ever considered, because to me, all life and consciousness ended at death. There was no heaven nor hell. But spouting my disbelief wasn't going to help Ingund.

She sat on the edge of my bed, her hands folded in her lap, her head bowed. "I wish I had someone to guide me in this struggle," she said. She paused but didn't look up. "I came to you because I know your secret. I know you can read, so it is possible you can also write. Will you write to the Bishop Cyprian for me? Perhaps he will give me some guidance. Some hope."

"I do not have parchment nor ink," I said apologetically. I didn't deny the ability to write.

Writing a letter would add more risk to those I had already taken. I had lied about who I was. I was making love with a servant on the king's own estate. I had intervened with Goswintha's baptism plans. And now would I write a letter that Goswintha could possibly intercept? If she did, she would be furious at Ingund's impudence and my interference. Pretty soon, my lies and sins were likely to be discovered, and I'd be doomed. Once that happened, would I have time to put on my dress and pass back through the portal to home and safety before I was marched to the rack?

But it occurred to me this was the second time in one day that I felt destined to be with Ingund in this place and time. Ingund *had* sent a letter to Cyprian, asking for his advice, according to Gregory of Tours' *History of the Franks*. Since Ingund couldn't write, and the Arian clerics were unlikely to help her, someone else had to have done it. Was that me?

"I will gladly write the letter if you can procure the materials I need." I had decided. Ingund was alone here inside the Arian Visig-othic empire, and I was the only one she could trust. She could trust me because she knew my secrets were worse than her letter would be. But I also believed she cared for me as much as I cared for her.

Two days later, Ingund came to my room before dawn. I heard the door open, and for a moment, I thought – wished – that it would be Sebastianus, even though I knew that could never happen. He did not live in the palace, and it would be dangerous, even life-threatening, for him to be caught inside the queen's quarters. I couldn't help feeling let down, even though I was happy to see Ingund.

"Cousin," she whispered, as I sat up and motioned for her to come closer. "I found what you need for the letter. Can we talk about it now?"

I shook myself awake and dispelled with the remnants of my disappointment. "Certainly," I said. "Let me put on my robe, and you can tell me what to write."

She rambled a bit, going back and forth, composing sentences and organizing her thoughts, but I got the idea, and told her I would put her words on paper as soon as it got light.

"How will you send it to him?" I asked.

"Sebastianus will deliver it to a courier who will carry it to Toulouse for a nice piece of gold," she said. "I have already talked with him."

I laughed quietly. We had become quite the conniving threesome, a threesome with even more conspiracies to come.

I decided to stick around long enough for the letter to get to Septimania, and for a response to come back, so I could read it to Ingund. Sebastianus and I had a few more daytime meetings in the stables, which didn't reduce my trepidation or confusion over our affair, but it did make the time pass more quickly, not to mention pleasantly. But a few days later, he left to carry out some undisclosed mission for Hermenegild.

When the Bishop's answer to Ingund arrived, the courier brought it to me, and I brought it to Ingund. I read it aloud to her. The missive was terse, and its tone was unequivocal. "You must keep trying to convert your husband," was the gist of it. "For your sake, his, and that of your children."

I knew this part of history, and I knew what was coming next. I needed a Minnesota break before I faced it. I wanted to come back if I could, but I had waited long enough to take care of things back home.

I told Ingund I would take her suggestion: I would recuperate for a while in a villa of her father's. I didn't, of course. I put on the dress and walked out of my bedroom into the corridor of a hotel in modern Toledo.

# XX

On the plane to Paris from Toledo, Nicole thought about how hard it would be for anyone to believe her stories. She didn't understand how she moved from century to century, and she wasn't yet convinced it was time travel and not an extended dream. For one curious thing, time passed at a different rate when she was in the sixth century than it did at home. When she had arrived in Toulouse, five years had passed in Ingund's life, but back in 2023 Minnesota, it had only been two months. And now, she had just experienced four years in Septimania and Spain, but only a week had gone by in modern Paris.

It reminded her of the movie "Contact." Jodie Foster's character traveled in an alien-inspired transport through a wormhole to a planet orbiting the star of Vega. Her headset recorded eighteen hours of travel, but on Earth, observers saw the transport crash in less than a second, and they were convinced that she didn't go anywhere. Nicole wondered what the scientist Sébastièn had thought of that.

But on the other hand, her portal, the dress, seemed like anything but a time machine. It was rather like an emotional trigger that could bring on dreams that she was experiencing as reality.

How did the dress "know" what she needed to research? How did it land her in precisely the place and time she needed to be? It was all so incredibly unlikely that she decided she'd never mention it to anyone but Katie, her mother, and Sébastièn, if she ever saw him again. She certainly wouldn't tell her dissertation committee, even if they questioned how she could explain all the historical detail that she would now incorporate in her novel.

Since she had no control, as far as she knew, over when and where she landed, she didn't know where she would end up if she decided to don the dress for the third time. Could she possibly end up further back in time? In ancient China? In some paleolithic cave? It seemed that anything was possible, as long as the second law of thermodynamics didn't seem to be holding.

NICOLE SPENT TWO DAYS IN Paris, supposedly doing more research at the Cluny and the Sorbonne, but in fact, she was only faking it. If she came back after only a week, it would look suspiciously like she hadn't done any research at all. And since her ticket was booked for two days later, she could see no reason to rush home.

Time travel was exhausting, she realized. She slept twelve hours a night in Paris and didn't remember a single dream from all that slumber. The rest of her time there, she sat at outdoor cafés, discreetly looking for the Sébastièn doppelganger she had seen on her last trip, jotting down memories from her trip to Toledo with Ingund in her notebook, hoping to capture enough detail while it was still fresh so that her novel would write itself when she got back. She'd learned long ago, as far back as high school, that whenever writing was hard, it was because you didn't know enough about what you were trying to write.

She returned to a quiet St. George. Katie was still off on her tour of literary sites in the UK, and her mother wasn't answering her phone. Justin was staying in Oklahoma until school started late in August, not that she would have told him much anyway. So, Nicole felt she had no choice but to try to reach Sébastièn. Even though he had explained the impossibility of time travel, he'd been politely curious, encouraging her to describe her experience. She needed someone to hear about the latest one.

He was off on a trip to a conference at the Hadron supercollider in Europe, the physics department admin told her. "He should be back in a couple of days. Do you want me to have him call you?"

He called three days later, by which time she'd written as much as she could remember, worrying less about the sentences and the paragraphs and concerned more about preserving detail before she forgot it. In putting it down, she realized she now believed it had happened, and if she put on the dress, it would happen again. It wasn't just a dream.

They met at a bar just off campus, a place where they could have been recognized if seen together. But few students hung around for summer school at MacIntosh. Most were off on European vacations, internships, or back home entertaining younger siblings. According to the calendar, she'd only been gone nine days, and he'd only been gone two weeks. It was still the middle of July.

Nicole had planned to tell him about Sebastianus, perhaps to coax him into admitting he was her sixth-century lover, but when she saw him, she changed her mind, as unsure as she was about everything that had happened.

"How was the supercollider?" she asked after they ordered their drinks.

"Meh," he said, shaking his head. "You've seen one, you've seen them all."

She laughed dutifully, but when he followed that up with "I have to admit something, Nicole," she thought he was going to confess he been in Spain on his own time-travel adventure. That he was Sebastianus, just as she was the ersatz cousin of Ingund. He would say that he hadn't been in Geneva at all, but he'd been with her in Toledo just days ago.

"You have opened my eyes to something I'd never realized before: that the dark ages could be interesting," he said instead.

"I always thought nothing much happened except for a bunch of peasants mucking around in the dirt and nasty kings and queens and their armies going at each other with battle axes. Oh, and the plague."

"It's a lot of all that," she said, smiling broadly to hide her disappointment and suspicion. How had he found out that the Middle Ages weren't boring? Wasn't it from her naked history lesson on the hay bales in Toledo? "Have you been reading up on it? I have lots of books you can read, if you're interested."

He nodded and declined the offer. She couldn't help but stare at his face, trying her best to imagine him with a full beard, and when he glanced over at her, she looked away quickly. She leaned over the bar looking for the bartender, who appeared to have left without delivering their drinks, and she wondered if she could go behind the bar and help herself. A drink to hold onto might help her feel a little less anxious.

"I heard about the department's investigation," Sébastièn said, putting his hand on her arm and squeezing lightly. "I'm sorry. But you'll finish your dissertation soon and find somewhere much more suitable, I'm sure."

"I suppose the news is all over campus," she said. He mumbled an affirmation.

"What do you think about these things?" she asked, looking down at his hand on her arm. Did it look familiar? Was it the same hand that had rested on her breast fifteen hundred years before? "Do things like that happen in the physics department or are you safe from censorship there?"

"Oh, there are plenty of opinions about scientific theory that can collide and cause enmity. You know, the strings and the particles things. And always, there's jealousy over grants and journal publications that causes sniping, usually among the faculty though, not between students and professors. The censorship afflicting history departments and the other humanities hasn't happened to us yet."

"You should be grateful."

"I am." He gave her the half-smile she had come to anticipate. It softened his eyes, and she had to turn away to keep from thinking even if he wasn't Sebastianus … well, then what? Maybe the spark wasn't irresistible, but it was still there. She feared she might lean over and kiss him, just as she had his doppelganger.

"Still," he continued. "A lot of professors in sciences worry about what they can teach or say in their classrooms, especially, I think, in organic chem and biology, you know, evolution, adaptation, and natural selection. And whether the world is only eight thousand years old. It seems that all the power is now in the hands of students who get to tell the professors what they should teach instead of the professors deciding what the students should learn."

Nicole let his empathy sink in a minute, as she sipped from the glass of wine the bartender had finally delivered.

"You know," she said, "I know so little about you. Are you married? Kids? Ex-wife, grandkids? Serious girlfriend?"

"It's hard to say," he said. A half-smile snuck up one side of his face as he looked off.

"Hard to say? Those questions pretty much call for yes or no answers, don't they?"

"Right," he said, meeting her eyes again. "You're right."

He told her about his marriage: he was twenty, she was twenty-one. She was an artist, he was still in undergraduate school at the University of Wisconsin, and they had met during a spring party on the lawn in front of the main administration building, Bascom Hall. The party was a vestige of the Pail and Shovel Party, which had won the student government election in 1978 by promising such absurdities as a half-submerged Statue of Liberty in Lake Mendota and a flock of pink flamingos on the Bascom Hill lawn, both of which they delivered.

Sébastièn and Lydia were high when they met, and high when they got married after three weeks in her small bed in an artist cooperative. Sébastièn worked in the physics lab to earn his tuition and took more than a full load of heavy science classes, trying to graduate early. In Lydia, he saw a way out of the gloom and tedium he'd created for himself since coming to campus from a small town in northern Wisconsin. His father was an engineer and his mother a full-time housewife, and up to when he joined that party on the steep grassy slope of the Hill, he'd done nothing his parents wouldn't have wanted or expected, except smoking pot with his friends in the dorm.

They were married for six months, all the time sharing a bedroom with three other artists who were more likely to be sleeping there during the day than at night. The first two weeks were glorious. Sébastièn felt liberated from his strict upbringing and his studies. She introduced him to her favorite science fiction and fantasy novels, and he tried to talk to her about physics. But she quickly tired of the physics lessons, and he tired of the silly, impossible stories she read aloud to him. They stuck it out for another five and half months, mostly for the sex, partly because he was afraid to admit the mistake to his parents.

The divorce was quick and easy; neither of them owned anything of value except textbooks and novels. He moved back into the dorm, and his parents wrote to him of their relief.

"There," he said. "I've confessed. And you? Tell me about your fiancé."

"That's quite a story," she said, avoiding his question about Justin. "No one since then? Girlfriends? Lovers."

"Nothing serious."

No sex, no love interest for eight years? Nicole found that hard to believe. He was a little too attractive to have not encountered plenty of willing companions. But then he hadn't said "no sex," only "nothing serious."

"So, what did you do after Lydia?"

"Head down. Graduated from the UW, went to MIT, dissertation, PhD, job hunt, here." Anticipating her next question, he explained that he had chosen little, unimpressive MacIntosh over better offers because he liked to hunt and fish, which he'd indulged in for the first couple of years.

"But then I got tired of waiting for fish to bite and hauling a rifle into the woods. I realized I preferred to paddle around in a canoe and walk around the lakes without an agenda. I could just let my mind wander."

"And think about string theory."

"Right, and lately, time travel." He grinned.

She socked him in the arm and companionly leaned her head onto his shoulder. She quickly straightened up. What was she thinking? He had given no indication that he was interested in even a low level of physical intimacy.

"Time travel?" she asked, sitting back to distance herself from her uninvited gesture.

"You seem so sincere," he explained, "so I've been looking to see if there are any serious scientific theories that might explain what you've experienced."

"And…?"

"Well, nothing so far. But I may try to develop my own theories to get around the second-law problem."

"Oh." She thought about what that meant. Did it indicate he might be open to hearing the story of her latest trip?

"I went back." She surprised herself by blurting it out. She didn't look to see his reaction. She was afraid he'd smirk or shake his head with derision. "I went back to the sixth century. I'd like to tell you about it, but I imagine you probably don't want to hear it until you have worked out your theory."

"Yes," he said quietly. "I do want to hear about it. I'm all yours for the evening. I'm very intrigued."

She looked up and his open expression convinced her he was serious.

"Okay, but it's a pretty long story this time. I was there for about four months."

It took her nearly an hour, and Sébastièn listened intently, asking only a few questions now and then. As she continued, she felt ratified by his attention. If he found the story engaging, perhaps her dissertation committee would, too. And her novel readers after that.

But even more heartening was his lack of incredulity. He didn't suggest that it hadn't really happened.

At the very end, she told him about Sebastianus, how the sixth-century man was cagey about his life as Sébastièn had been until now. But she said nothing about their trysts.

"Did he believe you when you told him you came from 2023?"

"I couldn't bring myself to tell him."

Sébastièn nodded and rubbed his chin using the same motion that Sebastianus used to stroke his beard. Maybe all men did it the same way.

"I'm starting to wonder if you are one and the same," she said, lightly.

"I love your story," he answered. "But I'm afraid you're starting to take this time travel thing a bit too personally."

"Personally?" she asks, a bit miffed. "It is happening to me. Why wouldn't I take it personally?"

"Well, perhaps you are not really traveling there physically," he said. "Perhaps it's someone else's life, and you're just inhabiting it now and then. That is one of the things I'm considering."

"That's even harder to understand than time travel."

He paused and locked eyes with her. "I suppose it is." He stood up and put his hand on her elbow, as if to help her up. Despite an inclination to ignore the gesture, she rose with him.

He leaned down and brought his lips to hers, and she knew.

His kiss wasn't exactly the same. There was no scratchy beard adding to the drama. But otherwise, he was Sebastianus. How much more room was there for doubt?

# XXI

They didn't sleep together. Nicole couldn't do it. She was back in the "real" world, and her engagement still meant something here, even if it didn't in the sixth century. She hadn't figured out what to do about Justin, and having him away made it both easier and harder to decide whether it was unavoidably over between them.

Sébastièn had asked her to come home with him. She didn't fool herself by thinking she turned him down because she didn't want to sleep with him. But it was Sebastianus she was in love with. Even if they were the same man in two different centuries – could she imagine having thought something so irrational six months ago? – she wasn't going to have sex with him until he admitted it.

Partly to have time to sort out Sébastièn and Justin in her head, and in part to check in on her mother, she drove down to Iowa City the next Saturday.

She parked in the driveway and walked into the house through the open garage door. Her father's car was gone. He was probably at one of his many coffee klatches her mother had told her about. "They aren't just for old ladies anymore," she had said, chuckling.

Her mother was snoozing on the couch in the family room, PBS on the TV, the sound off. Nicole tiptoed into the kitchen and poured herself a glass of water. Just then, it occurred to her that she had never gotten sick from drinking water in Toledo. She'd gotten sick a year ago going only as far as Mexico, and in the same century. Perhaps this was an indication that her time travel wasn't real. Or maybe it wasn't physical. Maybe there was something to what Sébastièn had hinted at: it was only her mind or her soul that was traveling. But she didn't believe in souls, so that didn't make sense. And how was she ending up in a body and face that was just like hers? And how did he?

Her mother stirred on the couch and opened her eyes. She blinked, sat halfway up, and looked at Nicole, confused.

"Mom?" Nicole asked. She walked to the couch and sat down next to her. "It's me. Nicole."

Her mother swatted her on the leg. "I know who you are. I am just wondering why you are here." She struggled to sit up straight but gave up. She lay back, exhausted.

"Mom, why are you so tired? I've never seen you like this. Especially in the middle of the day." Nicole leaned over and put her hands on her mother's surprisingly bone-thin knees. "Is there something wrong you haven't told me about?"

Grimacing, her mother looked away. "You just got here. Do we have to talk about it?"

Her look was so pleading that Nicole gave in. "Okay. No, we don't. Where's dad?"

"I have no idea," her mother said, finally managing to push herself up to sitting. "He's gone a lot these days, and I can't really blame him. I'm not much for company."

"Is he having an …" Nicole couldn't bring herself to suggest he was having an affair.

"That's the last thing I'd guess," her mother said, chuckling. She reached for Nicole's water. "My guess it's another gossip session with the boys. Just because he has a PhD doesn't mean he's any different from any other old man at the coffee shop."

Nicole relinquished her water glass and got up to get her own.

"Have you been teaching summer school?"

Nicole sat back down on the couch. "I haven't told you what happened," she said. "I forgot you didn't know."

"Know what?"

"I'm being investigated by the ethics committee for embarrassing some young men in my class with my feminist theories." Nicole relayed what her mother would call the Reader's Digest version of the story: short, sweet and devoid of animosity, which made her realize how little she cared about MacIntosh University and the history department now.

"Odd that they're okay with teaching about bloody battles and decapitations and god knows what else is in their lectures," her mother said to Nicole's delight. "But talk about women, and it's 'oh my God, how disturbing!'"

"Exactly!" Nicole agreed.

"And you're almost done with your dissertation, anyway, aren't you?"

"Well, yes. No. I mean, Mom, I'm not sure I'm going to go through my orals."

"What?" That gave her mother the spark to sit up straight. "After all you've been through? You're not going to get your PhD?"

"Relax, Mom," Nicole said. "I'm going to finish writing the novel. But I think I may just decide to stick with that. With writing, that is."

Her mother held her eyes for a moment and nodded. "Well, you certainly can't make any less money than you did teaching feminist history at a military school."

Nicole laughed. "Not actually a military school, but it might as well be."

They sat and sipped their water companionably, and Nicole looked around the room. It hadn't changed in the twenty years since she'd been in kindergarten. Same shag carpet, same cheap wainscotting, same popcorn ceiling. Same brick fireplace that hadn't held a fire in at least a decade.

"When are you going to get this room remodeled, Mom?" she asked. "It looks like it was transported out of the Brady house when they were done with it and ended up over here."

"Well, dear." Her mother paused. "I think it's probably a little too late for redecorating."

Nicole poked her arm. "You're still young, Mom. Lots of time." "Not really."

The sadness in her voice made Nicole set her glass down on the end table, afraid she'd drop it.

"What are you talking about?"

"I have pancreatic cancer. Stage four."

Her mother said it bluntly. Flatly. As if it was happening to someone else. Had she already worked through the shock of the diagnosis, or was this how she was handling it, by separating herself from the emotion of it?

"Oh, Mom. I'm so sorry."

Her mother looked back at her with weary eyes, deep, purplish hollows threatening to suck them down her face. "At least it will be quick, if ugly," she said. "They say probably six weeks."

"I should stay here." Nicole's reaction was instinctual. She didn't need to think about it.

"No!" her mother's response was as quick. "That is not going to happen. I want you working on your dissertation, er … your novel, not hovering over me, making me feel worthless and like a burden. If I have to hide somewhere where you can't find me, I will. But you are not going to ruin your life thinking you can save mine. Mine's a lost cause."

"I can write while I'm here." Nicole swiveled away to wipe her eyes. "It won't ruin my life."

"Crying is okay, Nicole," her mother whispered. "I don't expect you to be stoic about this. I just don't want it to take up the next two months of your life nursing me."

"How is Dad taking this?" Nicole asked.

"I wonder if he isn't a bit relieved."

Nicole twirled around. "What? What do you mean?"

Her mother shrugged and slumped back into the couch. "You know things haven't been so nice between us for some time. I think he's thinking about how things will be better with me gone. He goes out a lot. I think it's like practice for him."

"Don't say that!" Nicole nearly shouted, even as she considered the possibility that it was true. She reacted by whispering instead. "I know you two have, well, what you used to call an 'interesting' relationship. But you've stuck it out this long. He'll miss you terribly."

Her mother's mouth smiled, but her eyes didn't brighten. "But enough. Nicole, really. With so little time left, I'd rather talk about something else. Why don't you fix me a decent martini, and we'll talk about that time-travel thing some more. Okay?"

DRIVING BACK NORTH THE NEXT day, Nicole wondered how her father was going to manage without her mom cooking, cleaning, and washing clothes for him. He'd always had it easy, working just one job while she had two: teaching; and taking care of the house, Nicole, and him.

When he came home earlier that afternoon, he behaved himself. He didn't argue with her mother, disagreeing with everything she said just to prove himself the smartest one in the room, like he used to.

After dinner, Nicole washed the dishes, and her dad dried them while her mom went to bed.

"She told you, I assume?" he asked her, dishtowel in hand, waiting for her to finish scrubbing the last pan.

"Yes. Is it really two months?"

"Probably. Maybe less. These things kill quickly."

"How are you taking it?"

"Okay," he paused. "You know, when you get to be our age, it's probably easier. It's not like any of us thinks we're not going to die.

You get closer to it, and it's easier to take than you'd think."

Nicole was surprised. How could his reaction be so rational, so cold? She placed the pan in the drainer, and her father grabbed it and started wiping. She turned to see his eyelids had turned red, even though his jaw was set.

"But do you now wish you guys had gone traveling the way Mom wanted to? Remember how badly she wanted to go to Greece and see the islands of the Greek myths? Do you wish you'd done some of that?"

"Me? No. Maybe she does. But it was never my thing."

So that was that. Even with his wife nearing her death bed, he was unrepentantly selfish. It wasn't what he wanted, so it was fine if it hadn't happened.

In her childhood bed that night, she could see her mother's tired face and her father's stubborn one, and wondered if this was really the marriage they had wanted. Or at least the marriage she wanted. Had they married because their best friends had married each other? Was it just as predestined – okay, arranged – as hers and Justin's?

Falling into easy marriages, taking the well-travelled path, going with the flow. Lots of clichés seemed to apply. Some turned out okay, of course. Some people loved each other passionately, right up to the end, like Ingund and Hermenegild might. But no, it wasn't going to be that way for her. Regardless of what happened to her in the sixth century or here in the twenty-first, with Justin or somebody else, it was going to be adventurous and spontaneous, she decided. Scary as that might be, at least she wouldn't be bored. It was time to talk to Justin.

SHE WAS BACK WORKING AT her desk, fussing with her uncomfortable chair Tuesday when her father called. "Your mother is in the hospital. She doesn't want you to come."

"But I want to——"

"If you come," her father interrupted, "she'll refuse to see you.

She doesn't want you leaving your work to watch her get needles stuck in her arms and bedpans pushed under her butt."

"But I'd hate it if I missed—"

"Missed what?" He clearly didn't want her to argue. "Miss her final breath? I don't think she's at that point yet. Anyway, you and she had time together when she felt well. This is not her at her best."

Nicole got up and walked outside to the deck with the phone to her ear and sat down under the shade of a big maple.

"Then why did you call?"

"She insisted I not keep any secrets from you. We discussed this when you left last weekend. She wants to make sure you don't rush down here, but she wants you to know what's up."

Nicole didn't know how to respond. Why did her mother want her to stay away so badly?

"What are they doing for her?"

"Medical stuff. Transfusions, IV medications. I don't know. It's all so vague. You know how abstruse doctors like to be. Like we would never understand even if they tried to explain."

Nicole had to smile at that. Only her father would throw around words like "abstruse" when "unclear" would work. Again, the smartest man in the room.

"So as long as we're on the phone, how are things going with the dissertation?" her father asked.

"Amazing," she said. "My research has gone well. But I'm not convinced I need a PhD anymore, or to teach history."

She hadn't realized she had made that decision until she told her mother about it on Saturday. She hadn't been looking at the listings for openings in history departments, which she should have been doing, and now she knew why.

"I'm enjoying writing so much, I may just move onto another novel."

"Oh, novelist," her father said. He laughed. "Now there's a lucrative profession."

# XXII

Nicole was fired. She was working on lesson plans for the summer session a week after she returned from the sixth century when Timothy walked down to her office and handed her the letter that made it official. She hadn't even been allowed to defend herself before the ethics committee ruled. Without tenure, without a PhD, assistant profs like Nicole were easy to dismiss, per the university's rules.

"I'm sorry, but the ethics committee has recommended we don't renew your contract," Timothy said, standing in her doorway, as if he wanted to be able to make a quick escape.

"What does that mean? I'm fired?"

"It wasn't up to me, Nicolette," he said.

"I'm guessing it kinda was," she retorted. "They recommended, you and the dean ruled." He ducked as if she'd thrown something other than words.

"You guys were never fans of my research anyway," she said, shaking her head and looking at the letter again. The words swam on the page. Timothy had stood up for her in faculty meetings, which misled her. Feminist history was scary, and now she wondered why they hired her. Maybe the conservative bent of this faculty had limited the number of applicants, and she was just barely the best choice among many poor ones.

"I'm sorry," he repeated.

Yeah, yeah. Removing her from the faculty would not only eliminate a charge that MacIntosh was brainwashing kids in leftist ideology or broaching "divisive concepts," like nearly all universities were accused of these days, it would also help cut the mandated 10 percent from next year's history department budget. One less faculty member, especially at her salary, wasn't going to get Timothy there, but it would help.

"Just leave," she said, waving a hand toward the hallway, and Timothy quickly obliged. She shut the door after him.

Left alone to study the letter, she had about ten minutes to absorb the news before a reporter from Minneapolis called her to ask about it. Apparently, it took no time at all for someone in the department office or the ethics committee to spread it around. The debate over free speech at universities was hot news.

Someone knocked lightly as she was finishing her discussion with the reporter. Without waiting for an invitation, Jonathan opened the door just enough to stick his head in.

"Hey," he said.

Nicole nodded, and he walked in.

"I'm so sorry to hear what happened," he said. "You know I haven't always agreed with your theories, but this kind of censorship is wrong."

"What, has Timothy made the rounds?"

"Yeah, he came by my office a minute ago. Everyone is shocked."

"I suppose you should all look over your lecture notes. Any one of you might be next."

Again, uninvited, Jonathan sat in her guest chair.

"Why would you think that?"

"Well, you teach about Civil War battles, right?"

"Yes, and about the reconstruction," he agreed, nodding.

"What do you say about slavery? Any mention of racism? You

don't think that's risky in today's academic climate?"

"I don't know. Slavery was a thing. How can anyone argue with that?"

"A thing?" Nicole shook her head. "I don't know, but I'd guess you had better go back to your office and start thinking about how you talk about that 'thing' pretty seriously. No one is safe if they talk about it these days."

ONLY TWO HOURS AFTER SHE emailed the reporter a copy of the letter, the story showed up on the Star Tribune's website.

## MacIntosh Professor Fired for Feminist Lectures
## By a Star Tribune reporter

ST. GEORGE, Minn.–An assistant professor of history at a small university in Minnesota was fired on Tuesday after two men in a class she was teaching complained to the administration that her lectures were filled with "misandry and anachronisms."

In a letter assistant professor Nicolette Larson shared with the Star Tribune and the Associated Press, MacIntosh University Dean of Letters and Sciences wrote that its ethics committee had reviewed the students' complaint and found it "contained ample examples of statements that were likely to embarrass and demean the male students in her class."

(Misandry is the male-directed equivalent of misogyny, or an expression of antipathy or disrespect for men.)

Ms. Larson will not be allowed to complete her summer teaching assignment. She said she has not yet decided what her next steps will be.

Reached in his office by a reporter, Dean Dr. Dan Danforth declined to comment on the dismissal other than to say he was "surprised" that Ms. Larson had shared the letter with the media. "This is not something she should be proud of," Dr. Danforth said. He also declined to provide the Star Tribune with a copy of the complaint or disclose the names of the student complainants.

Ms. Larson's history class, "Women in the Middle

Ages," was typically filled with female students only, Ms. Larson said in an interview. The two male students who filed the complaint didn't raise their concerns in the classroom, nor did they share their discomfort with her outside of class. "I've only had two other men take the class over the past two years, and they had no complaints that I know of."

"I believe that I should have been given an opportunity to answer the complaints," Ms. Larson continued. "There was no due process here. An accused person is usually granted an opportunity to face her accusers and answer them. This decision was made based on a one-sided argument, most of which I found superficial and petty."

Asked if she would provide a copy of the complaint, Ms. Larson said that she was only allowed to read it in the department head's office and wasn't permitted to make or receive a copy. "There's something very odd about the way this was handled," she asserted.

In a similar case at Hamline University, a small private school in St. Paul, an adjunct professor was fired for showing images of Muhammad among other religious leaders, which Hamline president, Fayneese L. Miller, called "Islamophobic." In that case, the student who filed the complaint about showing the depiction of Muhammad, an act considered sacrilegious by Muslims, did not respond to prior warnings by the professor that the images would be shown or to the professor's request that anyone who would be offended by it should let her know.

Referring to Ms. Larson's dismissal, Geraldine Cameron, a first-amendment attorney and an advocate for free speech in higher education at the American Civil Liberties Union, said it is "another example of the stifling of ideas and opinions and free discussions in precisely the kind of place where such concepts should be debated."

MacIntosh is non-religious, private university based in St. George. It has 2,225 full-time students, most of whom graduate from the School of Letters and Sciences or the School of Engineering.

"Hey, you're big news." It was Katie who saw it first and called her rught away.

"Oh, Christ," Nicole said, calling up the story on her computer while on the phone. "Justin is going to have a fit."

"He knew about this, didn't he?"

"Uh, no. I never told him."

"'Oh Christ' is right," Katie said. "Why not?"

"I was kinda hoping it would just go away. And Justin already thinks I'm nuts. Now he's going to think I'm nuts and irresponsible."

"But he supports your research, doesn't he?"

"I used to think so. Now I don't know."

# XXIII

A "fit" was expected. But Justin's reaction was more judgmental than emotional.

He hadn't seen the newspaper article, or heard the news, so for a moment, Nicole hoped that she could deliver it in a way that might soften his reaction.

"We need to talk," she said when he got home from student golf practice late that evening.

"We need to talk" has never been a signal of good things to come in any situation, anywhere. Justin put down his cellphone and frowned.

"About what?"

"Well, something happened today. Something horrible. Let's get a glass of wine and sit down."

"I don't need a glass of wine," he said, his voice a bit too loud for their small kitchen. "Just tell me. What's going on?"

"Okay. At least sit down."

Justin sat on the nearest bar stool, folded his hands on the bar, and stared at her.

"Well, I'm going to have a glass," she said. Nicole pulled a bottle from the rack and searched in the utility drawer for a corkscrew.

"Would you just get on with it?" Justin demanded, not a whiff of sympathy in his voice.

"Well, it's not easy," she said, abandoning the bottle and sitting next to him. "I got fired."

"You what?" He half stood up and then sat back down.

"I got fired."

"Why." He made that one word sound like an accusation, not a question.

"Apparently two young men in my class in the spring thought I was being too hard on men in general. That I was being misanthropic. Really misandrist."

Justin jerked his head back as if he'd been slapped. "What's that?"

"It means hating men. It seems they think I have been too hard on their little male egos. They think I've made them feel bad about themselves."

"You've got to be kidding," Justin said, getting up and going to the drawer where she'd been searching, finding the corkscrew. He tore the seal off the top of the bottle.

"I wish I were kidding," she said. "It really seems outrageous, but I guess students get to decide these days what they want to hear in their classes from their teachers, and if they don't like it, they can silence us. These guys didn't like my theories about feminism, apparently."

"Well, that's ridiculous."

For a moment Nicole thought he was taking her side.

Until he continued. "There has to be more to it than that. They chose to take a class on feminism. Why would they want to get you fired?"

She was puzzled. Was he questioning the ethics committee's logic, or was he questioning her version of the story?

He answered without her asking. "Did you do something inappropriate?" he asked. "Cross someone's personal boundary?"

Spoken like a high school teacher steeped in workshops about "appropriate" student-teacher relationships! She hadn't expected this reaction or the anger that boiled up inside her.

"Hell, no!" she shouted. She stood up and grabbed the wine and corkscrew from him. She uncorked the bottle, her hands shaking.

Justin walked to the breakfast room window and stuck his hands in his pockets, looking out at the back yard.

"You don't believe me?" Her voice shook with anger. She poured herself a large glass, some of it slopping over the edge onto the counter.

"I don't know what to believe," he said, continuing to stare into the distance. "You've been so caught up in your weird history stuff lately, I don't know what code of ethics you're following. Is this some kind of medieval thing? Queens soliciting their subjects for sex?"

"Where is this coming from?" she shouted at his back. "It's insane! I was fired for teaching feminist history that hurt a couple of conservative boys' feelings. That's what the letter says. Here. I'll show it to you."

She dug it out of her purse, unfolded it, and held it out to him. He turned around and walked past her outstretched arm.

"I guess this is a good time to tell you I'm going back to Oklahoma for the rest of the summer to help with the golf program," he said, opening the refrigerator. He didn't look up at her until he'd emptied a can of beer into a glass. "I will be leaving tomorrow."

"This is your response to my dismissal?" she said. "You're just going to leave?"

"It's not a response to your firing. I just think we need some time apart. I'll be gone a couple more months, and by then maybe you can figure out if you really want to get married and what you're going to do with your life. Apparently, this feminist shit isn't going to get you anywhere."

"Feminist shit? That's what you think of my work?" Now Nicole's entire body was shaking. She sat back down on the bar stool to steady herself.

"Work?" Justin scoffed. He shook his head and left the room.

Two days later, after getting advice from an attorney recommended by Katie, who had yet to need one, Nicole called Justin in Oklahoma to tell him she was calling off the engagement. The conversation was easier than she expected. She still didn't know, and she no longer cared if he was having an affair. She knew she was, although in the sixth century, not in this one.

"It's not your fault," she said quickly, although he hadn't suggested it might be.

"Is there someone else?" he asked, calmly, as if an affirmative answer would be fine with him. "You've met someone?"

"I'm not sure how to answer that," she said.

He laughed. "Well, it's not that difficult. Either you have met someone who changed your mind about us, or not."

Nicole tried to figure out what to say. Could she simply say she met someone while doing research in Europe? It was technically true, but it was quite a bit more complicated than that. Or should she tell him that just days ago, she was making love with someone named Sebastianus in the sixth century? If she did, he would probably be relieved she was calling things off. She was deluded at best, perhaps psychotic.

"Let me say this," she said instead. "If I ever do get engaged again, I'll be the one who chooses. Not my parents and not his."

Justin didn't respond. He might have been thinking the same thing. Or he might not have understood her. Maybe he didn't see their engagement the same way she now did.

"Are you coming back soon?" she asked, filling the uncomfortable silence.

"In time for school." His voice had dropped. Perhaps he was more disappointed than he had let on. Or perhaps he was thinking about how they had decided to marry.

"Look. I've got to get to work," she said. "My dissertation deadline is coming up, and I've got a bunch of research to incorporate. We can talk when you're back. We'll need to decide what to do with the house, how to tell our parents, and things."

Again, silence on the other end of the line.

"Okay, then. Talk to you later." Nicole tried to keep from sounding cheerful. But she failed.

With the engagement off, Nicole had less reason to avoid Sébastièn, but she did. At first, she was tempted to walk over to his office and tell him what she'd done. But something about a relationship with him in the twenty-first century didn't seem right. Whether he and Sebastianus were one person or not, the man she loved was the one with the beard and the scar on his arm. She didn't know why, but she wasn't finding it that easy to transfer that feeling to his contemporary iteration, despite his Sebastianus-like kiss.

And, by avoiding him, she wasn't as distracted as she would be. She could work. She and Sebastianus had made love in the sixth century nearly every day. She couldn't do that with Sébastièn now and keep her mind focused on her novel.

Katie returned from the UK. Once she and Doug got caught up, she called Nicole for drinks at the same bar where Sébastièn had kissed her. Nicole decided it was time to tell her best friend about her time travels to the sixth century. She was going to leave again soon, and if she didn't return, she wanted someone to know where she had gone. Someone besides Sébastièn. Even if no one else would believe it.

Katie's eyes grew wider as she listened, and when Nicole got to the part about her affair with Sebastianus, Katie's smile widened.

"Oh, you have to make this a time-travel novel, not just historical fiction," she said. "It's better than Outlander! Much sexier! Every modern woman will be trying to figure out how to go back in time and find her own Sebastianus. What a great name, by the way. How did you come up with it? Were you thinking of Sébastièn?" She teased me with her grin.

"Katie! I'm not making any of this up."

"Oh, right." Katie nodded, miming sincerity. "All of this really happened. You're not making any of it up."

Nicole sat back and took a big swallow of wine. It did sound fantastic. But even if she were the only person in the world to believe what she was experiencing, Nicole had stopped doubting. It wasn't a dream. It wasn't her imagination. It was as real as the dress that hung in her closet.

WHEN NICOLE HAD WRITTEN ALL she knew about Ingund's journey so far and was finally ready to return to Spain, she hoped it wasn't too late. Had Ingund and Hermenegild left for Seville? Or was it even later than that? Had Ingund left for Constantinople? Had she died in Carthage?

To prepare for the trip, she reread the portions of the history books that detailed the last years of Hermenegild's life as a substitute for the lack of information about Ingund. She bought a large road map of Spain and studied the geography of the regions she would pass through if she got to Toledo in time to travel with Ingund to Seville and later to Córdoba.

But as she prepared, she worried about two things. First, her mother. Would she die before Nicole got back to see her again? And second: what if the portal didn't open? Katie's disbelief and Sébastièn's denial continued to work on her certitude. Back and forth, she believed in her own stories, and then, briefly but often, she doubted them. But she had to try. If she didn't get back to the sixth century, she'd miss the rest of Ingund's story.

She boarded the plane to Toledo with little more than the dress in her suitcase and the travel clothes on her back. If she passed through the portal and stayed long enough to learn of Ingund's fate, she wouldn't waste time in Spain or in Paris coming home. She'd rush back and finish her work.

Unless, she admitted, Sebastianus convinced her to stay.

# XXIV

Once I got back to Toledo and the sixth century, I wrestled with my foreknowledge of Ingund's death. I was already mourning her demise, which was still a few years in the future. I had no right to warn her. I had no right to interfere with history unless I was convinced that I was destined to do things like save her from drowning in the fountain or writing the letter to Bishop Cyprian.

Regarding her death, historians didn't know much. The Spanish playwright that I had read on the patio at the patisserie in Paris attributed her death to her sorrow at being separated from Hermenegild by the Byzantines. Most historians attributed it to the plague and postulated that she died in Carthage, but oddly, considering she was a Visigothic queen, no one knew where she was buried. But a few scholars speculated that she had not died in Carthage but had secretly accompanied her son on the ship to Constantinople. I didn't know if I would get to witness what really happened, but I hoped the latter was true.

It turned out that I had missed only six months of time in the month I was back in the twenty-first century. In that time, Leovigild had wisely decided to physically separate his wife and Ingund, restoring the peace to the palace that had been shattered by the fountain incident.

King Leovigild was getting old and tired of long absences from Toledo, so the solution to the bickering in the palace served more than one purpose. He sent the young couple to Seville, capital of Baetica, the southern part of the kingdom that Leovigild expected his son to rule after his death. Meanwhile, he sent Reccared, Hermenegild's younger brother, north to govern over the northern border and Septimania and repel Frankish incursions. Leovigild, then, could stay home and let them manage his far-flung armies.

When I woke up in the palace in Toledo, grateful to find the dress still worked, I immediately went looking for Ingund, not knowing I'd missed her departure by a couple of days. A handmaid spotted me and hurried me along to Goswintha, who told me the young couple had been sent to Seville, known then as Hispalis.

"I hope my son can beat some sense into that woman's head," she hissed. "I am tired of her obstinance. Obviously, Leovigild is, too." I wanted to suggest that maybe Leovigild was more interested in stopping her bickering, but I knew better. I'd seen her exercise her temper, and I didn't want it directed at me.

"When she's got her own sovereign duties to attend to, she'll drop her plot to convert him," Goswintha continued. "They'll have the brutal Byzantines to deal with down there. Maybe that will teach her that Catholics are no friends of ours."

I nodded servilely and waited for the tirade to wear down. "Is she expecting me to follow her?" I was finally able to ask.

"Yes," she said, sighing. "Hermenegild knows how much she has come to love you. He has arranged for a horse and an escort to take you to Seville. When you're ready to leave, the man will meet you in the stables."

"Is it Sebastianus?" I asked, and immediately blushed. I should have simply waited to see for myself. But the queen took no notice. She had already turned to lecture her handmaid about something else.

It wasn't Sebastianus waiting in the stables, but he had chosen my horse, a gentle mare on the small side, and the groomsman who would accompany me. I was glad I wouldn't travel alone. The roads were full of highwaymen and physical dangers, too treacherous for a woman traveling alone, even one who had taken self-defense classes since kindergarten. I recognized the man but had never said a word to him before. He looked me up and down, as if trying to decide what Sebastianus saw in me. I hoped he had no theories that came close to the truth.

Even with an escort, I feared making the entire trip by horse. To steel myself, thought about Margery Kempe, who in the fifteenth century had gone on a years-long pilgrimage to the Holy Lands, leaving her husband and fourteen children at home, traveling over snow-packed mountains on foot, visiting pilgrimage sites, mystics, and anchoresses along the way. That pilgrimage had been far more grueling than my trip would be, and she had returned home safely.

Ingund had left for Hispalis only two days before, and it was likely we could catch up with them before we got there. They'd be traveling in a slow-moving caravan carrying goods and servants. My escort and I would only have a small bag of personal things and some traveling clothes astride our horses. They could cover the equivalent of twenty miles a day, while we could cover more than thirty, at least until we came to the steep foothills.

We started out the next morning, taking a route to the southeast, even though Hispalis was slightly southwest of Toledo. I questioned the choice, and the groomsman grumbled an answer: it was to avoid the highest of the passes through the Sierra Morena. We could have taken a more mountainous route, but then we'd not catch up to the caravan.

The first day, despite my trepidation, I had grown excited about the adventure, but by noon, my thighs and my butt hurt so badly, I considered walking the rest of the way, even if it took me three times as long. But even on horseback, it would take ten days to get to Hispalis, and, until we caught up with Ingund's carriage, I would have no choice but to suffer the pains.

We stopped for the first night as the sun was sinking through clouds toward the hills in the west. I dismounted stiffly, landing painfully; I could barely walk. I remembered why I had never become a horsewoman. If horseback riding didn't start when one was young, abductors and adductors in the thighs never got used to sitting bull-legged atop a jostling horse. I stumbled into the modest inn and collapsed on the first stool I could find. The groomsman followed me in with the saddlebag that carried my possessions. He looked at me, not with sympathy, but with derision. He, no doubt, hated having to accompany me, and now his suspicions of my ill-suitedness for the journey had been confirmed: I was neither strong enough nor tough enough to make this trip.

I looked at his sneer and decided I would not let Sebastianus down. I would get back on the horse the next day, no matter how much it hurt, and prove his faith in me. After a small bowl of watery soup, I retired to my bedroom, which I was sharing with three other women, all strangers. None of us spoke. I was so exhausted, I wasn't interested in conversation, although I was interested in what they thought of Ingund and Goswintha and the entire Visigothic ruling clan.

I knew it would hurt getting back on my horse, I had no idea how excruciating it would be. My eyes crossed as I pulled myself up into the saddle with the grudging help of the groomsman and felt every nerve in my ass react with shock. My pelvic bones felt like knives sticking through my flesh. I knew that I would have blisters on top of blisters by the time we finished that day. I wondered if their sting could be any worse than the pain I was already feeling. Stirrups might have allowed me to take some weight off my butt and carry it on my feet, but they had yet to be invented. I wondered if I could risk changing history by suggesting some kind of workaround resembling a stirrup. But as I was pondering that, the groomsman took off down the road, and I had to hurry to follow him, no matter my misery. He wouldn't have listened to me anyway.

I HAD NO WAY OF knowing how far we traveled each day. For the first few painfilled days, most of the trail we followed could only charitably called a road, It was in the sun, as we traveled through the southern half of the Meseta Central, the great plateau of central Iberia that in my time produced the lesser wines of Spain. Even as we passed through on horseback, I could see indications of what was to come: vineyards, unkempt and looking nothing like their manicured modern counterparts, clung to dry hillsides. Harvest was just starting, and mule-drawn carts laden with grapes met us, blocking our passage from time to time. We led our mounts onto the side of the roads to let them pass. The uneven borders of the fields were littered with flowering Spanish broom and yellow asters that looked much like the goldenrod in Minnesota, signaling that autumn was arriving. It would be good to be in southern Spain where winters were milder than here in the high desert.

My escort didn't talk to me. He signaled our brief rest stops by pointing into a copse of Holm oak trees or Aleppo pines, or by just turning off the road and expecting me to follow. I stopped behind him, hobbled off my mare, found the best cover I could where I could pee, and then grimaced as I climbed back on. None of our stops correlated with the names of the towns I had memorized from either old Roman maps or my modern road atlas. And most of the inns we stopped at were in nothing one would identify as a town anyway. A stable, a few outbuildings, maybe a stone square that looked like it could be either a house or a shelter for livestock. On our sixth day, as we started to climb over the edge of what I believed were the Sierra Morena mountains, the air got cooler, and our progress slowed. On the seventh night, we were told the prince and princess were less than a day ahead of us and on the eighth day, to my relief, we caught up with the rear guard of the royal caravan and, shortly after that, with Ingund's carriage.

I MIGHT HAVE BEEN SADDLE sore, but I didn't feel half as bad as little Ingund. When Sebastianus climbed down from his seat at the front of her carriage, and opened her door for me, with a surreptitious squeeze at my elbow, I had expected her to be as happy to see me as I was to see her. But instead of hopping up to greet me, she lay slumped on the seat cushion, her skin greener than the parched grass under the carriage wheels.

"Cousin," she whispered. "I am glad you are here." She struggled to sit up and fell back before I could catch her. I didn't know if she was suffering from exhaustion, motion sickness, or her pregnancy, but it was apparent no one was doing anything to help her. I suspected at least one of her problems was dehydration. If she was still throwing up with morning sickness, she was probably drinking too little water or juice to replace the lost fluids while on the road.

Before the door closed behind me, I stepped back out. "We need water," I said to Sebastianus. He didn't ask why or hesitate but strode to the wagons behind us and returned with a small tankard. I hoped the water wasn't contaminated enough to make Ingund sicker.

"Has it been boiled?" I asked Sebastianus.

He nodded, again without questioning me. Another clue. Like me, Sébastièn wouldn't have lost his twenty-first-century medical savvy, however uncredentialed.

"Could we wait a few minutes before moving on?" I asked him as he handed me the water. I climbed in the carriage. I pushed Ingund to a semi-sitting position and opened the tankard.

"Here, dear," I whispered. "You need to drink."

She shook her head and tried to lie back down. I tightened my hold on her shoulders and held her upright.

"You must," I said, sternly. "Your baby needs water."

Making it about her child helped. She nodded slightly, and I helped her pull the tankard to her lips. She took a couple of small swallows but started to slump again.

"Not enough," I said. "Come on. Try!"

"I will vomit again," she said, shaking her head.

"That is okay," I countered. "If you keep any of it down, it will help you feel better."

Finally, she managed to drink a couple of ounces. I held her against my shoulder. I would try to get her to drink again in a few minutes. I wondered how the handmaids had been so neglectful. Surely someone should have noticed how sick she was. Why wasn't anyone riding in the carriage with her? And where was Hermenegild?

The carriage started moving again with a lurch. Ingund opened her eyes, and I helped her drink a little more.

"Thanks," she said, weakly. "No one would help me."

"Why?" I was furious. Goswintha had sent Ingund's Merovingian maids back to Metz after her arrival and replaced them with her own servants. Why would they ignore a pregnant woman who was suffering this much? Did they think pregnancies were supposed to be miserable and that was fine? Or did they simply not care because she was a Frank, and not one of them?

"Where are Goswintha's handmaids?"

"They are not here."

"Where are they?"

"Goswintha would not let them come. She said we could find our own when we got to Seville."

Of all the things that woman had done to punish Ingund for her religion, that was the second most outrageous, next to pushing her into a fountain. "You have had no one tending to you the whole way?" I calculated how long they'd been on the road. If we had been travelling for eight days, they would have been on the road for eleven.

"Only Sebastianus," she said. She let out a little sigh that sounded like an attempt to laugh. "I should have married Sebastianus."

"Maybe we all should have," I said without thinking. She looked up at me and nodded. I wondered again how much she knew.

Then my thoughts turned selfish. How long would it be before I could be with him again?

# XXV

The former Catholic monastery in Hispalis that served as the new palace for the prince and princess was humble as palaces I'd seen in the sixth century went. But we were a small entourage, at least at first, and we didn't need as much space. Ingund asked me to help her acquire the handmaids, cooks, gardeners, and other servants that she needed to run her household. Hermenegild drafted Sebastianus to hire stable hands and organize the palace guards.

We were both swamped with work for the first few weeks in our new capital, and we rarely had a chance to even see each other, let alone rendezvous for repeat performances on bales of straw. Besides, it took a week or so for my butt to heal from riding. I missed him, but I had my hands full with Ingund's prenatal care and the household management, which was left to me while Ingund recuperated from the journey, able to do little as the baby grew.

Athanagild was born four months after we arrived in Hispalis. I avoided the birth room, not knowing the first thing about that business, but confident that the old woman and her assistant — I was told they were the best midwife team in all of Baetica — could handle the situation better without me. I had never fainted at the sight of blood, like my mother did, but watching someone writhe in pain wasn't something I needed. Especially when I'd probably be worthless and in the way.

As soon as I heard Ingund's first pained outcry, I put on a cloak and walked out into the frosty morning air. I told myself I wasn't looking for anything or anyone in particular, but I walked toward the stables. It would be okay to run into Sebastianus. We had not had a chance to be alone together since our arrival from Toledo, and although I had gone months without sex with Justin without falling apart, going much longer without Sebastianus's attention loomed as intolerable.

As expected, I found him in the stables. Once he had finished his assignment to hire the team of groomsmen and stable muckers, and organized the guards, he had relinquished control of them to more experienced officers and managers and receded again to the background. He preferred horses to soldiers, and when I walked in on him grooming his favorite mare, I found myself seething with jealousy.

"I think you love that horse," I whispered. His back faced me, but he didn't turn.

"Indeed, I do," he said. "She is dependable, obedient, and docile; all the things a horse should be, but a woman should not." He turned then and grinned at me.

"What should a woman be, then?" I asked, surprised at my flirtatious tone. It didn't suit the woman I thought I was.

"Hmmm," he said, stroking his bushy beard and holding my eyes with his. "A woman should be whatever she wants to be, but always strong and capable."

"That's incredibly articulate for this early in the morning," I replied. I fought the urge to reach up and touch his face. "And have you ever found such a woman?" I was still flirting, ashamed of myself for it, but unable to stop.

"Come back when the sun peaks, and we'll see," he said.

"You mean noon?"

"Is that what you call it in your world?"

"What do you mean by 'my world?'" I stopped being coy. I thought he was finally going to admit that he came from St. George, Minnesota, in the twenty-first century, just like me.

"We can talk about that at 'noon,'" he said, turning back to his mare.

We didn't talk about anything at noon. When I walked in, he took my hand and led me to his cot in a small alcove at the back of the stables, and in less than thirty minutes, we made love twice. Naked and lolling under a moth-eaten blanket afterward, we still didn't talk. Sebastianus slowly stroked my back while he held me close, my breasts to his chest. I nuzzled my face into his neck and replayed every minute of the last half-hour in my mind. I knew how difficult the next few months and years were going to be. Quite likely, these assignations would be hard to reprieve among the chaos. I was going to need these memories to make it through.

THE BIRTH WAS EASY, THE handmaids told me. Named after Ingund's grandfather, Athanagild was small, only about five pounds I guessed when holding him, which had made it easier for Ingund's tiny body. Her breasts had filled so much that they looked too heavy to carry, and the baby suckled nearly constantly. In just a few days, he grew heavier and taller.

He was a cheerful baby, only crying when he had dirtied the rags that were tied like a sling under his crotch. Due to his healthy appetite, the handmaid who did the washing was busy, rinsing, scrubbing, and hanging the cloths out in the sunshine every day, finally folding them into neat piles and delivering them to the nursery. I helped change Athanagild a few times, just often enough to wish for safety pins, if not for disposable diapers.

Word spread quickly through Baetica, where Ingund was popular, as much of the population of Hispalis and the southern provinces of the peninsula had been Catholic since the Roman days. Hermenegild, still an Arian, was tolerated as long as he, like his father, allowed for Catholic services and Catholic baptisms. We heard the noise of celebrations of Athanagild's birth wafting down the streets for days. The people had very few occasions that permitted them to put off farmwork and cobbling and gather for a party. This was, apparently, one of them.

The news quickly reached Toledo, and soon Hermenegild heard back: Goswintha was coming to Hispalis. I knew she would stay for a long time, although she didn't admit it in her letter to Hermenegild, and I didn't burden Ingund with the insight. Despite the cruel way she had treated Ingund in Toledo, Goswintha's heart softened with the arrival of her first great-grandson. But it wasn't just that; Athanagild also strengthened her place in the kingdom. He was heir-apparent to the Visigothic throne, and a potential heir to the Merovingian empire, depending on what happened in the wars the Franks were forever fighting against each other up north. Goswintha was coming to secure her place alongside the baby.

A month after the birth, I was helping Ingund get ready for dinner with Hermenegild—a duty that typically would have fallen to one of her new handmaids, but Ingund didn't feel comfortable with them. She preferred to have me brush her hair and help her dress. She said our time together helped her reclaim her image as an intelligent woman after spending hours of the day with a non-verbal, suckling baby. She and Hermenegild had been close and much in love before Athanagild's birth, and I sensed that she wanted to regain that affection and passion.

During the day, she had been more attached to the newborn and less solicitous of Hermenegild than I had expected. I thought she would delegate the baby's care and feeding to wet-nurses and governesses and a handful of others. But as much as Ingund craved Hermenegild's love, she also understood that it was Athanagild who would secure her position among the Visigoths. She'd learned from the best: Her brother Childebert was Brunhilde's key to authority and survival in Austrasia, and Fredegund had retained her power in Neustria after her husband's death by acting as regent for her young sons and grandsons. Heirs were a mother's greatest asset.

When a trumpet signaled visitors, we stopped our quiet gossip and looked up. A racket of wheels and horses rocked the courtyard, and I went to the window. It was no surprise. A half-dozen wagons rolled in behind Goswintha's carriage, filled, I expected, with presents and treasures for the newborn. I wondered if anything of value had been left for Leovigild.

After our confrontation at the fountain, I mostly avoided Goswintha in Toledo. I wanted to do so in Seville as well, and it turned out to be easy. She wanted to be around Ingund and Athanagild for hours every day, which relieved me of my duty to keep Ingund company most of the time. I focused on managing the household, monitoring the cleaning and cooking, and supervising the gardening. But since I was managing and not actually doing the work, I had enough free time to join Sebastianus on his stable cot nearly daily. Oddly, I realized later, I never worried about getting pregnant. Perhaps I assumed that I couldn't; that somehow, time travel made me infertile. It was a senseless excuse for our recklessness. But I never missed a period, and I forgot about the risk we were taking.

Risk, however, was in the air, and soon Hermenegild took the second biggest gamble of his life, one that led directly to his biggest. And being there when it happened gave me an answer to a question I and every historian before me had never been able to resolve.

# XXVI

I had never found an explanation for Hermenegild's decision to declare himself a king of the Visigoths. Historians had theories and guesses, but none of them seemed satisfactory. Hermenegild's move seemed needless and foolhardy. He would eventually, on his father's death, inherit his half of the kingdom anyway. He didn't have to instigate a civil war to achieve that.

But those historians didn't see what Ingund saw or hear what she heard in the palace in Hisplis. If they had, the mystery would have been cleared up long ago.

It was a dreary night in the middle of winter. I had gone to bed, having pulled the covers up over my ears. The palace's fireplaces couldn't keep up with the unseasonable, unusual cold spell we were having. I wished again that I had Sebastianus next to me, keeping me warm.

Again, someone snuck into my room, raising my hopes that my wish had come true. And again, it didn't.

"Cousin," Ingund said quietly. I sat up and wrapped my blanket around me.

"What is it?"

"Were you asleep?"

"No," I assured her. "It is too cold."

"Move over," she whispered. "We will keep each other warm."

"Why are you not with Hermenegild?" I asked, scooching over to make room for her. I opened my blanket and enclosed her with me.

"We had an argument," she said, sniffling now. I almost said, "Aww, your first argument. How sweet," but I'm glad I didn't. That would have been trite, and the argument was anything but that.

"What about?"

"His mother. Or stepmother. She has talked him into declaring himself king of the southern half of the kingdom, and I am afraid what this might mean."

Aha, I thought immediately. It was Goswintha's idea! Finally, I understood why Hermenegild did something so inscrutable, so unnecessary, something that led to civil war with his father.

"How do you know this?" I asked.

"I was there at dinner when she demanded it."

"And he argued?"

"No." She was clearly disappointed with the husband.

"Do you know why she wants him to do that?" I asked. Here would be the second half of the answer to the question that had hung in the air for fourteen hundred years. "Why would she want him to defy her own husband?"

"She suspects there is a son from Leovigild's first marriage, one he fathered before his first wife died. She fears he may show up some day and claim the right to the throne."

"Ah, primogeniture," I said. Ingund looked at me quizzically, and I realized the term had probably never been used around her, even though she knew it by principle: oldest sons were the first in line to inherit the throne.

"But I thought that Visigothic kings were elected by their military leaders," I said.

"Not if the kingdom has already been promised to Hermenegild and Reccared," Ingund said. I wanted to argue that Leovigild did not necessarily have the power to do that, under Visigothic tradition, but it seemed silly to take the conversation down that path. What I needed to understand was what this:

"Why does Hermenegild have to declare himself king?" I asked. "How does that solve the problem?"

"Goswintha wants little Athanagild to inherit an empire," she said. "If Hermenegild has his own kingdom, then Athanagild won't have to compete with anyone for the throne. He will have his own empire."

It made sense. Goswintha's wish for a union between her daughter Brunhilde's Merovingian kingdom and the Visigoths would be more likely to come true if her stepson and grandson were kings.

Now the difference between Brunhilde, Goswintha, and Fredegund on the one hand and Ingund on the other saddened me. The older women were the feminists I had lectured them to be: independent, strategic, willing to use violence to secure their own agency. They didn't want to be ruled; they wanted to rule, even if their sons or grandsons or great-grandsons were nominally kings. If Ingund's role as a queen of Iberia had held, would she have turned out like them? But knowing in advance how short her "reign" would be, I lamented how little control she and most women of arranged marriages of Ingund's time had over their own lives despite their value as diplomatic fodder for their families.

"Well, we do not know what will happen," I lied, finally reacting to Ingund's statement. "We" didn't know, but I did. "Maybe Leovigild will be fine with Hermenegild taking the reign. That was going to happen eventually, anyway."

And for a while, it did seem fine. Hermenegild's declaration of kingship was met with silence. Leovigild did nothing to reproach him, seemingly ignoring it, even with the cities of Hispalis, Coruba (modern Córdoba), Italica, and Mérida all pledged their allegiance to Hermenegild.

But two years later, Hermenegild took another step that his father couldn't ignore. And this time it was Ingund's fault.

Since it seemed that Leovigild was not going to do anything to resist his son's kingship, Ingund had stopped worrying about the consequences. Over the next, quiet six months,  Sebastianus and I continued to see each other, although less regularly, as he went to Corduba or Cadiz frequently to oversee palace business with merchants and horse dealers. At least that's what he said he was doing. I was puzzled by the leap in responsibility from his humble origins as a stable servant, but he took it on with little fanfare.

I considered sticking around longer, but I worried about my mother. The possibility that she had died before I could say goodbye, even if she didn't want me to say goodbye, weighed on my conscience. And I knew that in Baetica, not much of consequence would happen for three more years, when all hell would break loose.

I decided to go home now and get back to Seville in time to follow the rest of Ingund's story. I wondered what I should tell Sebastianus and what excuse I should make to Ingund for my absence. In the end, I decided to tell Sebastianus nothing; he would figure it out, eventually. And I told Ingund the truth: I was going home for a while because my mother was sick. Ingund didn't know where and when "home" was for me, but that didn't mean it wasn't the truth.

Judging from my earlier trips to the sixth century, I expected that if I stayed in Minnesota for a month, I would be gone from Seville for around two or three years. Since I couldn't time it exactly, I'd just have to take my chances.

# XXVII

Nicole had only been gone for a week in Minnesota time. Justin was still in Oklahoma for the last two weeks of summer. In an email, she told him she wanted to put the house on the market and asked him to sign the real estate agency papers she would send to him. He agreed.

She called Sébastièn's office and found out he had applied for and received an extended leave to conduct some research.

"What research?" Nicole smirked. Did it have something to do with time travel and the second law of thermodynamics?

"I have no idea," the admin said. "Would you like to talk to the department head?

"No, it's really none of my business." She concluded that she shouldn't see Sébastièn until she finalized things with Justin and got back from her next trip to Seville.

She called Katie and planned to meet her for dinner at a Scandinavian restaurant halfway between their houses. She smelled the kumla and lutefisk when she walked in and would have turned around and walked out to avoid smelling more of it if Katie hadn't come in behind her and blocked her exit. Nicole was half Norwegian, but her mother was Irish and refused to cook Scandinavian foods, even those that were Nicole's father's favorites. Perhaps that had something to do with her parents' tenuous relationship. She knew couples who had divorced over less substantive matters.

Nicole chose a Reuben sandwich, which seemed a little out of place in a restaurant called Syttende Mai, Norwegian for the day Norway declared its independence from Sweden. Although it wasn't her favorite food, Nicole could stomach sauerkraut long before she could eat fish balls, potato dumplings, cod soaked in lye, or sheep's head.

"Justin and I are splitting up," Nicole said after they had ordered. She knew how dispassionate she sounded, but she couldn't get emotional about something that made so much sense. "We're going to put the house on the market as soon as Justin gets home."

"Don't you think you're being a little hasty?" Katie asked. "All of the sudden, you aren't getting along. This isn't about Sébastièn, is it?"

"No, it's not. Why would you think that?" Nicole was a little miffed. She hadn't told Katie anything about her last meeting with the physics professor or his kiss. "It has nothing to do with him. Maybe it has something to do with his sixth-century doppelganger, but not him."

Katie laughed a bit too hardily in Nicole's opinion. But she let it go. "The thing is, Justin and I haven't gotten along that well for a very long time," she said. "We've just been good at covering it up. It's been six months since we've had sex."

"Sex isn't everything in a relationship," Katie said, her head tilted down like she was sharing a secret. "You have history. You have a lot of things in common."

"History, yes. Perhaps too much. Like way before kindergarten. But things in common? Like what?"

"Like golf. You both like golf."

"No. Justin loves golf; I tolerate it. That's not the same thing. I haven't played in more than a year, and I don't miss it. Every time I trip over my clubs in the garage, I think about taking them to the used sporting goods store. Now I might. No, now I will."

"Well, you both …" Katie drummed her fingers on the table as she searched for another example.

"See. That's what I mean. Nothing. And what's worse, before he left for Oklahoma, he called my research and my theories 'feminist shit.' How do I live with that?"

Katie didn't have an answer. As long as she had the upper hand in the argument, Nicole took the opportunity to venture further. "And I besides, I went back to the sixth century again, something I will never be able to tell him about."

Katie turned her head away for a long moment before looking back. "Do you know how crazy that sounds? 'I went back to the sixth century again.' It's nuts."

"Absolutely. Yes, I know." Nicole nodded. "If it weren't happening to me, if it were happening to you, and you were telling me about it, I'd think you were nuts. Or very badly in need of a fantasy."

"And you wouldn't believe me, right?"

"I don't know."

"Why should I believe you?"

"I don't know. Maybe because of how crazy it sounds? Like I wouldn't be telling you about it if I had any doubts that it really happened? If I didn't need someone to share it with?"

Katie looked at her over her wine glass. She took a long swallow. "Okay, Nicole. Lay it on me. Tell me all about it. There's nothing I like better than a good story. I'm all ears." To prove it, Katie picked up her cell phone and turned it off. "Go."

Nicole got through most of what had taken place in Toledo before their food arrived and finished telling it by the time she polished off her sandwich and Katie got her kumla into her stomach and away from Nicole's nose.

"So, when things settled down in the kingdom, I decided to come home," she concluded. "I'm going to work on the novel for a few days, and then, maybe I'll go down and see Mom before I go back."

"Go back? Go back to the sixth century?" Katie shook her head and tipped her wine glass up to her mouth to drain it. She waved at the waiter who was serving the table next to them with their food. "We'll have another. The same," she said, wiggling the near-empty bottle. The waiter nodded approvingly. Another forty-five dollars on the tab would amplify his tip.

"What do you think?" Nicole asked, tipping the last of the first bottle into her glass.

"I think you are crazy, but it is a good story. And the way you tell it makes me want to believe it. Maybe you should quit this history thing and write novels."

"Yes. Actually, I've been thinking the same thing," Nicole said just as the waiter arrived with their second bottle of wine. He pulled a corkscrew out of his apron pocket and took his time sinking it into the cork. He popped the cork out theatrically and poured a couple of ounces into each of their glasses with a flourish.

Katie seemed to not notice the minor drama and waited until he walked away before adding: "What I don't understand is why you are trying to convince me it really happened. You can just tell me you've thought up a great story, and you'll turn it into a novel."

Nicole felt let down. She shouldn't have expected her friend to believe the outlandish things that had been happening to her. But on the other hand, she hoped that their friendship would mean Katie would be doubtful instead of dismissive. If Katie had just said "I don't know," instead of "No way," it would help.

"I understand," Nicole finally answered. "It is something you would have to experience yourself, or it sounds too outrageous. I get it. I'm sorry I wasted your time."

"Well, we have an entire bottle of wine to finish now, so let's waste some more time," Katie said, perhaps recognizing Nicole's disappointment. "Tell me more about this Sebastianus. I think I like him. But isn't it odd that the name Sebastianus is so similar to Sébastièn?"

NICOLE TOOK THE NEXT WEEK to flesh out some chapters of her novel, incorporating what she learned on her latest trip, checking in with her father every other day to see how her mother was doing. She suspected it was her father, more than her mother, who didn't want her there. When she finished emptying her notes into the computer and fighting with her uncomfortable desk chair, she decided not to wait until her mother slipped into a coma before rushing home just in time for the funeral. She packed up her car with enough clothes to last for a month and drove down to Iowa City.

When she got there, her mother had just been moved from the hospital into an in-patient hospice for her last few days on Earth. Nicole offered to drive her father over to make sure she was settling in comfortably.

"I didn't think it would be this soon," she said as she drove to the house that had been turned into a hospice residence. It looked like a private home, not a nursing facility, which Nicole appreciated. Who wanted to die in a hospital bed in a sterile room off a noisy hallway?

"Yeah," her dad said. "These things are fast. Good thing. This place costs a fortune."

Nicole turned into a parking space, braked hard, and turned to look at him. "What did you just say?"

Her father answered her frown with raised eyebrows. "What do you mean? I just stated the truth. It's really expensive."

"Well, the truth is my mother is dying, and you only seem to care about how much it's costing you."

"That's not fair, Nicole. You haven't been around. You don't know what it's like to take care of someone who can't do anything for herself. She couldn't even go to the bathroom. I couldn't do it anymore. I had to get help."

"Dad," Nicole shook her head and put the car in park. "You complain about how much it costs to put her in here, and yet you hate taking care of her on your own. It seems that it's one or the other, isn't it? Are you okay? Have you had a cognition test recently?"

"I'm not senile. Don't you dare go there." He unfastened his seat belt and opened the car door. "And if you mention any of this to your mother, I'll kill you."

He got out and slammed the door. Nicole dropped the keys into her purse and followed him to the entrance, seething. She caught up with him. "And you're the one who didn't want me around here," she said, walking past him and opening the door. "It wasn't Mom, was it." It wasn't a question.

He walked in without looking at her.

"Oh, you are here for Mrs. Larson," the receptionist greeted Nicole sweetly. "Yes, she's just now getting settled. I'll have someone escort you back to her." The woman donned a headset to make a call, and Nicole braced herself for what was likely to be her mother's shocking appearance. Her father walked over to a row of chairs, grabbing a magazine off an end table as he sat down.

Down a corridor to the right, four doors were propped open with rubber stoppers. A fifth door was equipped with the big square button of an automatic opener, which Nicole guessed would be the visitor's restroom. She hoped her mother would have her own bathroom. She'd never liked using public ones, and Nicole remembered rushing home from shopping more than once because her mother wouldn't use the women's room in the mall.

"Have you been here before?" Nicole asked her father.

"No," he said, not looking up from the old New Yorker he'd opened.

"Well, you seem awfully ready to make yourself comfortable."

He looked up at her with a scowl. "What do you want me to do, Nicole? Stand around and weep?"

"I should have come a week ago," Nicole said under her breath. "God knows what Mom has been through with him."

A middle-aged woman in a neat shirt dress belted at her narrow waist walked down the hallway toward Nicole with a smile. Her plastic name tag said simply "Hostess."

"You are Nicoletta?" she asked.

"Yes, and this is my father." Nicole pointed at him.

"I'll come later," he mumbled, not looking up from his magazine.

The women exchanged glances. "Come on down with me," the hostess said. "My name is Beth. Your mother is having some soup for lunch. She'll be getting ready for a nap soon."

As they walked down the hall, the hostess pulled Nicole close, nodded back at the reception area, and whispered. "It is often this way. It's hard for some men to handle the imminent separation. Don't be too judgmental. How long have they been married?"

Too long, Nicole thought. But she answered, "I think it's about thirty-five years. They were college sweethearts. They and their two best friends were married at a dual wedding."

"Oh, how sweet," Beth said. "Are the best friends still around?"

"They live a few blocks away. They were my fiancé's parents. I mean my ex-fiancé."

"Oh, now that's got to be a story," Beth said. "That's a whole lot of togetherness."

"Very insightful of you," Nicole said with a laugh. "It took me about twenty-six years to figure that out."

They turned into the last open room at the end of the hall, and Nicole saw a vestige of her mother in a chair, nearly bald, skeleton-thin, leaning to one side like a willow on an eroding riverbank. Beth helped her sit back upright. "Someone here to see you," she said cheerfully. "Your first guest."

When her mother looked up, Nicole saw something that made her sadder than her mother's weak body. Her eyes were clear and her smile quick. Her body had failed her, but her mind was still sharp. How hard it must be to know what's happening, to be so cognizant of your own impending demise! Meanwhile, her father's mind seemed to be slipping inside a strong, healthy frame.

Nicole remembered her mother's spirited fight for her own tenured position at Iowa. She took the study of paranormal literature to new heights; what became a legitimate and popular genre in 2023, fantasy fiction, had not always been. In her childhood, Nicole listened to her mother's impassioned debates with her father over the dinner table. He, a classic Shakespearean scholar, looked down on her work. What had impressed Nicole was her mother's refusal to back down and change her focus. She never stopped believing or teaching that myth, legend, and superstition contributed significantly to shaping cultures through literature.

Only recently had Nicole realized that her mother had the same arguments in her English department as Nicole had in history. The debates she had faced every day at MacIntosh over her theories of early feminism echoed her mother's over speculative fiction. But her father never embraced either of their studies.

"You weren't supposed to come, Nicoletta," her mother said. "I'm not much to look at these days."

"You look beautiful to me, Mom," Nicole said, feeling budding tears sting the corners of her eyes and leaning down to kiss her mother's pale forehead. "I'm sorry it took so long for me to get here. Dad kept telling me to stay away."

"Yes, he thought it would be for the best."

Nicole was about to ask "what did you think?" but she stopped herself. It was not the time to wade into their marital dysfunction. She wiped her eyes dry and sat down in the chair next to her mother as Beth excused herself.

"Don't you have work to do?" her mother asked.

"Well, I just got back from France. And I got fired."

"Oh. But you're still working on your novel, aren't you? Have you been back to the sixth century?"

This was not fair, Nicole thought. The one person who unequivocally supported her and believed in her time-travel was the person she was about to lose. Justin and Katie thought she was crazy, and she couldn't even imagine telling her father. Even Sébastièn equivocated, although she suspected it was a cover.

"Oh, Mom. I have. And I can't wait to tell you about it. But you look tired. This was a big move today. Maybe I should come back later when you've rested a little?"

Her father, who had slipped unnoticed into the room behind her, answered instead. "You're right, Nicole. We should go. Your mother isn't up for this right now."

"How would you know?" Nicole asked, her voice rising. "You just got here. And now, I suppose you're in a hurry to leave."

"Don't argue with me, Nikki," her dad said sternly. The nickname jarred. He hadn't called her Nikki – no one had – for years. Decades. Was it more evidence that his mind was slipping? This and his recent volcanic temper?

A nurse cut around him. "Sandra, I'm going to help you get into bed for a short nap," she said in a normal voice, pulling the lunch tray away from Nicole's mother's chair. Nicole had expected to hear the staff talk to her mother like she was a child, or at least an invalid—baby talk. But apparently, they realized people in their care were adults and wanted to be treated as such.

Her mother nodded and blew a kiss around the nurse at Nicole. Nicole turned to see her father had already left.

Nicole didn't get a chance to tell her mother about her last trip to the sixth century. The cell phone buzz woke her up the next morning, and she got the news from Beth before her father did. Her mother had died. Nicole expected her father would be pleased. The hospice bill wouldn't be that bad after all.

# XXVIII

I walked into Ingund's bedroom, hoping to find her before I ran into anyone else in the palace. I wasn't sure how long I'd been gone so I had no way of knowing what had happened in my absence.

"Cousin!" she shouted. She was resting on her bed, little Athanagild lying beside her. He looked to be a little over two years old, maybe even three, my first indication of what year it was. She jumped up and embraced me. "You have been gone far too long? I take it your mother has passed?"

I nodded. For once, I could tell the truth, even if my mother had died in Minnesota and not in Carthage.

"I just got back," I said reciprocating her warm hug. "I cannot believe you left my room just as it was. Thank you!"

"I'm so glad you're here," she said, backing away and picking up her waking son. "You won't believe what's happening. But first, tell me, how was Carthage? Is it teeming with the plague like they say?"

"Yes, it is," I lied. Or, to be more accurate, I had no clue. But I stuck with my Carthage story. "I had to be careful to keep myself as far away from other people as I could. And the rats, those nasty plague-carrying rodents."

I slapped my hand across my mouth. I had just told her something that doctors and health officials wouldn't figure out for centuries. One of the tragedies of the plague was that the authorities had eradicated from the streets the very predators that might have helped stem the disease. It was spread by the rats the cats would have killed if they hadn't been killed first.

"No, it's the cats," Ingund said. "I don't want to talk about the plague, though." She grabbed my hand and pulled me over to sit on the edge of the bed beside her. "Tell me how you have been. Have you found love yet? I thought you'd never get back!"

"I know it has been too long." I reached for sleepy little Athanagild, who slumped into my arms without a fuss and fell back to sleep. "I wasn't sure you would welcome me after such a long time. Athanagild has grown, and you look well. Pretty as ever."

"Oh, no. I'm getting old!"

"No, remember you told me I was getting old."

"But it doesn't look you have gained a year!" she exclaimed. She pushed my face to one side and then to the other with a finger. "Not a wrinkle anywhere."

I smiled. I had only spent two months in Minnesota. I was still twenty-six. I hoped I didn't have many more wrinkles, even though my mother's death had been difficult to accept. As was my father's reaction to it.

"Sebastianus will be happy to see you. He was gone, too, but he got back yesterday." She gave me a sly smile and tipped her head. "You two did not run off together, did you?"

"No, we did not." I wanted to halt that rumor before it had a chance to spread. Of course, Ingund wouldn't be the only one to notice he and I had been gone at the same time.

"But tell me, is Hermenegild well? Has he communicated with his father?"

"No, his father has been in the northwest, trying to pacify the Suevi, from what we hear," she said. Athanagild started to wake again and squirmed in my arms. Ingund reached over and took him from me. "Baby," she said, putting him on his feet. "Run along now and find your nanny. She will get you something to eat."

Ingund walked to her dressing table and pulled a few pages of parchment from the drawer. I wondered what she was doing with it. She didn't read or write.

"My mother has sent these since you were gone. I have the Bishop Leander's scribe read them for me and respond, but I cannot trust him. I do not know what he may be leaving out or adding in to conform to his idea of proper topics. Can you read them to me?"

I couldn't imagine anything more like a gift for a historian than handwritten letters from Brunhilde herself! I reached over to grab them out of Ingund's hand, and realizing how rude that was, I pretended that I had stumbled.

"I am so clumsy," I said. "It must be from the long trip. Please forgive me."

"Will you read them?"

"Of course, I will. Do you want to do it now, or can you give me some time to read them first, so I don't stumble over the language?" I wanted time to memorize as much of them as I could so I might reconstruct them when I got back to Minnesota.

"Timotheus told me the language is 'vulgar,'" she said. "I am not certain what that means, but I suppose it means that it is not up to his standards." Timotheus? I chuckled thinking what Timothy back in St. George would think of a sixth-century scribe sharing his name.

I TOOK THE LETTERS TO my room, feeling as if I had contraband in my hands, as precious as they were. Ingund told me they arrived only about a week after they were dated. I wondered if that was true. I knew a fast horse and rider could cover about fifty kilometers in an hour, which meant that a courier could travel the distance from Metz to Seville in about forty hours, if he and his horse never stopped. With rest and changes of horses, I figured a one-week delivery was indeed possible.

The date on the top of the first letter was "spring," which meant it had been sent about a year ago. The last of the three said "spring" again.

"*My dearest Daughter, Queen of the Visigoths,*" Brunhilde wrote at the start of start each.

At this point, Brunhilde would have known Hermenegild had declared himself king of Baetica. In her first letter, Ingund's mother wrote that she had received news from Goswintha that Leovigild wasn't happy about it but was too distracted by border issues with the Suevi to react. And she urged her daughter to continue to pursue her husband's conversion.

Brunhilde had converted to Catholicism when she married Sigibert, and tradition called for Ingund to convert to her husband's faith as well. While Brunhilde had accepted her conversion, she didn't want Ingund to do so. She made it clear she expected Hermenegild to be the one to convert.

*Has Athanagild been baptized?* Brunhilde asked in the letter. I tried to understand her urgency and figured she wanted her grandson to be welcome in her version of "the kingdom of God," the Catholic one.

Her letters contained domestic details like the start of Chlosinda's menses and Childebert's growth spurt. I was surprised she had not written anything about her half-uncle, Gundovald, who was building an army in Aquitaine to challenge her rule in Austrasia and Fredegund's in Neustria. He had some support among the nobility in Austrasia, tired of Brunhilde and Fredegund's constant scrimmages and drama. But Brunhilde didn't mention it in her letters.

I was disappointed not to read more first-hand information about the politics in Gaul, but at the same time, it was eye-opening to see that even in times of great political upheaval, letters between mothers and daughters were much as they were in modern times: full of domestic details and gossip, and little about the outside world.

Returning to Ingund's dressing room later, Ingund nodded

along as I read the letters aloud. "Not much different from what Timotheus read." She seemed relieved that she hadn't missed anything. Timotheus had not yet come to take dictation for her response to the last letter, so we sat down at the dressing table, and I wrote as she dictated. Like her mother's missives, Ingund's letter was filled with family news: Athanagild's childish antics and assurances of Hermenegild's continued affection.

When we finished, I set aside the parchment to dry, and Ingund turned toward her mirror and handed me her brush. I stood to gather her long hair back behind her shoulders and started brushing it from the bottom, working my way up to ease the tangles a few at a time.

She smiled at me in the pewter. "No one else brushes my hair like you do."

"I am certain no one else loves you as I do." I said it without thinking and wondered if it was true. Certainly, Hermenegild still loved her, in a more intimate way. But brushing her hair? Unlikely.

Just as we finished, a maid delivered a sleepy Athanagild to the room. He staggered on chubby legs toward Ingund, and she pulled him into her lap. She closed her eyes, leaned her chin on his head, and stroked his curly, blond hair until he fell asleep.

She opened her eyes, now wide with excitement. "Oh, I was going to tell you my good news," she said, waking her son.

"What—"

She didn't give me a chance to ask.

"The Bishop Leander has just returned from Constantinople, and he has spoken to me."

Aha. That bit of news helped me narrow down the date of my arrival even more precisely. It had to be 582 if Leander had just come back.

"What did he say?" I asked, reaching for sleepy Athanagild, who slumped into my arms without a fuss and fell back to sleep.

"He talked with Emperor Tiberius," Ingund said excitedly. "The emperor said he will support my husband's sovereignty in Baetica over Leovigild's, but that Herme will have to convert to the ortho-dox religion first."

"Has he talked with Hermenegild about this yet? What does Goswintha think?"

"No, he has not talked to either of them yet. He just came to me, Christian to Christian. He thinks I have enough conviction in my faith to persuade my husband to convert."

"Do you?" I asked.

She winked at me as she stood up and flopped down on her back on her bed. "You know I do," she said coyly. I got the gist.

"What about your grandmother?"

Ingund propped herself up on an elbow and hesitated. I won-dered if she was worried about revealing what was on Goswintha's mind. "She supports Herme because she wants Athan to be king of his own empire," she said, finally. "You know that. But I can imagine her husband is furious about it. She may never be able to go home." She lowered her voice. "And I will never be rid of her."

I nodded conspiratorially. "I imagine she is quite difficult at times."

"Yes. Just like my mother."

"When is Leander going to talk with Hermenegild about Tibe-rius's offer?" I couldn't bring myself to say "Herme," which she pro-nounced like "HER-me." She pronounced "Athan" like "AY-then." I could handle that, but not "HER-me."

"He wants me to talk with Herme first. He asked me to re-port back to him after I do. With the Byzantines sitting beside us along the sea's edge, I cannot imagine that Herme will disagree. He has the support of many in Baetica, but Leovigild has a much big-ger army. With the Byzantines on our side, we would have a better chance."

"You have become quite the politician, just like your mother," I said.

"No, that is only what Bishop Leander told me. I will go slow, though. I do not want to push my husband too hard."

"I think you sell yourself short."

She squeezed her eyebrows together. "What does that mean?"

I laughed at myself. I had to drop my twenty-first-century idioms if I wanted to be understood.

# XXIX

I caught up with Sebastianus the next afternoon. As much as I wanted to lie in his arms instead of talking, I first needed to find out if he knew anything about what the Byzantines might be planning. He saw me coming across the yard and walked out of the stables toward me.

"You have returned," he said, his eyes smiling.

"And I heard you have just come back, too," I said. "Where have you been for three years?"

"How time flies." He ignored my question. Where had he been? In the sixth century his answer probably would be Corduba, or some such place, on orders from Hermenegild. In the twenty-first century would it be the Hadron supercollider again?

"Can you come back tomorrow to discuss working on your carriage?" he asked, slyly. "Maybe about noon?"

I thought his metaphor was clever. "I believe so," I said, choking back the anticipation. I looked around to see who was within earshot. There were a couple of groomsmen in with the horses, but they were having a loud discussion that bordered on an argument.

"Do you know what the Byzantines are planning?" I asked in a near whisper. "Leander has been sent by Tiberius to bargain with Hermenegild. Do you know what the plan is?"

"I was just down in Cadiz, and there is a lot of activity down around the seaport," he said, his back toward the stables. "But I don't know what it means. It could just be some uprising in North Africa or more trouble with the Lombards in Italy."

From my historical research, I knew that Tiberius had been begging Ingund's brother, young Childebert, to help him battle the Lombards in Italy, but that the Frank wouldn't feel pressured enough to do anything for a while, at least not until the Byzantines had their hands on Athanagild.

"What do you think will happen if Hermenegild converts?" I asked, even though I knew the answer.

"Why do you think he'll do that?" Even if Sebastianus was Sébastièn, he wouldn't know that answer. It was a legitimate question. He didn't know the history of the next three years like I did.

"That is part of Leander's bargain. Or I should say Tiberius's bargain." I hoped I wasn't leaking a detail of the future that would matter.

"Aha." Sebastianus nodded. "Perhaps there is more to what is going on at the port than I thought. You have great insights, Cousin." He wiggled his eyebrows. "Why would a woman in Visigothic empire need to be so smart?"

I almost punched him in the stomach. The real question was: Why wouldn't he just admit who he was?

The next noon, we met on Sebastianus's narrow cot just like before. The lovemaking was only getting better, more nuanced, at times more adventurous, at times more emotional. But after a few days, I was frustrated with having such a profound connection with Sebastianus in his bed but not having a meaningful relationship with him in a vertical position. He was smart and strategic and even funny at times, even in bed. But we only shared a few minutes of the day. I believed he would make a great friend the rest of the time. But this was the sixth century. Outside of marriage, men and women didn't hang out together.

That wasn't 100 percent true. Radegund the nun and Fortunatus the poet had been close friends, meeting over several years at the Monastery of the Holy Cross in Poitiers that she had founded. But to pull that off, I'd have to be a nun, and he'd have to have some reason for visiting a convent on a regular basis. And sex would be out of the question. Or we'd have to get married, something I was sure neither of us contemplated.

I'd never appreciated living in the twenty-first century with its more relaxed social conventions as I did then.

SHORTLY AFTER MY RETURN TO Hispalis, the Bishop Leander arrived at the palace in a flurry of horses and carriages worth of a royal entourage. Ingund expected him to meet with Hermenegild alone, but shortly after the cleric arrived, she was summoned to her husband's throne room as well. I wished I could go along, not only to offer her emotional support, but also to watch and listen. But I was not invited.

The bishop stayed for a couple of hours, and when Ingund returned to her rooms that afternoon, she was smiling.

"What did your husband decide?" I asked excitedly, ready for history to start moving forward. I was tired of the stalemate we were in, waiting for either Leovigild or Hermenegild to make a move.

"He listened, but he did not choose Christ," Ingund said, but her happy demeanor indicated that the conversation was cordial and gave her hope. "I will have to keep talking with him. I need him to join me and Athanagild at the foot of the temple in God's kingdom."

I realized her focus was more far-sighted than mine. While I didn't wish for the worst to happen, which it inevitably would, at least for Hermenegild, I wanted this stalemate between Hermenegild and his father to end.

Before the bishop came to visit again, Sebastianus was sent to Cadiz by Hermenegild to evaluate the mutual defense agreement between the Byzantines and Baetica, anticipating Leovigild's eventual reaction to Hermenegild's usurpation. I didn't think the prince, or king, as he called himself now, would entrust such a sensitive mission to a person who was little more than a groomsman. I had underestimated Sebastianus's true position within the palace.

At first, I hated the way this new understanding of Sebastianus's rank made me feel. I realized that the more power Sebastianus had, the more I was attracted to him, which was not the way I thought liberated feminists should feel. What did his rank in a militaristic culture have to do with me? Why would his relative power in any society, especially a medieval society, affect the way I felt about him?

I thought about this a great deal while he was gone. I decided, eventually, that if I wanted to be a powerful, autonomous woman, then I wanted to align myself with – who was I kidding? Align? – then I wouldn't want my partner to be anyone but an equally powerful, autonomous man. I wanted to find my equal. I wanted to be his equal. I wanted us to deserve each other.

I wanted him to come back.

While Sebastianus was gone and I was musing about such silliness, the bishop came for a second visit, and Ingund was even more excited about this one than the last. I knew she had been playing on Hermenegild's conscience, working to convince him that not only would an alliance with the Byzantines further his ambitions, but his conversion to her religion, Orthodox Catholicism, would ensure they would spend eternity together in the kingdom of heaven.

When she returned from her meeting with the bishop and her husband later that afternoon, she was giddy. "Now I'm sure he will renounce his Arian heresy," she said as she floated into her chambers where I was waiting. "I want to write to my mother and tell her the good news."

I took a sheet of parchment from the dressing table, and we sat down to compose the short missive. Then I helped her prepare for the evening meal with Hermenegild. She dabbed rose and lavender oil on her neck and wrists, and I helped her dress in her most feminine shift and silk vest. I fixed her hair with ribbons and jewels, and she colored her lips with a pink tincture of berries and pork fat. She was always beautiful, but we made her stunning.

As she left for her evening meal, she curtsied flirtatiously, as if practicing for her husband or, perhaps, her grandmother. "I hope that tonight I can seduce him with my love and win him over to God's love." I wondered what the hagiographers who later canonized Saint Hermenegild would have thought if they had heard her say that.

# XXX

It was probably as much the promise of support from the Byzantines in the war with his father as Ingund's flirtations or Leander's pressure to convert that made up Hermenegild's mind. In the end, the impetus mattered little. It was unfair, but it was Hermenegild, not Ingund, who was first sainted for turning the Visigoths from Arianism to the orthodox religion, Catholicism, paving the way for much of the Iberian peninsula to be united in faith for another one hundred years.

While Leovigild had ignored Hermenegild's ostentatious grab at the title of king, he couldn't accept his son's conversion. He needed Hermenegild to remain Arian. Little rebellions among nobles and would-be royals were a constant irritant in the loose union of territories that constituted a kingdom anywhere on the continent. Steadfast allegiance to Arianism was one of the few things that held the Visigoths together. Leovigild had to know that the Catholic Byzantines would celebrate Hermenegild's conversion and ally with him to solidify their hold on the southeast coast of the peninsula.

Leander was baptizing the kneeling Hermenegild in the Cathedral of Hispalis when his father, having successfully pacified the Suevi, began mobilizing his army to quell his son's rebellion.

We had no trouble getting up-to-date news of Leovigild's march into Baetica. Even as the Visigoths took most of the peninsula from the Romans, they had accommodated the peninsula's religious majority, tolerating both Catholic churches and Catholic baptisms. Therefore, Leander and his brother, the Bishop Isadora, had clerical contacts throughout the territory between Toledo and Hispalis who could forward them news of the approaching army.

At first, Ingund could "hear no evil, see no evil" about the impending military confrontation. She was so ecstatic that her husband would now join her for eternity at Christ's feet that she had no interest in bad news. She floated around the palace with Athanagild in her arms or toddling behind her, ignoring the defensive preparations: barricades around the palace, the frequent meetings of Hermenegild's top military commanders, and her husband's frequent absences. Apparently, she needed him less in the present, knowing that he'd be with her forever in the hereafter.

I wasn't so sanguine. I wanted Sebastianus to return and assure me that Leovigild's inevitable conquest would be less bloody and less violent than I feared. I was hoping that it would turn out to be the kind of victory for Leovigild and loss for Hermenegild that my old colleagues at MacIntosh would ignore for its lack of protracted, gruesome battles. As much as I loved medieval history, its conflicts and bloodletting weren't my thing.

As Leovigild's armies swept south, Goswintha told us that she was writing nearly daily to her daughter Brunhilde and her grandson, Childebert, for assistance. I was biased, I suppose. But when Sebastianus returned from Cadiz with news that the Byzantines were mobilizing an armada to travel up the Guadalquivir River to help Hermenegild defend Hispalis, I was predisposed to think that it had more to do with his charismatic diplomacy than any long-distance communications between Goswintha and Brunhilde.

While pleased with Sebastianus's status as a key advisor, I discovered the price of his palace status was his frequent absence. As soon as he returned to Seville, he was sent north to assess the accuracy of the reports we were getting of Leovigild's army's progress.

I put my romantic interests aside and focused on the day-to-day history I was witnessing. I knew that Hermenegild's rebellion was a lost cause, and I suspected that Sebastianus did, too, but he attended to his duties, and I respected him for that, even though it meant that I was left alone.

Eventually, the reality of Hermenegild's gamble penetrated Ingund's eschatological fog, and one of her handmaids called me to her room to answer her questions.

"What will happen if Hermenegild is defeated by his father?" she asked as I walked in and her handmaid was dismissed. "What will happen to us?"

"Why do you think I would know?" I asked.

She shrugged. "My baby boy must not suffer from my obstinance," she said, scooting back on her bed and patting a spot next to her.

"Your adherence to your faith is not obstinance, is it?" I asked, sitting on the edge of her bed. "It is faith."

"True. But what if Leovigild takes Hispalis What will happen to us then?"

"I suppose it depends on what your husband decides to do. If his father demands that he renounce the faith he has just accepted, he will have to choose. You know him better than I do. Will he bow to his father to save his life on earth, or will he be more concerned with soul?"

Of course, I knew the answer. And I didn't believe any of this life-after-death mythology I was alluding to. I didn't believe in a soul separate from the body. But I wanted to comfort her by reminding her that Hermenegild had traded his worldly surety for the promise of spending eternity with her, as she said often, at Christ's feet.

Ingund was not placated by my equivocation. Hermenegild was gone most of the time now, out commanding the troops who stood to stop his father's advance. And what we heard from the battlefields told us it wasn't an even fight. Several cities had pledged their allegiance to Hermenegild and his orthodoxy, but under the threat of siege or pillaging, they backed down quickly and switched sides. Religion may have been a cause célèbre for Leovigild and his son, but for most of the inhabitants of Baetica, the religious preference of the Visigoths was mostly an abstraction. Once the armies passed through, they could get on with their lives and let kings and princes settle their religious differences somewhere else.

When Sebastianus returned from the north, Ingund sent me to bring him to the throne room.

"What is your sense of the situation?" she asked him bluntly, no pleasantries exchanged.

"It is hard to say this early in the campaign," he said.

"No," she said. "I did not ask you to tell me what you think I want to hear. I want to know how likely Hermenegild is to prevail."

Sebastianus looked at me sadly. I had the impression he wanted me to bail him out, but my love for Ingund was too great. I couldn't allow anyone to lie to her.

"Tell her the truth," I whispered. "She will know soon enough."

He turned to her, his hands clasped behind his back. "Many small cities have surrendered and switched allegiances," he said. "There were very few casualties. That is the good news."

"Mérida?" she asked.

"Catholic stronghold. It should buy the Byzantines some time."

"What about Italica?"

"Even though it is staunchly Catholic, I suppose it will be easy for Leovigild to pacify. Hermenegild has a small legion holed up inside the fortress there, but it won't be hard for his father to breech the weak walls."

Ingund took in his analysis quietly. She wrung her hands in her lap but didn't argue for a better prediction. "Hispalis and Corduba?" she asked.

"If the Byzantines get up the river soon enough, we may be able to hold Leovigild outside our city walls until additional troops arrive from Carthage. Corduba is less vulnerable than Hispalis because Hermenegild has allowed the Byzantines to move in and billet there, but it likely won't matter. If Seville falls, it will be over."

Ingund nodded, calmly. At that moment, I saw the queen she had matured into. Working behind Hermenegild's back with Leander had been risky, but it had proven to her that her commitments meant something. And now she was committed to helping her husband, or his legacy, by ensuring Athanagild's safety. She respected the truth.

"Thank you for telling me." She stood and Sebastianus humbly backed out of the room. He never looked at me, and I didn't expect him to.

I went to the stables the next day at our usual hour, and he greeted me warmly, but he didn't take my hand, and we didn't retire to the hay. Given the tense atmosphere, our focus was elsewhere. I wanted to find out what his plans were and hoped he wasn't going to end up on the battlefield himself. He quickly quieted my fear.

"You and I will escort Ingund and the little prince to Córdoba if it looks like the Arians will take Hispalis," he said. "Hermenegild believes the Byzantines will be able to hold Coduba, even if Leovigild manages to breech these city walls."

"What do you think?" I asked.

He paused, his face betraying his first inclination: to lie to me to keep me from worrying. I shook my head, and he understood.

"Okay. The truth? Hermenegild doesn't have the resources to prevail."

"Okay." I nodded. I was sad, but it wasn't like I didn't know that. I couldn't tell anyone, not even Sebastianus, although if I had thought he was in danger, I would find it hard to hold back.

"Let me know when you know," I said. Our eyes met and I realized that Ingund wasn't the only one who had grown through these troubled times. I believed that if Sebastianus and I were still able to see each other after Hermenegild fell and Ingund escaped from Spain, we, too, had a chance of developing that relationship beyond his small cot that I had wished for.

# XXXI

Ingund had lived through civil wars between her parents and their relatives in Gaul. In her youth, she and her sister were shuttled between one safehouse and another and from one imprisonment to another, collateral in the non-stop Merovingian wars. She knew how quickly the momentum on either side could change and wasted no time preparing for the worst. She sent some of the local servants she hired home. "Go take care of your families," she told them. I could see the fear in their eyes. If the queen was willing to do without them, things must have been very bad. She sent word to the stables to prepare a few necessary carriages and wagons for departure, although Sebastianus had already done so. Sebastianus reported that the request had the same frightening effect on the groomsmen, and a few left shortly after to return to their homes.

Goswintha had supported Hermenegild on behalf of her wishes for her grandson, but I could tell she was conflicted. If Leovigild succeeded in taking Baetica back from Hermenegild, she would be caught on the wrong side of the conflict. She didn't know if her husband would forgive her, forgive Hermenegild, or permit Athanagild's eventual ascension as heir to the throne. Her fate was unknown, to her and to me.

Mérida proved to be more of an obstacle to Leovigild's advance than I had expected or read about in any of the history of the conflict. Mérida had been held by Leovigild for six or seven years, but the local population was still largely Catholic. The bishop there was a close ally of Leander, and he urged the community to make a stand for orthodox Christianity and Hermenegild. But in the end, the Arians were too strong.

After word came of Mérida's surrender, and shortly thereafter, of the destruction of the fortress at Italica. Hermenegild still believed that, with the Byzantines on their way up the river to help, the substantial city walls of Hispalis would hold. It would leave him with a diminished kingdom, but he could retain the loyalty of a substantial military force and some portion of his reign. Sebastianus told me that Hermenegild knew that if Hispalis were lost, the cause of Chalcedonian Catholicism in Iberia would be defeated.

Goswintha came to Ingund's dressing room the evening after we heard about the fall of Italica. The palace was chillingly quiet, and Hermenegild, out on the battlefield, trying to hold off his father's advance, no longer dined there.

"Daughter," the queen said, taking Ingund into her arms. I had never heard her call Ingund "daughter" before, but things between them had improved significantly since Athanagild's birth. "I believe you should leave the city with your son as soon as you can. I have consulted with Hermenegild's advisors, and they agree."

"But what does Hermenegild think? Does he want me to go now?" She knew she might have to leave but she wanted to stay close to her husband as long as she could.

"I do not know," Goswintha conceded. "But it is not safe for you or Athanagild here with Leovigild's army so close. You must protect the only legitimate heir to the throne."

"I do not want to go without Herme," Ingund said, sinking into the chair at her dressing table. She turned to me.

"Would you find out? Talk to Sebastianus. See if he can find out what Hermenegild thinks. Find out if we need to leave soon."

I nodded and left the room. I already knew the answer. But I had to make a show of finding out. I had only about an hour before dusk set in to find Sebastianus.

I reached the stables just as Sebastianus rode in on his favorite mare with three other men I didn't recognize. He dismounted next to me and frowned.

"What are you doing out here?" he asked me gruffly. I took a step back, surprised by this treatment.

"Ingund sent me to find out whether Hermenegild thinks she should leave Hispalis." I nearly stammered in the face of this new attitude from the man I had shared a bed with so often.

Sebastianus shook his head and looked away, as if trying to calm himself.

"I am sorry. I did not want to be so rude. I am coming to the palace now to deliver a message from the king."

"You mean Hermenegild?"

"Yes." He smirked as if he found my question absurd. "I do not speak with Leovigild very often."

"And the message?"

Sebastianus put his hand under my elbow, threw his riding gloves toward one of the men who had accompanied him, and we strode together to the palace. I left him in the throne room while I retrieved Ingund and Goswintha.

"His Highness wants me to take you to Corduba, where you can take refuge in the Cathedral," he told the women as soon as they rushed in ahead of me. "You should be ready to leave at dawn. The bishop has assured the king that you will be granted sanctuary there."

"And my son?" Goswintha asked. "Will he come with us?"

"Not unless Hispalis falls. And then he will have to decide. He may meet with his father and reach a truce."

"But he cannot denounce his faith," Ingund nearly shouted.

"I will leave that matter to you and the bishop," Sebastianus answered quietly. I was impressed by his composure. Delivering such shocking news was one thing; standing calm in the face of Ingund's panic was another.

"I will stay here with my son," Goswintha announced. That surprised me as well. Historians had not known what had happened to her once Leovigild prevailed. We knew what happened to Hermenegild, and we had some alternative theories of what eventually happened to Ingund, but Goswintha had disappeared. No historian knew if she would die in the fall of Hispalis or if she would end up back in Toledo with Leovigild.

Ingund didn't react to Goswintha's decision. She thanked Sebastianus, grabbed my hand and pulled me away. Upstairs, she rang the bell outside her bedroom door for a handmaid, and sat on the bed, wordlessly, pensive. When the maid entered, Ingund asked for Athanagild to be brought to her.

"The governess has put him to his bed," the maid said, bowing her head. "Do you want her to wake him now?"

Ingund reconsidered. Her face was drawn with worry. "No. We will need to rouse him early tomorrow. Please let his governess know that she should have him ready to travel with me before dawn. And alert my other handmaids that I will be leaving in the morning with my son and my cousin."

It was the first I knew I would be going with her.

"And in a moment, come back for a letter I will ask you to send to the bishop for delivery to my mother."

"Yes, Your Highness," the maid said, curtsying quickly and leaving us alone.

Ingund turned to me. "Will you write again?"

I pulled a sheet from the dressing table and prepared my quill. Ingund told her mother that she was going to Corduba with Athanagild. She could be reached through Bishop Masona there.

I handed the letter to the maid waiting outside her door and hurried to my room to pack for our departure. I didn't have much, but as always, I took my special dress. I never knew when I might need to leave the sixth century in a hurry.

WE LEFT EARLY, RODE FAST, and arrived in Corduba in the evening. The bishop knew we were coming, and the guards were waiting at the Cathedral gate. Sebastianus handed our few bags to a waiting cleric and waved to us as he jumped back on his seat and drove the carriage away, leaving two of Ingund's guards at the gate with the bishop's men. I supposed he was returning to Seville, regardless of the hour.

We were escorted to a small building that stood so close to the back of the church it might as well have been attached. We were safe within the cathedral grounds' walls, I knew. Sanctuary was only rarely breeched in early medieval times, and when it did happen, it was to capture enemies far more dangerous and treasonous than Ingund. Certainly, Leovigild may want to retrieve Athanagild and bring him back to Toledo, but even if that happened, it would be done without bloodshed.

Inside the tiny wood hovel were two narrow beds, a wood stove, a small desk and chair, and a table big enough for two bowls and cups, and nothing more. A cross was nailed to the east wall above a kneeling bench for prayer. We were in the quarters for visiting clergy. Simple and clean. It would be fine for me, but it certainly didn't look like a place for a queen or an heir to the Visigothic throne.

A man dressed like a monk knocked on the door shortly after our arrival and handed me a pitcher of water, and a basket with bread, fruit, and a small greenish glass bottle of milk. Although glass bottles had been made for a couple of thousands of years by then, I had never seen one in my sixth century visits. I wondered where it had come from.

The monk handed me a lantern and a flint and turned to leave.

"Excuse me!" I called after him. "Does the bishop expect the queen to remain here during her sanctuary?"

"I will come for her in the morning," he answered. "The bishop will show her where she will stay."

So, the queen was destined to stay in little more than a hut, but perhaps for only a night. I looked around and realized it wasn't much worse than many of the inns we had stayed in on our journeys from Toledo, although with substantially more meager provisions. I knew that bishops were fed better than we were that night, but perhaps the monks and lesser clerics were accustomed to austerity.

Without a handmaid to help us, I pulled our bags inside the house. Ingund had set the grapes on the table and poured half of the milk into the cup for Athanagild. The little boy sat on the chair and solemnly drank. He looked around curiously but didn't say a word. When he finished with the milk, he held out the empty cup to his mother.

"Sleep?" he asked his mother, holding out his arms to be picked up. His mother laid him on one of the beds and pulled the lone, scratchy blanket up over him.

"Where do you suppose we relieve ourselves?" she whispered, turning to me.

I shrugged. "I will go investigate before it gets too dark," I offered. I walked out and closed the door behind me.

The cathedral grounds were beautifully manicured. A row of benches ran along the wall at our end of the garden, and in the back corner stood a small wood house I assumed was our outhouse. I walked toward it down a path of stones lined with phlox and vinca vines and shaded by huge chestnut trees. In normal times, I would have found this place a peaceful retreat, welcoming rest and contemplation, but our hasty exodus had left me unsettled.

I knew what would happen eventually to Hermenegild, and I expected I would be able to put on the dress and return to my life any time I needed to, but I didn't know the fate of the two people I had grown closest to, Ingund and Sebastianus. I also wondered when we would get news of what happened to Seville.

I took my relief in the outhouse and returned up the path. A guard had moved from the gate to our front door, and he nodded at me as I returned. I was glad to see he was nearby. I wondered if he had to stand awake all night. I appreciated our walls, roof, and beds.

<h1 style="text-align:center">XXXII</h1>

I awoke at dawn and lay still while I worked out where I was. I had slept well despite the strange circumstances. Ingund and Athanagild were sitting on their bed, sharing the last of the milk and eating bread.

I hadn't heard a peep from Athanagild all night, and it made me wonder if I'd been wrong about kids all along. A little guy who looked like Sebastianus wouldn't be so bad, I found myself thinking. Without the beard, of course. But raising a child in the time of smart phones and the internet would be as different as the twenty-first century was from the one Athanagild inhabited.

I laughed at myself and sat upright. I was still wearing my traveling clothes, and I wondered how long it would be before we would find a wash tub and some warm water to wipe off some of the road filth.

Athanagild slurped the last of the milk from the cup, and Ingund took his hand to help him slip down off the bed.

"We're going down to the latrine," she said, and they left hand-in-hand. I heard the guard greet her, and I got up. I was amazed at her equanimity with the situation. She didn't cry or complain or moan about her treatment. She had always been a princess, and now a queen, and she was taking her misfortune with grace. As I had thought before, perhaps being shuttled from town to town as the Gauls switched allegiances and won and lost territory had steeled her for this life.

I ate the last of the bread and drank some water straight out of the pitcher while I waited for Ingund to return.

"Stop!" I heard the guard shout, and I opened the door to be sure he wasn't holding Ingund and Athanagild back.

A trio of large men in strange helmets and heavy tunics stood in front of our guard, whose back was to our door, arguing. I was about to close the door for our safety when a man in flowing clerical robes strode down the path toward them. He stepped between the guard and the helmeted men. The trio quit talking and lowered themselves on a knee.

The Bishop Masona, I realized. He was not as well-known or powerful as Leander or his younger brother, Isadora, but he had the respect of the Byzantines for his efforts to convert Visigoths to the Catholic faith in both Corduba and Mérida.

He motioned for the men to stand, and after a brief discussion, they walked back around the cathedral. I doubted they were leaving, but I was glad they took their attitudes elsewhere.

The bishop turned to me. I didn't know whether I should kneel like the soldiers or cross myself or do something else, so I just stood with my mouth open.

"The queen and the prince have been given sanctuary in the cathedral," he said. "They asked for you. Please follow me."

Inside a small room at the back of the cathedral, Ingund and Athanagild were talking with a tall man dressed in the same fashion as the trio I had seen outside. Like theirs, his Latin was strange, and I realized they were Byzantine soldiers. But what were they doing there?

Ingund waved for me to sit with them when she saw me at the door. I quickly took a seat on the bench next to her, while the man continued to speak. Although he was hard to understand, I thought the gist of it was that the bishop's sanctuary no longer meant much. We were now under the protection of Maurice, the new Roman Emperor in Constantinople, and we would remain so as long as our lives were threatened by the Arian Visigoths. I doubted I was included in the protection, but I didn't ask for clarification. I didn't say anything, and neither did Ingund.

Eventually he finished his speech, bowed tersely, and left.

I looked at Ingund, and she looked back as Athanagild crawled into her lap.

"Did you understand him?" I asked. Just behind him, the cleric who had been standing in the back of the room started to walk out.

"What has happened?" Ingund asked him.

"The bishop will come to address you," he said curtly over his shoulder.

Hell of a way to treat a queen. I was incensed, even though I had never held much love for modern-day royals, anachronistic in the twenty-first century, but not in the sixth. I remembered the disgust I felt at the over-the-top celebrations of Hermenegild's wedding and Athanagild's birth, but there was a great deal of moral distance between extravagant waste and disrespect.

The bishop who had escorted me to the cathedral came back into the room and stood before us, his hands clasped in front of his white robes. Ingund stepped forward and knelt. He held one hand out to her, and she kissed it.

"Bless you, child," the bishop said, and Ingund sat back down with us. He spoke directly to her. "Emperor Maurice has extended his greetings to you. You will be under his protection as long as the Arian heretics threaten you and your child. Be assured that your sanctuary here is respected by the Byzantines. As I receive news from Seville, I will bring it to you."

"Thank you, Your Eminence," Ingund said in a near whisper. "Do you have any news of my husband?"

"Not yet. I will bring you any news I receive, my child. Meanwhile, my servants have prepared a room for you in the clergy house next to my residence. A steward will arrive presently to escort you. He will transfer your possessions for you." He nodded slightly and left the room.

Our new abode was considerably more comfortable than the one-room cabin we'd spent the night in. It had a small sleeping room with four beds and a larger living room with a dining table and a desk with a lantern, as well as an attached toilet—a true luxury in those days. We wouldn't have to run outside to relieve ourselves, which was especially nice, knowing that the scary Byzantine guards might be lingering around.

As soon as we entered, Athanagild ran ahead of us into the sleeping quarters and jumped on a bed. The servant brought our bags and set them down. "I will bring you a basket soon with bread and cheese and some fresh water, My Lady," he said to Ingund, bowing his way out the door.

I didn't mind being ignored by both the bishop and the servant, concerned as I was for Ingund. I had hardly been aware of the change in my attitude and purpose over the past month. When I first arrived at Ingund's side, my goal was only to observe and learn enough to help me write my dissertation. But as she came to depend on my friendship, and I became attached to the young woman, I now felt more like a real cousin to her. I knew the heartbreak that was coming, and I wished I could do something to prevent it. Hermenegild should leave Hispalis and come to Corduba now, if he wanted to survive. But that wasn't going to happen.

Burdened with that knowledge, I found it hard to put on a cheerful face. That, however, only made matters worse.

"Cousin," Ingund said with alarm when she saw my eyes fill with tears. "What is wrong? We are safe! Don't worry. The Christian Byzantines are our allies. They will take care of us."

How I wanted to warn her of their intentions! That I couldn't only made me cry harder. I shook my head, waved off her proffered embrace and closed myself in the closet that served as our toilet. I sat on the bench to think, but nothing came to me but the wish that

Sebastianus could have stayed with us.

But with that thought, I began to worry about him as well.

Sᴇʙᴀsᴛɪᴀɴᴜs, ᴀs ɪꜰ ᴄᴀʟʟᴇᴅ ᴛᴏ us by my thoughts, came the next day. He pulled me outside of our little house to share the news from Hispalis before the bishop informed Ingund. Just south of the city, Leovigild's forces had dammed the Guadalquivir River, effectively prohibiting the Byzantine fleet from reaching Hispalis from Cadiz. Hermenegild was on his own.

"It is likely that Hispalis will fall to Leovigild in the next couple of days," he said. I looked back at the house to be sure I'd closed the door and Ingund wouldn't be able to listen in.

"The citizens may be Catholic," Sebastianus continued, "but they have little appetite for another siege. And I am concerned that the Byzantines have ulterior motives for letting Ingund stay here."

I could see his point. The hatred between the Byzantines and the Visigoths was raw. Only ten or eleven years ago, the Visigoths had seized Hispalis from the Byzantines. Since then, no Visigoth, by birth or marriage, could step foot in Byzantine Corduba and expect to survive. And now Ingund was supposed to trust them to protect her?

"What ulterior motives do you suspect?" I knew he was right, but what could he do to help her? And should he? I had become so attached to her and her son, I was starting to lose my determination to keep from messing with history.

On the other hand, I had felt this before: this impression that I was meant to be here, that I was in fact part of the history that in my world had already been written. And since I suspected that if Sébastièn was Sebastianus, perhaps he was part of that history, too. I prodded him for his theories.

"If the Byzantines hold Ingund and Athanagild, they can demand that Brunhilde and Childebert help them repel the Lombards in Italy. They've been asking for Childebert's help for a long time, but he has had little incentive to agree. Now he does. Athanagild is his nephew." Sebastianus looked to me for confirmation. "Right?"

He was asking me. He knew that I had a grasp of the future that no sixth-century cousin would have. He knew where I was from. Now I was sure of that.

"That sounds very plausible," I said, trying to keep a straight face. "How did you come up with that?"

Sebastianus lowered his voice. "Perhaps we will have to discuss this further sometime, sometime when we have a bit of time to relax and reprise."

"Reprise what?" I asked, surprised at how easily I had learned to flirt. I checked the house door again before I rose up on my toes and met his lips. It was a bad idea, because then all I wanted was to pull him back into the deep bushes of the property and lie with him.

We pulled ourselves apart and took a deep breath while holding each other's eyes.

"I certainly hope we will be able to see each other when this is all over," I said. It was clearly a wish we shared, and I didn't need to say it. But when Sebastianus nodded and pulled me close, I was glad I had.

# XXXIII

According to the letter Ingund received from Brunhilde a week later, Childebert had asked the Byzantines for help returning Ingund and Athanagild to Gaul, where they would be safe until the battle for Baetica was over. But Brunhilde was no fool. She knew that the Byzantines weren't protecting Ingund and Athanagild; she recognized a hostage situation when she saw one.

As Sebastianus had predicted, and as I had already known, the Byzantines wouldn't give up their captives without compensation. They promised to keep Ingund and Athanagild safe, if Childebert would attack the Lombards in Italy. Brunhilde promised Ingund that Childebert would do what the Byzantines wanted in Italy, although his legions weren't really motivated. What was in it for them? They weren't likely to gain any new territory or find much to plunder in northern Italy where war after war had already ravaged and impoverished the countryside.

There was a little good news in the letter: Ingund's remaining uncle, King Guntram, who controlled Burgundy, was helping Hermenegild by attacking Reccared's Visigoths in Septimania, hoping to divert some of Leovigild's attention and military power from his efforts in Baetica.

Reading her mother's letter aloud to her, I realized this could be the first time Ingund knew for sure that she was a prisoner and not a guest of the Byzantines — that to the emperor in Constantinople she was only a bargaining chip in a bloody contest for territory and power. I felt horrible for being the one who brought her that certainty. Would she be better off knowing the truth of her captivity?

She had just dictated a dispirited response to her mother when a knock on the door of our house made us both jump up from our seats. I waited to answer it until she had pulled Athanagild into her arms and ran into the sleeping room and closed the door.

It was the steward who worked for the bishop. "His Eminence wants Queen Ingund to meet him in the cathedral," he said.

"Of course," I said as Ingund emerged from the bedroom with Athanagild clinging to her neck. The boy was too big for her to carry. I pulled him into my arms, and we headed across the lawn for the side door to the sanctuary.

The bishop stood at the door of the small room where we had met with him a couple of weeks before. He waved us in, and I was surprised to see Sebastianus waiting there.

"The king's messenger has news, dear child," he said. "I am afraid it is not good."

Sebastianus looked like he would rather be anywhere in the world but here, presenting the news he'd been sent to deliver.

"Your Grace," he started, which was in itself alarming. He and Ingund had stopped such formalities long ago. Perhaps he said it for the bishop's sake. Masona was unlikely to approve of familiarity.

"Your husband has been taken captive in Hispalis. He is to be transported to Valencia where he will be held, awaiting Leovigild's judgment."

Ingund sank to her knees, and Athanagild struggled out of my arms to embrace her huddled figure. She sobbed, her face in her hands. She didn't look up for a long minute, and Sebastianus waited. When she finally turned her face back to him, he continued in somber tones.

"The city has surrendered, and the Byzantine navy has returned to Cadiz. The war is over, but you are still safe here, protected by the sanctuary granted by Bishop Masona and the Byzantine army."

"What will happen to my king?" Ingund pleaded, still on her knees, Athanagild clinging to her neck.

"We will hope for mercy and understanding," was all Sebastianus had for her. I pitied him for having so little to offer. I wished I could stand by him, embrace him, in some way show my support. But I stood, feeling worthless and impotent. History had played itself out, and if there was anything that could have made me feel better, it was this: clearly neither Sebastianus nor I had changed it in any meaningful way. At that moment, it was hard to celebrate that.

Ingund's only worth to the Byzantines now was as a pawn in their chess game in Italy. Chess had not yet reached continental Europe from its origins in India, but that didn't keep me from thinking of it in those terms. The battle over Baetica wasn't as important to them as their troubles with the Lombards. Even Corduba could fall to Leovigild, and they would waste no resources defending it as long as they still had what they needed most: the southeast coastline of the peninsula, from which they could control their territory in Northern Africa as well as organize and launch assaults on the Lombards in Italy.

INGUND AND I HAD LITTLE to do while we waited for news of Hermenegild. Summer had turned to fall nearly overnight, and the cooler temperatures were a relief as we holed up in our clergy house. I asked the steward who delivered our daily provisions for a book, and of course, he delivered a bible. I tried to find the less apocalyptic and tragic stories to read aloud to Ingund, and finding little that wasn't about conflict, war, and dire predictions, I settled mostly on the Psalms and poems in the Song of Songs. I was surprised how many love songs there were in the latter.

Song of Songs is a short chapter, and Ingund asked me to read it over and over. I didn't find the verses terribly inspired, accustomed as I was to modern poetry, which is less flowery and quite a bit less emotional. I hadn't read any of the bible for a long time, and I was a little surprised how mushy some of it was.

But Ingund loved it. Her favorites verses were 4:9-16 and 5:10-161.

The first starts "*You have ravished my heart, my sister, my bride, you have ravished my heart with a glance of your eyes, with one jewel of your necklace.*"

It got even sweeter as it went.

Her other favorite started: "*My beloved is all radiant and ruddy, distinguished among ten thousand. His head is the finest gold; his locks are wavy, black as a raven.*"

I was relieved to have a way to calm down her anxiety, even if it was only temporary. So, I reread the eight short chapters until I nearly had them memorized.

"I wish I could read," Ingund said, sighing after one of our sessions. "I suppose there is much more beautiful poetry in the great book."

"Song of Songs is unique in the bible," I said, not wanting to pop her bubble, but also not lying to her about the book's content. "Psalms also has beautiful poetry, but not so much about love between men and women."

"Perhaps I will learn to read. Perhaps you can teach me?"

I wished that I could do that.


WE GOT LITTLE NEWS FROM Hispalis, Toledo, or Valencia for weeks. We grew bored, I grew anxious, and if I hadn't felt so attached and somehow responsible for Ingund and Athanagild, I would have donned my time-portal dress and left. But she had no one else.

Sebastianus visited us occasionally, and although I would have liked a chance to be alone with him, Ingund craved his visits so much, I couldn't take him away from her. He wouldn't tell us where he was staying or what he was doing, other than to say he was ensuring that the queen's carriage and horses were kept safe so she would be able to travel back to Hispalis or to Toledo, whatever her father-in-law decided for her, once the kingdom had settled down.

Most concerning was the lack of news about Hermenegild. His brother, Reccared, Sebastianus told us, was pressuring him to renounce his faith and reconcile with his father, but Ingund's husband wouldn't budge. A week later, Sebastianus returned with news about Hermenegild that he didn't want to deliver to Ingund. He came to our door and, once again, asked me to step outside. That alone frightened Ingund. I saw her eyes widen and start to water, but she grabbed Athanagild and sat with him while I went out to talk with our messenger.

"There are conflicting reports," he said. "We heard that Hermenegild was imprisoned by Leovigild in Valencia. But now we hear that he took sanctuary in the cathedral in Hispalis, and that his brother has been visiting him there, not in Valencia. And now, his messengers have brought us the news that he was lured out of sanctuary by his brother who promised a reconciliation with Leovigild, and a man named Sisbert murdered him as he emerged."

I had known this would happen, but I nor any other historian had known who killed him. "Who called for his murder?" I asked.

"That, too, is a mystery. Some think it was his father, some think Reccared masterminded it so that he would be first in line for the kingdom. It's also said that Reccared then had Sisbert executed, but we don't know whether it was for the murder or to shut him up and cover up his complicity. It will be impossible to know the truth now that Hispalis is controlled by Leovigild. There are even rumors floating that he was in Caesaraugusta all along, not Hispalis or Valencia. But there is no doubt that he was murdered."

"And buried…"

"I have no idea."

So, despite my proximity to what had occurred, I wasn't any closer to the truth than any of the writers of the histories I had combed through in my research. That disappointment paled in comparison to my grief for Ingund.

"Now what happens to Ingund?" I asked, my own eyes filling with tears. Watching Ingund listen to the love poems in Song of Songs, I knew her love for Hermenegild had only strengthened since their separation.

"She is now solely in the hands of the Byzantines."

"Can't the bishop protect her? Doesn't she have sanctuary?"

He shook his head sadly. "The bishop is taking orders from Constantinople now. What the emperor wants …" He left his sentence unfinished.

I wiped my face with the back of my hand, and Sebastianus stepped forward and put his arms around me. He kissed the top of my head, and when I looked up, I saw his eyes reddening with tears as well.

"I miss you," I whispered.

"I will come with more news, if I hear any," he said. "Right now, I must tell the bishop about Hermenegild. Best if she hears it from him and not me. I can offer her no comfort but your love and my love; he will offer her God's love, which is much greater."

I looked at him sideways. Did he believe in "God's love?" That would be the first I had heard of any religious belief on his part—his or Sébastièn's.

"You think God's love—" I didn't have to complete the sentence when he held up his hand.

"I am referring to what the bishop and she believe."

He gave me an unsatisfactorily quick kiss on the lips and turned to walk to the cathedral. I did not want to go into the house and face Ingund's questioning. She had a right to know, but she shouldn't hear it from me, as Sebastianus said. I waited outside and hoped the bishop would send for her soon.

I heard Sebastianus address the steward at the door and enter the cathedral. As I waited, I watched a few leaves fall from the tree branches and float to the ground. The breeze made the ground rustle softly and kicked up the scent of fall. My tears grew and I blinked them away. I knew for the first time what it meant to have a heavy heart. I felt a weight I hadn't even sensed at my mother's death. Her life had been long and largely comfortable and free of adversity. Ingund was young and had already endured so much. She deserved more than this. Her courage, her energy, her love for her husband and her son, her love for me, even her love for her difficult mother all deserved some kind of reward, and not the ending the historians had recorded for her.

The side door to the cathedral opened and the bishop walked out, flanked by an acolyte and his steward. I was glad he wasn't going to make Ingund come to him. It was right for him to go to her.

# XXXIV

They didn't give Ingund a reasonable amount of time to grieve in peace. A day later, Sebastianus returned under orders—now from the Byzantines—to bring her and Athanagild to Malaca, which I knew as Málaga, where she would board a ship to Constantinople. Once again, the Byzantines framed the kidnapping as "protection," but she was no longer so easily fooled.

The bishop did not show up to bid her a safe journey, but his steward filled our carriage with a small cask of wine, jugs of water, and baskets of cheese, grapes, apples, and dried meat. No one gave me permission to go along, but no one stopped me either.

I carried Athanagild out to the carriage and waited beside it for Ingund to gather the strength to walk out of the clergy's house that had been our refuge and her prison for weeks. When she emerged, her face sober but tearless, she stumbled on the stone walk, and Sebastianus jumped to catch her. She leaned against him and walked with his arm around her shoulders. He helped her into the carriage, and Athanagild and I stepped in after her. As we settled in, she pulled her son to her side and reached across to hold my hand. She nodded at me, which I took as a sign of resignation. She would never again control a moment of her life or her son's, and she knew it.

Our entourage for this final journey in Iberia was made up of Byzantine soldiers, not the  queen's retinue. For all I knew, the queen's men might have been executed by Leovigild as traitors or simply sent away to find new employment. Other than Sebastianus, we knew no one. I imagined how abandoned Ingund felt. Hundreds of kilometers from her family, her husband dead, her mother-in-law missing, and her father-in-law blaming her for her son's insurrection, all she had was Athanagild, Sebastianus and me, and two of us were bound to leave her soon.

The road was more primitive than any I had been on since Toulouse. The empire had not built a road that led directly from Córdoba to Malaca, as most traffic in and out of the ancient Phoenician city of Malaca was by water, not land. At times it seemed like we were following deer and horse trails more than a road. The trip took four days, and on the third night out, there was no inn to house us. The soldiers staked a crude tent under a heavy cover of trees, laid rugs over the dirt, and tossed a couple of straw mattresses inside. We were not invited to join the men by their smoky campfire, although Sebastianus was. I watched out of our tent opening, curious about what a Byzantine army camp looked like, and saw him sitting silently among the soldiers as they passed tankards of wine back and forth. He got up and retired to his own bedroll early, while the soldiers drank and laughed late into the night.

I was tired and was thinking about ending my sixth century adventure. I knew Ingund had no such choice, and until she reached Constantinople, if she ever did, it would be a rough journey. Earlier that evening, Sebastianus had tried to dissuade me from traveling to Carthage.

"The plague is ravaging the Carthaginians," he said. "I have been commanded to accompany her by the Byzantines, and I can watch over Athanagild. Go back wherever you came from. You do not need to put your life in danger."

By calling it the plague, Sebastianus had again hinted at his real identity. No one called it "the plague" in the sixth century. Then, it

was known as the "blue sickness" because of the black-blue swell-
ings, or bobos, that gave it the name bubonic later in later medieval
times. I didn't call him on his subterfuge; it had become a kind of
flirtation for us, I believed, despite the serious and dangerous situation we all faced.

But I had made up my mind to continue the journey. I had
come to think that whatever happened to me in the sixth century
wouldn't hurt me in the twenty-first—even the plague. I wouldn't
abandon Ingund until I had no choice.

We reached the port city the next day and went straight to the
harbor. The docks swarmed with chaos. Men and animals and crates
and barrels crisscrossed noisily in front of us as we made our way
toward a huge sailing ship that towered over us. Men ran up and
down the planks onto a narrow deck about halfway up the side of
the vessel. Two rows of holes along the side served as ports for oars
that would propel us when winds weren't favorable, and the mast at
the middle of the ship looked to be half again as tall as a smaller one
at the front. Two large buildings of sorts sat at either end of the main
deck. Knowing nothing about medieval sailing ships, I considered
how I would describe this hulking behemoth in my novel.

We were hustled up the plank, led by one of our Byzantine es-
corts and followed by Sebastianus. I had asked him whether he and
I would be allowed to make the trip with Ingund, and he said the
Byzantine authorities welcomed us, as they did not desire to staff
the queen's ship quarters with servants of their own. I didn't mind
being referred to as a servant as long as I could stay with her.

Ingund, Athanagild, and I were led down a ladder to a tiny room
with two bunks somewhere below the deck and shown the latrine
and the dining hall. In his strange Latin, our escort informed us we
would not be allowed on the main deck. Sebastianus would be next
door in an even smaller cabin that had just enough room for him to
walk in and fall onto his bunk.

Only after our escort left did I realize we would not see day-
light until we reached Carthage. I immediately felt claustrophobic.

Saliva filled my mouth, and my heart pounded against my ribs. I had no idea I had this problem, but then I had never faced the probability of being confined to such small, dank quarters for what could be weeks ahead. And I didn't know how much worse I would feel once we sailed away from the shallow waters of the harbor.

"You have been on one of these ships before," Ingund said, looking up at me from the bottom bunk where she sat, holding a drowsy Athanagild. "On your passage from Carthage, right?" I saw the small smirk on her face and remembered she knew I was neither from Carthage nor a cousin.

I swallowed and waited for more, but she simply held my eyes, and I knew she was asking me for the truth.

"You want me to tell you who I am and where I come from?" I asked. She nodded as her son yawned and fell back on the mattress and curled into a fetal ball.

I considered my choices. I could make up another story – one more likely, such as I was from Hibernia, which became Ireland (hence my red hair), and I had been sent by Columbanus to help her convert her husband to Christianity. It seemed like a good story, I thought as I was searching my brain for ideas. It would explain my ability to read and write. Then I considered telling her I was sent as a spy from Fredegund, but that I had abandoned my mission as soon as I met her and never communicated with her evil aunt again.

I was in part frantically trying to weave a plausible tale, and in part I was thinking maybe I had a knack for making up medieval tales. This dissertation-turned-novel wouldn't be my last foray into writing fiction, just as I had told my father.

Finally, watching her eyes turn from teasing back to sad, I sat down beside her and put my arm around her shoulders as I had seen Sebastianus do.

"I will tell you my true story," I said, "but I do not expect you to believe it."

"Anything will be more plausible than a cousin from Carthage," she said. "I could see you were just as intimidated by this conveyance as I was. You have never been on a big ship before."

"Well, I have," I said. "But not one that looked like this."

"Go on." She shrugged my arm off her shoulder and pushed her butt back on the mattress to lean against the wall. "We are going to have plenty of time to talk this over."

I inhaled, thankful that she was making me forget the tiny space and the prospect of getting seasick in such confinement. I pushed myself to one end of the bunk and rested my back against a wall, too.

"Okay." Still, I hesitated. How crazy this was going to sound to a medieval woman, even one as worldly as Ingund. On the other hand, if a person believed in the resurrection of Christ and a place called Heaven, believed in eternal life and the creation myth, why couldn't they believe in time travel? "Okay," I said again.

"What does this 'okay' mean?" she asked, scrunching up her eyebrows, and I realized I was using an English word right in the middle of our Latin conversation.

"It means I will try. I will try to tell you, but I know it is going to be hard to believe, maybe even to understand."

"I am a woman of the world," she said, echoing my thought.

I took a deep breath and thought about where I should start. I'd seen enough time travel movies – those that attempted to be serious and those that were comedies – to know that the explanation always begins with "I'm from the future." It seemed so lame.

"I am from the twenty-first century," I started. Just as lame, but I didn't know where else to begin. "I live in a place that has not yet been discovered by people of this continent. It is a place far beyond the sea, far west of Gaul, far west of Brittania or Hibernia. I came to what is Gaul to learn about your life."

I paused to wait for her reaction. "My life? Why would anyone want to learn of my life?"

"I will get to that in a moment," I said, holding up my hand to encourage her patience. "I thought I would find what I needed in Lutetia. When I got there, I ended up travelling back in time to your century, and your dressmaker met me and took me to you. She is the one who thought I was your cousin, and I did not correct her. I was excited to meet you."

I paused for a moment, realizing something I hadn't thought of before. Perhaps I was the cousin from Carthage, or at least the cousin who was supposed to be from Carthage, the one who played this role in Ingund's life all along. Again, I considered that I was always meant to be here, I always was a part of history, and anything that I did or said now wouldn't change things in the future. It was a lot to get my head around. But I'd have plenty of time to work it out here in this claustrophobic ship cabin, and so I pushed ahead with my explanation.

"You may remember that in the beginning, I only stayed for a short time, but returned a few years later," I continued. Her eyes didn't leave mine. "You thought I'd been hiding from your uncle Chilperic in Lutetia. Actually, I went back to my life in 2023 and then came back here to find you again. I had discovered a way to go back and forth in time and was lucky to meet you in Tolosa. Then, when things settled down in Toledo, I went home again for a while. Remember I went to take care of my mother? I got back here in time to watch you and Bishop Leander talk Hermenegild into converting."

She shook her head and finally looked away. "I do not understand why you wanted to learn about my life." I nearly laughed. That's what surprised her?

Researching a novel? Hell, the idea of a novel itself was hard to explain to a sixth-century woman. Reading made-up stories instead of scriptures? That nearly everyone where I lived was literate would be fantastic as well.

I paused because I was about to reveal to her something about the future, which I had assiduously avoided. But now that I believed I was always a part of this history, I didn't think there would be much harm. And I thought it would be better that her life ended knowing she had made a difference in the world.

"In the future, many people read manuscripts about things that happened in the past. They do it for fun and sometimes as part of their work. For me, it is part of my work. I write stories about the past so people can learn something about their history."

Now she looked disappointed. "You have been here all along because you want to write about me? I thought you cared for me. But you have been following me around so you can share my secrets? Who will know these things?"

"I do care about you! I have come to love you as a sister—even more than a cousin. I hope many people will read my manuscript and know how meaningful your life was, and what a great impact it had on Spain."

"Spain?"

"On Visigothic Iberia. It's called Spain in my time."

"Oh."

Silence followed. Ingund's face revealed how hard she was trying to understand what I had just said. I thought she might be flattered, but instead, she was intrigued.

"If you can come back in time to me, can I go forward in time to you?"

"I certainly wish you could," I said. "But I think it would be quite overwhelming."

"You think I am stupid?"

I'd already violated my vow to not reveal anything about the future, so I went for broke. "Not stupid," I said. "But so much has changed over the centuries. We have machines that fly, and we ride in them. We can send messages from Lutetia—we call it Paris—to Seville in less than a second over what some people call tubes. We don't ride horses, but we drive machines that can go 100 kilometers in an hour. Women can do the same work as men. We live, on average, more than eighty years. Doctors take hearts out of people to fix them, and then put them back in. We choose our leaders, instead of living under kings."

She sat wide-eyed and a smile built across her face. "I would like to see that world," she said. She looked down at sleeping Athanagild and stroked his hair lightly. "But I cannot leave my son. And I must see what God has in store for me next."

"I understand," I answered quickly, glad she wasn't going to insist I take her back with me. I had no idea how to do that. Despite my insistence that I had figured out how to go back and forth in time, I had no idea how it worked.

# XXXV

The next week and a half were lost in a blur of nausea and stench. The three of us in our cabin could do nothing but retch and lie around, waiting to retch some more. The stewards kept telling us we were lucky, that the seas were quite gentle. The notorious Meltemi winds had been calm so far that year, and our voyage was much more pleasant than it could have been. But that only meant that we were tortured day and night by the rhythmic beating of oars on the water and the drone of the coxswain.

The mariners on the ship were accustomed to the rolling and swaying, and so apparently  was Sebastianus, who shouldered the smelly task of emptying our buckets of vomit and bringing them back to us rinsed in seawater. He made us drink from the ship's supply of rainwater, knowing that dehydration was the greatest risk of our illnesses, even though we didn't want anything more to throw up.

Finally, after ten days at sea, we arrived at Carthage, another busy port bustling with soldiers, merchants, and stevedores and their cargo. We were led out of our dark, odiferous cabin onto the dock. My eyes watered with the shock of the sunlight, and as much as I hated the rocking of the ship, my legs fought the steadiness of solid ground. I walked as if I were drunk, and I watched Ingund and Athanagild struggle, too. Even Sebastianus had trouble getting his land legs under him.

We stumbled behind a Byzantine soldier entrusted with getting us to our lodging, which was in the back of a modest church in the center of town. I had never been to Carthage's ruins or had studied much about North Africa. But I did know that Carthage's importance as a center of religious thought had not been diminished by the Vandals' interceding 100-year reign, due to the influence of the early Christian author Tertullian. The Vandals were expelled from the city a couple of decades before our arrival with minor damage to the metropolis, and Carthage had grown to become a major center of trade between the Roman Empire and the breadbasket of Northern Africa.

The house was like the one in Córdoba, except that it had two sleeping rooms—one for Ingund, Athanagild and me, and one on the other side of the house for Sebastianus. It was a relief to have him so close.

Sebastianus asked the Byzantine soldier escorting us how long we would be staying in Carthage, but he just shrugged. The bishop, he said, would visit shortly. Waiting for him, we settled in. I was so glad to get out of the hold of the rocking boat and on land that even before we knew when we would depart again, I was dreading it. Sebastianus noticed.

"I tried to persuade you before, but now I insist you stay behind. Sailing to Constantinople will be far worse than our short trip so far," he said.

Thinking about a journey, possibly one four times as long as the trip from Malaca to Carthage had been, terrified me. I had what I needed to finish my dissertation cum novel, so there was little benefit of following them all to Constantinople. I would end my story with Ingund and Athanagild boarding the ship for their final destination, wherever that might be.

"I will think about it," I told Sebastianus. But I had already decided to go home.

THE BISHOP MADE A CURSORY visit and told us the palace in Constantinople had arranged for us to sail in fourteen days. He did not address Ingund as queen; to him, she was not a member of a royal family, now that Hermenegild had been deposed. Only Athanagild held any value to the Byzantines as Brunhilde's grandson.

He bristled with attitude: Ingund was excess baggage.

"I fear they are going to kill her," I confided in Sebastianus that night after Ingund and Athanagild had gone to bed. We sat out on the stoop of our cottage, watching the sky darken. The grounds of the church were nothing like those in Seville. The part of the city where we were staying was like a desert: cacti and succulents struggled to find enough water to survive in the dry, packed sand of the garden. A lone Holm oak tree with its shiny, holly-like leaves provided little protection from the heat during the day. But that night, a comfortable breeze blew the choking smoke of the city away from us toward the ocean to the north.

"But she's Brunhilde's daughter," Sebastianus said. "The Byzantines need Brunhilde and Childebert to continue to back them in Italy against the Lombards."

"True. But you saw the way the bishop treated her. Like a common peasant. They probably only care about Athanagild, and him only for his value as a hostage. Is this what her life will be like in Constantinople?"

"Possibly," he said. He sat, his eyes focused on the far horizon for a long minute. "Perhaps it would be better for everyone if she is *thought* to be dead. The Byzantines can still use Athanagild for leverage with Brunhilde."

And so, we came up with a plan that would change history.

Or would it? I had begun to accept that we were always part of this time and place. Perhaps, I thought, time is circular and not linear, or perhaps for some of us, it staggers back and forth. Perhaps we were always part of the past and the present and the future, and so was Ingund and everyone else on earth. Maybe the dress I thought was transporting me through time was only a red herring. Maybe there was something more ephemeral that effected the transition.

It was too much to think about. I would bring it up with Sébastièn when I got back to Minnesota. Meanwhile, I worried that questioning the dress might undermine its power.

TWO DAYS AFTER THE BISHOP'S visit, Sebastianus and I visited the bishop and told him that Ingund had taken ill.

"We have quarantined her in a sleeping room," Sebastianus said. "If it is the blue sickness, only her handmaid and I will travel with Athanagild to Constantinople." I nodded to show agreement. The bishop rarely looked at me, let alone encouraged me to talk.

The bishop stepped back from Sebastianus as if afraid of contamination. "If you are ill, any of you, you will not be allowed to board," he said sternly.

"We are taking all precautions. If we have caught the sickness, we will stay here as well. If she dies, I will bury her myself. Tell me where I can place her to rest."

Ingund was relieved that we had a plan. She would dress like and become me. I would stay behind. The bishop would never see me or her again.

"I will miss you, Cousin," she said. "But I know you want to go home. You have been away too long."

"I will miss you, too," I said sincerely. It was sadly, horribly true. "But Sebastianus will accompany you to Constantinople. You will be safe with him."

I planned to see them off, don my own time-travel dress, and hope I would spin back home again. If I didn't … I couldn't even think about that.

After our meeting with the bishop, a sign was nailed to our door warning of the sickness inside. From then on, any time a Byzantine came to deliver food and water, I would close myself in our sleeping room, and dressed in my clothes, Ingund would answer the door as me. None of our Byzantine captors knew what either of us looked like, but over the fortnight, they came to know her as the handmaid. They never saw me again.

Two days later, we sent him the news that Ingund had died, and Sebastianus had buried her in a pit far behind the church walls and burned her clothes atop the grave. The bishop could find the grave later, if he dared to go near it, by the cross we had placed atop the burial. Of course, we had placed no such cross. No wonder historians could never determine where Ingund had supposedly been buried.

The next ten days would have been excruciating if Sebastianus and I, with Ingund's tacit acceptance, had not been able to share his bed at night. I felt guilty, not for sleeping with him, but for having companionship that Ingund had lost. On top of that, none of us could leave the house, and the daily rations of bread and water never varied. We didn't starve, at least, but Ingund and Athanagild were miserable from monotony and claustrophobia. Sebastianus had the benefit of being able to read, and although the only manuscripts in the house were religious writings, they kept him occupied during the day, and we kept each other occupied at night.

From time to time, Ingund and I would sit together in her sleeping room, and I would tell her more about my life back in Minnesota. For her, my stories were like fairy tales from a make-believe world, better than the faeries of Ireland or the gods and goddesses of Germania. If Sebastianus listened in, he never let on.

When the time came for Sebastianus, Ingund as the "handmaid," and Athanagild to leave, a doctor came to the house and called them outside so that he could attest that they were well, plague free, and could travel. They came back inside to get what little they were bringing with them. I had just a moment with Sebastianus to say goodbye. If it had been hours, it would not have been long enough.

I gave him my most sincere kiss, backed away, and looked him in the eye.

"Will I see you again?" I asked.

He smiled and flashed me his crooked-faced wink. "I believe you will," he said, and gifted me his most sincere kiss.

With little chance that I'd ever see her again, letting Ingund walk out of my life was harder. As Sebastianus left the house to give us some privacy, I wrapped my arms around her tiny shoulders and buried my face in the hair piled on top of her head. I tried to stop my tears, but they flowed, unbidden and uncontrolled.

"Will I reach Constantinople?" she whispered into my shoulder, and I realized that she now believed in my grasp of history. "Will you come back to see me there?"

"Dear girl," I said, stifling a sob. "I must confess I don't know what happens now. History loses track of you because everyone thinks you died of the blue death here. So, I believe you live a long and peaceful life, but I won't know where to find you."

She pulled herself back from my arms and looked at me with dry eyes.

"History, as you call it, may forget about me, but I will never forget you," she said, shaking her head. "How could I have survived without your love?"

I smiled through my tears, amazed at how much she had grown, what a strong woman she had become, and thankful that I had a tiny part in making that happen. She leaned forward, reaching up to touch her lips to my wet cheek.

"Goodbye, dear Cousin," she said, grinning slyly. "Wherever you go from here, you can now truthfully say you came from Carthage."

She turned and walked out, closing the door softly behind her. I sank into the small chair by the table. I knew little more about where my life was headed than she did about hers. We were both at the end of one journey, and although I had no reason to believe my life back in Minnesota would be filled with the kind of danger she faced, my next journey was just as clouded in uncertainty as Ingund's. I assumed Justin and I had no future, and the two young men with their burnt egos had eliminated my chances at a professorship, but rather than clarifying things, those endings had only expanded my choices, and nothing pointed me down one path over another. But at least I *had* options. I could live anywhere, pursue any of myriad careers, commit to Sébastièn/Sebastianus or leave him. Ingund may have had feminist yearnings for significance and agency, but she had no options. The Byzantines now controlled her future, even if they didn't know she was the one carrying Athanagild to Constantinople.

I reviewed the past several months and tried to project myself into some kind of future. I stayed hidden in the house for a safe amount of time before I slipped out, carrying my time-travel dress in a cloth sack, and following my friends to the pier. I watched them walk onto the ship, noticing for the first time that Sebastianus limped. I smiled, recalling Sébastièn's limp that day, so long ago, in the student union. I wondered how long it would take him to get back to St. George.

# XXXVI

At the airport in Seville where she had been just a week before in the twenty-first century, Nicole bought an overpriced composition book and a pack of pens, and on the long plane ride, she wrote down as much as she could remember. She searched her memory for words and sentences from Brunhilde's letters, conversations she had with Ingund and Goswintha, details of the visits from the bishops in Seville, Córdoba, and Carthage. She left out Sebastianus; she'd have to figure out how to fill in the gaps in her story caused by his absence later.

After landing in Minneapolis and retrieving her car, she merged onto the highway to St. George before realizing she was crying. Was it happiness for being home, worry for Ingund, or the loss of Sebastianus that brought the tears? She concentrated, trying to sort it out, finally accepting that it was all three.

The house was empty of all but a few pieces of furniture and her personal possessions. In the week she had been gone, Justin had moved to Oklahoma to teach and coach golf at the university. He had said goodbye in an email she found in the dozens she'd scrolled through while waiting for her luggage at the airport. He took his golf gear, his clothes, one of their two TVs, a stereo system, and half of the pots and pans, plates and bowls, and flatware. In clearing out, he'd been judicious and fair, leaving Nicole the artwork and books she had purchased, as well as her favorite linens, casserole dishes, and all the rugs. He'd always preferred the wall-to-wall carpeting in the house in Iowa where he grew up.

That evening, she called her father to check in with him. He sounded stoic as ever, never alluding to his wife's absence from his life.

"How is the novel business going?" he asked.

"Very well."

"What does that mean?"

"It means I'm getting ready to finish up my draft and see if I can find a publisher."

"I suppose you can always self-publish," he said, sniffing a bit. She knew how he and other English professors at Iowa felt about self-publishing: Only losers go that route.

"I suppose," she said, unwilling to engage on the subject. She'd heard him rant enough about how KDP and Amazon had ruined the book business. And she was tired. She needed a nice glass of cabernet and some sleep.

The next day, she surprised herself by waking up at dawn. Usually, it took her days to readjust from jet lag. But knowing she had enough detail now to finish her novel, she couldn't wait to get started. She walked two blocks to the Casey's General Store on the corner to pick up some milk, eggs, butter, and bread — all sold at "convenience" prices — and a Star-Tribune, and headed home to make breakfast and get to work.

It was evening before she finally limped out of her uncomfortable desk chair, poured another glass from the bottle of wine she'd started the night before, and dialed Katie's number.

Fifteen minutes later, leaving the glass in the refrigerator, she met her friend at the Hyatt Hotel, which had the fanciest bar in town.

"How was the trip?" Katie asked.

"Great. I think I'm done with research. I made a lot of progress today on the draft." As an English professor, Katie should have understood what a big undertaking a novel is. But, nodding and looking away, she gave the strong impression that she had little respect for or interest in Nicole's work.

"Tell me something," Nicole said, wanting to change the subject. "What happened way back when between you and Sébastièn?"

Katie blushed so deeply that Nicole could see it in the dim lighting of the bar.

"Why do you ask?" Katie asked. "Are you seeing him?"

"Well, I don't know. He's on leave, the department admin told me. I have no idea if we will see each other. But clearly not right now."

"I wouldn't recommend it."

"What happened?"

Katie twisted her mouth and squinted. Nicole nearly laughed at the funny result.

"I made a fool of myself with him," Katie said. "That's the short story. The long one isn't worth telling. But before I met and married My Favorite Marxist, I met your favorite physicist. I liked him a lot, and I made a pass. He rejected it, I lost my self-respect, and I haven't been able to face him since."

"Oh. That is sad, but short of a tragedy, I think. But I'm sorry."

"You have nothing to apologize for. But if you called his office, you must at least want to see him."

Nicole tried to figure out how to respond. She knew Katie would roll her eyes if she shared her suspicion that sixth-century Sebastianus and twenty-first-century Sébastièn were one and the same. She certainly couldn't relay the well-above-average sex she had with him in the earlier century.

"I'll be honest," she said. "I like him. We've met for coffee and once for wine. He kissed me after the wine, and I wouldn't mind a repeat of that."

"Good for you," Katie replied. Now she looked miffed. "I guess you are more is type, a little more worldly than me. I just sit here in America, sleeping with a Communist, and teaching bored nineteen-year-olds Mark Twain."

Nicole didn't know how to answer that either. If Katie were jealous of her travels, there was no reason she couldn't undertake some of her own. She had plenty of money and a secure, tenured professorship, even if she didn't have the time-traveling dress.

Finally, she opted for humor. "Well, sleeping with a Communist can't be boring. Or is his idea of foreplay reading Das Kapital aloud while you undress?"

It was a weak joke, but at least Katie smiled at that, even if she didn't laugh.

Nicole said nothing about time travel, and Katie didn't ask.

BACK HOME, RETRIEVING HER WINE glass from the refrigerator, Nicole sat back in her recliner, thankful that Justin had left it, and thought about how her relationship with Katie had deteriorated. Maybe it was Nicole, herself, who had changed. Her center of gravity had shifted from the present to the past, and she guessed she could have trouble making close friends after what she'd been through in Europe. Who would believe she had traveled to the sixth century if they weren't predisposed to astrology, the power of crystals, reincarnation or chem trails, things that Nicole would never embrace? And how could anyone be a close friend if they didn't believe her stories, and she couldn't talk about them?

With little else to do until Sébastièn returned, she worked long hours the rest of the week, adding the detail of Ingund's story into the manuscript. Then, against her better instincts, she headed right into revision, starting at the first page, editing and rewriting sentences, shifting around paragraphs, and adding even more sight, sound, smells, tastes, and touch to the draft. It would have been better to wait a few weeks before revising so she could see her work with fresh eyes, but she wanted to get her advisor's feedback as soon as she could.

By the end of the second week, she was pleased with what she had in the second draft, and she sent it by email to Iowa. She prefaced the attachment with a note that was probably far more informal than it should have been, considering her advisor's investment in her degree:

> *I am sending this draft along now, but I know it won't be my final one. I want your thoughts about it, although I have decided I don't plan to submit it as a dissertation. I have decided that writing novels, not teaching history, is what I want to do with my life. No PhD needed for that! Please let me know what you think.*

It was late on Friday by the time she sent it, but the professor answered right away:

> *I'm disappointed, but I understand. History professorships are being cut right and left, so not a bad decision. Although I can't imagine that there's a lot of money in historical fiction either! I'll read this as soon as I can, and I'll talk to my friends at the Writer's Workshop and see if they can recommend an agent.*

# XXXVII

Sébastièn called Monday evening.

"You're back!" Embarrassed, she realized that she had shouted into her phone.

"Yes," he answered with a quiet chuckle. "Do you want to get together?"

She wanted to be coy, but how could she when her heart was pounding?

"Yes."

"Want to meet me over here?"

"Yes."

"I just got home. I'll text you the address." He added, "and hurry, please," which made her heart pound harder.

She changed her underwear, put the curling iron to her hair, and dressed in her nicest t-shirt and a short skirt. She didn't go overboard: no putting on makeup that he'd never seen on her, or dressing up like it was a date.

She ignored the thin ice on the windshield and pulled away.

On the drive to his house, Nicole was surprised that her thoughts were on Ingund. Her first question for him would be: What had happened after he and Ingund got on the ship? Would her question make him confess that he and Sebastianus were one?

That wasn't what happened.

She rang the doorbell, he answered, she stepped inside, he slid his hand behind her neck, pulled her gently to him, and kissed her, and she kissed him back. Two hours later, tangled in the messy covers of his bed, she was finally calm enough to ask about Ingund. "I turned in the manuscript to my advisor last week, but I can always rewrite the ending. Did she make it to Constantinople with Athanagild?"

He smiled, accepting that his ruse was over. If they had been strangers in bed, it would have been obvious. It wasn't even close. So, perhaps that was his confession. He had put an age-old writer's advice into practice: Show, don't tell.

He propped himself up on an elbow and traced a figure eight around her breasts with a finger. "Well," he teased, "are you sure you don't want to just make it up?"

She pushed his hand away. "No. Tell me."

"Okay." But first he leaned over and kissed her again, a deep, lingering kiss that made her consider postponing Ingund's story in favor of another repeat performance of their earlier repeat performance.

He pulled away, brushed her forehead with his lips, and flopped onto his back. "The trip across to Cyprus was much worse than the one from Málaga," he started. "I was glad you weren't with us. Those Meltemi winds were every bit as bad as advertised. Ingund was so violently ill, I didn't know if she would survive. Little Athanagild did better, and he stayed in my cabin so he could get some sleep.

"By the time we got to Cyprus, she was begging to get off the ship. We stayed in another church house, even more modest than the one in Carthage. She wanted Athanagild to stay with her on Cyprus until her mother could arrange for an escort through Italy back to Metz. The Byzantines were fine with her staying behind, as they still thought she was a handmaid, but they insisted on taking Athanagild with them to Constantinople. In the middle of the night, the little boy disappeared. They kidnapped him and the ship left before we knew what had happened."

"Poor girl! What then?"

"We talked to the priest. It wasn't easy because he was better at Greek than Latin. Hard to understand. But it didn't matter in the end. He could do nothing for her."

"So, you left her there?"

"Yes. It was her idea. Once letters from her mother convinced the priest that she was Ingund and not the handmaid, he agreed to take her to a monastery for women, and when I left, she had taken her vows and settled in. As royalty, she was welcome. The abbess, who is supposedly close to the emperor's wife, promised to get regular reports of Athanagild for her. Her last non-celibate act was to kiss me goodbye. Not like this…" He leaned over and kissed Nicole deeply again. "…but like this." He then gave her a peck on the cheek.

"Did she figure out you were from the twenty-first century, too?"

"Apparently once you told her about your time travels, she did."

Nicole lay quietly beside him for a few minutes, pondering how she would add his story to her novel.

"A nunnery is a much better than death from the plague," she concluded aloud. "I need to change my ending."

He put an arm under her back and pulled her on top of him. "How about you put that off for another hour or so?"

She didn't need words to answer.


THEY ALTERNATED BETWEEN SLEEPING AT his place and hers until she sold the house and got ready to spend the next few years traveling. Besides the proceeds she'd get from the house, her mother had left some money to her aside from that which was automatically transferred to Nicole's father. It was enough to wipe out her credit card debt and pay for some travel, and it bought her some time to finish her novel and decide what to do next.

"You know," she said between bites of toast at breakfast one morning, "it's sad that Catholics in France don't give Ingund credit for the conversion of the Visigoths to Catholicism, even though she is their native daughter. Some of the Spanish do, and they sainted her, but the French don't. Why is that?"

Sébastièn put down the newspaper and shook his head. "No idea. Not a historian."

"Ha! My guess is you now know more about medieval politics than most historians," she said. "But did you know that Reccared converted shortly after his brother's death, and there went the Visigoths? I give Ingund credit for that, and the Spanish do too."

He smiled and picked up the business section. No comment.

"You know, I have always wondered how we ended up in Gaul at the same time," she said.

Sébastièn folded his paper and laid it on the bench beside him, giving up on concentrating on the latest mergers and acquisitions. "After you asked me about time travel, I made it my business to be there."

"But you were there the first time I was in sixth-century Paris, before we had coffee when I told you about my travel back in time. I remember you helped me down from the carriage with the dressmaker. How could that be?"

His eyes squinted with humor. "If you can decide to go back in time to escort Ingund to Spain, why can't I decide to go back in time a year earlier?"

"Makes sense," she admitted, still with no idea how either of them had pulled it off. "But how did you learn Latin?"

"A classical education," he said. "Boring, but now I'm glad for it. I was in a Catholic prep school through the twelfth grade. My freshman year at the liberal University of Wisconsin knocked religion right out of me—although it had never sunk in very well to start with."

"But why did you hide your identity from me for so long? Why not admit we were going the same place at the same time?"

Sébastièn tipped his head as if trying to figure that out for himself. "I didn't want to admit it until I had a good scientific answer for what was happening. Stephen Hawking made a very sound argument that time travel is impossible, and he's a hard person to contradict. At first, I thought you had planted the idea in my head, and I was dreaming. I still don't have a sufficient theory that could explain it, nor do any physicists. But I've gotten past that."

"What was your portal?" she asked. "You know mine was the dress. What was yours?"

"Sleep. I went to sleep with the intention of waking up near you. If I were as articulate as Hawking, I could describe for you a wormhole or cosmic string or other things that have been proposed as possible time machines. But I'm not Hawking. My portal was simply in my head. Which is why I could be convinced it was just a dream, except that two people can't share a dream together, like we did."

Nicole nodded.

"Although," he continued thoughtfully, "perhaps sharing a dream is more likely than actual time travel. Who knows?"

Nicole got up from the table and retrieved the coffee pot. Sébastièn put his hand over his cup. "I need to get some sleep one of these nights," he said with a wink. "Less coffee, maybe."

"And less you-know-what?"

"Not for a long time." He shook his head convincingly. "Now my turn to grill you. I've been wondering whether Ingund proved your theories about feminism in the Middle Ages or arranged marriages."

"Ah!" Nicole replied. "About arranged marriages, I never really had a theory, which probably made it a bad focus for a dissertation, now that I think of it. I just find them an interesting artifact of the Middle Ages ... and some contemporary cultures as well. I'm glad I dodged that bullet with Justin. And in retrospect, I see that Ingund and Hermenegild were made for each other. They were certainly in love. But I think they were lucky."

"And feminism?"

"Yes, there I do feel vindicated. Of course, Ingund would never have called herself a feminist. She had no context for her feelings that would get her close to thinking about such things as equality or women's rights. But she wanted control over her life, and she had ambitious plans to convert Hermenegild and the Visigoths, and she carried them out. It was because of what she started that the kingdom converted just a few years later. So, yes, she had feminist qualities. Just like Brunhilde and Fredegund."

"Then congratulations are in order." Sébastièn lifted his near-empty cup in a toast. "I imagine not many historians have gone to the lengths that you did to prove a theory. Where do you want to go next?" That wink again. "I really like making love to you in a different millennium."

Nicole laughed and leaned over to kiss him on the cheek. "I've been thinking about writing a novel about Rigund's failed betrothal to Reccared."

"You realize that means running into Fredegund, don't you?" He laughed. "If you think Goswintha was scary, you haven't seen anything yet."

# AUTHOR'S NOTE

Gathered in Chalcedon in northwest Asia Minor in AD 451, bishops attending the fourth ecumenical Christian council convened by the Roman Emperor Marcian agreed that Jesus Christ was God, of the same substance as the Father, but also divine and human, and rejected the Arian belief that Jesus was two things, first a man and then a God. For this belief, the Visigothic Queen Ingund pledged her life.

That is a true story, and this novel is based on a true story. But, as with any fictionalized account, I had to fill in the blanks left by historians with my imagination, buttressed by many months of research and my liberal imagination.

In doing so, I came across four different historians' versions of Hermenegild's capture, imprisonment, and murder. Only his death at the end of the civil war seems to be undisputed. Where he was captured, where he took sanctuary – if he did – where he was imprisoned – if he was – where he was murdered and at whose direction were all described differently in every account. I avoided making a choice among the different histories. Therefore, when I have Sebastianus relay the news to Nicole, he lists all the theories.

There is little disagreement over Athanagild's arrival in Constantinople, but not much is certain after that. He never made it to Metz, but historians disagree about whether he ever returned to Spain.

When it comes to Ingund's death, however, I wasn't happy with the ambiguity left by historians. In some of their accounts she died in Carthage from the plague. In others she disembarked in Sicily and from there was lost to history, and in still others, she made it to Constantinople. I chose the story I liked best: she got off the ship in Cyprus and joined a female monastery. There is no historical record of that, but given her piety and royal blood, it makes sense to me that she would end up there. Imagine how painful it must have been to lose her son to the Byzantines.

Historians recorded two dramatic events that I included in this story that may seem apocryphal but appear to have been true: Hermenegild rode out of Toledo to meet his bride before his mother got the chance to welcome her; and Goswintha threw Ingund in a fountain as an attempted forced baptism. I am not sure she was pregnant with Athanagild yet, but the timing seems right.

In addition, Ingund's meetings with the Bishops Cyprian, and Leander were recorded in the nearly contemporaneous histories, including that of Bishop Gregory of Tours. Although Gregory exercised considerable historical latitude to promote his political and religious agendas, there is little reason to doubt that these meetings took place or that the subject discussed was Ingund's destiny in convincing Hermenegild to convert.

Ingund, the two Athanagilds, Fredegund, Brunhilde, Sigibert, Rigund, Chlosinda, Chilperic, Childebert, Guntram, Reccared, Leovigild, Luiva, and Goswintha; the bishops Masona, Leander, and Cyprian; and the various Byzantine emperors were all real persons, and I have tried to keep their stories here as true to history as possible while still writing fiction. All the conversations came from my imagination, thinking about how this history played out. Of course, Nicole, Justin, Katie, Sébastièn and Sebastianus are fictional.

I have adjusted many place names to reflect either their ancient nomenclature when the story is told in the sixth century or the modern names if the story is set in 2023. A caveat: There are many versions of these old names, depending on what sources are used. I had to make choices based on the information I could find. Historians disagree, and they're free to disagree with me as well. The map in the front of this novel should help readers adjust to the ancient names and place them in the context of what they know now. I didn't change some of the modern names to their ancient ones if the towns were less important to the story.

For example, these are the modern city names and their equivalents used in this novel:

Paris: Lutetia
Toulouse: Tolosa
Carcasanne: Carcasanne
Narbonne: Narbo
Castelnaudary: Sostomagus
Barcelona: Barcino
Zaragoza: Caesaraugusta
Toledo: Toledo
Seville: Hispalis
Córdoba: Corduba
Málaga: Malaca
Tunis: Carthage
Istanbul: Constantinople

For the background politics of the time, I relied on a few historians who have made the Merovingian and Visigothic Empires their lives' work, most notably Ian Wood, Peter Heather, Roger Collins, and Shelley Puhak. A few of their books are listed in the following references.

Collins, Roger. *Early Medieval Spain; Unity in Diversity, 400-1000.* 2nd ed. (St. Martin's Press: New York, 1995).

Crisp, Ryan Patrick. "Marriage and Alliance in the Merovingian Kindgoms, 481-639." Dissertation for PhD, Ohio State University: 2003. Accessed via www.academia.com.

Eckenstein, Lina. *Woman Under Monasticism,* Chapters on Saint-lore and Convent Life between AD 500 and AD 1500 (Cambridge University Press, 1896) Transferred to Print on Demand, 2015, Forgotten Books.

Gregory of Tours, *History of the Franks.* c.593. trans. Ernest Brehaut. (Cudahy, WI: First Rate Publishers. 2014).

Halsall, Guy. *Barbarian Migrations and the Roman West, 376-568* (Cambridge, UK: Cambridge University Press, 2007).

Heather, Peter. *Empires and Barbarians: The Fall of Rome and the Birth of Europe.* (Oxford, UK: Oxford University Press, 2012).

Hen, Yitzhak. *Culture and Religion in Merovingian Gaul AD 481-751* (Leiden, The Netherlands: E.J. Brill, 1995).

Kiner, Aline. T*he Mirror of Simple Souls.* Susan Emanuel, trans. (London: Pushkin Press, 2023).

Lerner, Gerda. *The Creation of Patriarchy.* (New York: Oxford University Press, 1986).

Lerner, Gerda. *The Creation of Feminist Consciousness.* (New York: Oxford University Press, 1993).

Mari, Jose. "Ingunda, la princesa franca que cambió la religión de los visigos," http://caminandoporlahistoria.com. 12 Abril 2008, accessed 5 June 2022.

Puhak, Shelley. *The Dark Queens: The Bloody Rivalry that Forged the Medieval World.* (New York: Bloomsbury Publishing Inc., 2022).

Salisbury, Joyce E. "The History of Spain." DVD set. The Great Courses. 2017: Chantilly, VA.

______. Song of Solomon, *The Holy Bible,* Revised Standard Version, New York: Thomas Nelson & Sons, 1952, pp. 524-527. The chapter is also known as Song of Songs.

Wood, Ian. *The Merovingian Kingdoms 450-751* (Routledge: London and New York).

# ABOUT THE AUTHOR

Marj Charlier is the author of contemporary women's and historical novels. Her novel *The Rebel Nun* (Blackstone, 2021) was named the best historical fiction and best fiction overall (Herb Tabac CIPA Choice Award) in 2023 by the Colorado Independent Publishers Association. *The Candlemaker's Woman* followed in 2023. She lives in Colorado Springs with her husband, the journalist Ben Miller.